THE L[

JIM WILSON

SPRINGBOARD

1994

Published by Yorkshire Art Circus
School Lane, Glass Houghton, Castleford
West Yorkshire, WF10 4QH
Telephone (0977) 550401

Events and characters in this novel are entirely imaginary. Any similarity to real events and persons is coincidental.

© Yorkshire Art Circus Ltd, 1994
© Text, Jim Wilson
Edited by Graham Mort
© Cover illustration by Rich Whale
Cover designed by Tadpole Graphics
Back cover photograph J S Waring

Typset by Yorkshire Art Circus
Printed by FM Repographics, Roberttown

ISBN 1 898311 01 3
Classification: Fiction

Springboard is the fiction imprint of Yorkshire Art Circus. We work to increase access to writing and publishing and to develop new models of practice for arts in the community.
For details of the full programme of Yorkshire Art Circus workshops and our current booklist, please write to the address above.

Yorkshire Art Circus is a registered charity (number 1007443)

Acknowledgements
Ian Daley, Fiona Edwards, Olive Fowler, Tina Kendall, Reini Schühle, Linda Smith

We would like to thank the following organisations for support towards this book.

To Maura

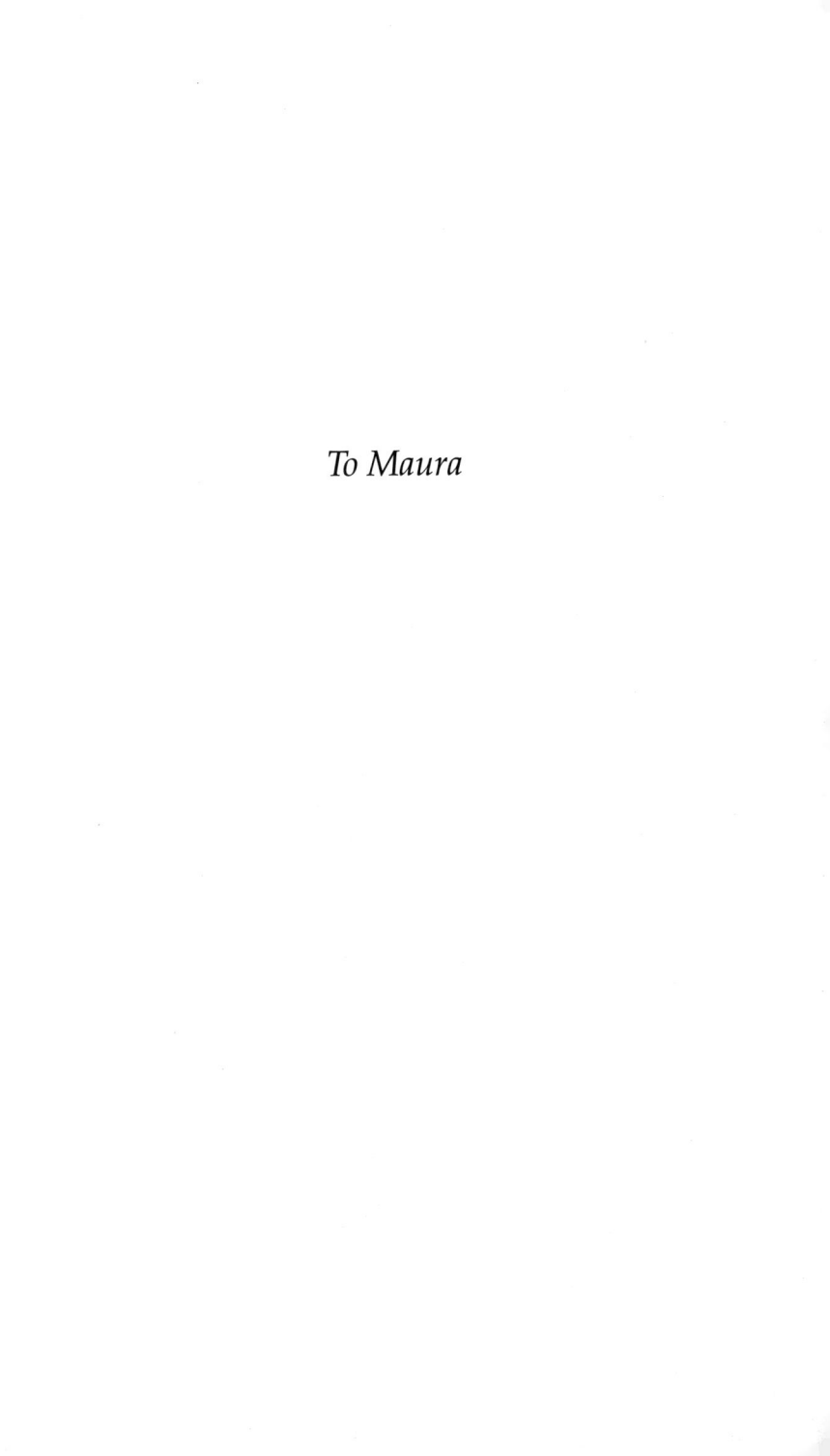

Chapter 1

Election day had fallen on the solstice and at noon the sun fell straight down between the walls of Perseverance Street and onto a group of mill girls, sitting on the car park wall. Two girls were swinging their legs in the air, sucking on melting ice-pops and chatting in the heat.

'You going to hear the Labour bloke in the canteen?'

'No.'

'I thought you were Labour.'

'I am, but it's too nice, innit?

Suddenly, from the Commercial Street end, they saw a middle aged man, red with terrible exercise, burst into the street and flap past them like a grey worsted bird towards Union Street. His red tie and thin hair trailed after him.

Had they been able to put together the words they caught in gasps as he passed, they would have heard him say, in an old Cockney accent.

'Sod this for a lark!' before he turned sharply through the car park and down the alley between Woolworths and the Italian cafe.

He had hardly disappeared from sight when two younger women skidded to a halt at the same place he had appeared. One of them was tall and powerfully built. Her breast rose and fell under a cotton suit as she looked all around her. The other woman was small and wore large glasses. She clutched her throat and gasped, desperate for air. She hardly had time to breathe before the big woman dragged her off in pursuit again, shaking the paving stones as she ran, shouting:

'Harry! Harry! Come back! Harry!'

The lunchtime traffic gobbled them up. The mill girls turned back to the Commercial Street end and waited.

An old Indian man in an expensive suit sweated onto the stage, mopping his bald, brown head.

'Hari!' he shouted optimistically. 'Hari!'

He limped on in pursuit, acknowledging the shouts of encouragement from the girls with a fly-swatting of his handkerchief.

He was followed by two slim young men in dark suits and floral ties who argued their way down the street, lost in altercation and waving pieces of paper at one another.

'The working class care about jobs man!'

'Oh, you'd know, of course. I suppose...'

Ignoring the workers' pointing fingers they wandered off the wrong way down Union Street.

'Europe! Europe! They don't care about bloody Europe...'

The mill girls waited patiently but the show seemed to be over. They finished their sandwiches and watched the wrappers float away on the shallow waters of the little culvert in the car park before drifting back to work themselves.

The two women and the Indian man met up in a small piazza in the town centre.

'Ah, we have lost him,' said the Indian man hopefully, his hand searching desperately inside his jacket for a heartbeat.

'I must take more exercise.'

But the women were not listening to him. They were tense and alert, their hawk eyes sweeping the streets that radiated into the town. The smaller woman had got her breathing under control and was polishing her glasses, misted by exertion. The larger woman absently flattened the lid of a bin with her knuckles as her eyes narrowed to probe deeper into the streets.

'No, there he is!' she said, and smashing a triumphant blow into the bin, pointed to a bald head bobbing rhythmically down Station Road.

'There!'

She tore off in pursuit. After she had settled her glasses back on her nose, the smaller woman shuffled off gamely too. The Indian man sat on the beaten litter bin and begged,

'Hari!'

But it was more to heaven than Harry, who was maintaining his lead and was almost at the station.

They thought they had him in the long straight. But despite his rasping gasps for air and the wobbling tear lenses that hung in his eyes and shook the images of his darting feet, his skinny legs bore him onwards.

'Harry! Harry!'

Recklessly his legs carried him across Burnley Road, through the screech of tyres and a small tinkle of headlamp glass, nothing serious, and into the station car park. Across the sun-softened tarmac, past the taxi rank where a cabby asked, amazingly:

'Taxi, sir?'

Into the station. Unflagging, he shot past the ticket office and clattered down the wooden stairs on flamenco heels and onto the platform.

'Harry!' echoed under the wrought iron roof. Down the platform. Past the dreaming porter with thin, oiled hair and the skinhead with soft, brown eyes. Down the slope and onto the forbidden cinders. Across the rails threatened with a rusty closure - no longer his concern. Down the dusty embankment. Through a corner of the toffee factory's lorry park. Over a trampled wire fence and onto the canal bank.

His legs galloped along the tow path and his spirit, hanging on like a novice rider, followed. With every thrust of his leading right foot he could hear himself saying:

'Sod this! Sod this! Sod this!' as tears streamed down his face and blew off his cheekbones into his slipstream.

Suddenly the town was gone and a primeval forest fell across his path. Blackbirds sang in the dark chestnuts and frightened moorhens burst from under the skirts of hawthorns into the scum-still waters, nodding their heads like clockwork. Yes, yes, yes.

Very distant, somewhere, 'Harry!' sounded. He galloped on. A hundred paces and the ash trees closed over the canal. In the shoals of their tropical shadows by the tow path, almost invisible, Harry saw the doorway to a neat brick building. He ducked under its rotting lintel and flattened himself against a wall in its shade. Inside, his heart pounded against his eardrums and his lungs raked the air for oxygen. Outside, the cicadas fiddled, the sun burned and howler monkeys screeched across the jungle top.

For some time he lay plastered against the wall, breathing painfully down a frozen windpipe. On the run down the thought had darted in and out of his mind that his phenomenal performance was being drawn from that legendary pre-death reserve of energy. The idea now terrified him so that his head spun. He dug his fingers into the crumbling brickwork for support. But after he had blown his nose on a final gas bill and wiped his eyes with the end of his tie, his heartbeat slowed. His breathing became regular and his terror subsided.

As his body regained its composure the features of the little building began to form themselves out of the grey light and shadows. He found himself considering what sort of building it was. Too small for a stables or a pumping station. Not a house or workshop, far too small. Very plain and symmetrical; a brick cube really; something to do with the electricity board perhaps or...

'Now then!' said a voice behind him.

An icy hand grasped his bowels. An apparition in a mildewed sports jacket pushed past him and out into the sunlight where it developed, like a photograph, into an old tramp. The tramp stepped out of sight and returned with the thick end of a hawthorn bough which he dragged in behind him and wedged in the doorway, fussing it into place with cautious plucks and prods of his fingers.

'There,' he said, nodding with satisfaction at the camouflage. 'They'll not find you here lad.'

A rabbity panic bolted across Harry's mind.

'Trapped!'

But the old man began chinking tea things in an corner and he heard the crinkle of a sugar bag and a tiny hail of grains and then,

'Will you have a brew?' in such lovely West Yorkshire tones that his fear melted.

'Aye, I will,' said Harry.

'Harry!' quite near, then a long pause.

'Harry!' right outside. Another icy panic. Harry commando-crawled up to the door on his elbows and peered at the broad back of Jo and the slighter, stooped profile of Heather, outside in the sunlight, looking for him everywhere, even in the tree tops.

The two women stopped almost outside the door. They shuffled round and round in the gravel looking for him, pretending, it seemed, not to see him in the doorway behind the hawthorn.

Jo made a megaphone of her hands and roared into the treetops:

'Harry!'

The two syllables rolled after one another through the foliage, flushing magpies from the elders. When they had gone there was silence.

Heather took off her sandals, neatly rolled the legs of her jeans up to her knees and then sat on the bank, soaking off the dust of the chase in the water. Once or twice she held out an open palm as a prelude to saying something, but nothing came. Jo remained standing, with her fists on her hips, looking after the word she had shouted into the trees as if the name might return with the man. Her lips began to form a smile.

After taking off her glasses and pinching the bridge of her nose Heather eventually said, 'He's gone.'

'Does he have to sign anything?' Jo asked, still staring into the trees.

'What?'

'Tonight, after the count. Does he have to sign anything?'

Heather replaced her glasses and Harry saw the back of her head rock from side to side as she considered the question.

'No, I don't think so. He has to take the oath at Westminster, of course, but I don't think he has to do anything tonight.' She shook her head and shrugged. 'But I don't know.'

Jo came and sat beside her, dangling her own legs into the canal.

'Well that's me done with the Labour Party,' she said, and kicked a shower of amber water into the air.

'Sod it!'

Heather laid a hand on her thigh and rubbed it gently.

'Me too. Harry was the last thing keeping me in. We could have had this seat for Ginny but we slaved away for that man. She stamped her foot in the water, soaking her jeans.

'Bastard!'

The old man nudged Harry's arm and with a silent nod passed him a mug of tea. Handleless. Harry nodded in return and turned his attention back to the women.

Jo was pitching stones with distracted regularity at a bobbing coke can, her forearm flicking out like a darts player's and the stones dropping badly off target. The pedantic science teacher in Harry, which three weeks of optimistic campaigning had only thinly buried, almost dragged him out to tell her to keep her forearm horizontal; the trajectory of the projectile being a parabola, initially, at least, tangential to the arc her arm was describing. But he restrained himself. Heather put an arm around Jo's shoulder, although she couldn't quite cover the full breadth, and whispered consolations to her which she revealed with little backward flicks of her hand.

The two men held their mugs and watched them until their tea went cold. Eventually, when she had used up her supply of pebbles, Jo clapped the dust off her hands and washed them in the canal. Then she stood up and shook the cramps out of her legs. She grinned at Heather and helped her to her feet. They set off together, back the way they had come. After a few paces they stopped and Heather said,

'Chilean women, Jo. That's where the future lies.'

And she sipped a little sob of Inca gold. But Jo was not listening. She was looking back and had made a half move towards the little cabin but Heather called her, irritably.

'Come on, Jo!'

When he was quite sure they had gone, Harry sat up and began to peck at his tea. It was strong and curdled with Carnation milk. It tasted of his boyhood.

'Aye, you're well out of it, Harry lad.'

Harry wasn't really surprised that the old man knew his name; Jo had arranged for it to be plastered all over the constituency after all. But he was grateful to him, so he pretended to be impressed.

'You know who I am then?'

'Aye, of course I do. You're Harry Beamish the Labour man. Oh I know you alright. I'd have voted for you myself, if I'd been on the roll, like. But I don't stay in one place so long these days. Floating voter.'

They both laughed. Harry gave the old man a toffee bar left over from the morning's visit to the sweet factory. The old man handed Harry a leather bound copy of the Communist Manifesto that Nikita Kruschev had given him thirty-odd years earlier in Tbilisi.

'Who gave me that then? Go on, have a guess. You'll never guess, never.' Before he could make even a futile guess the old man told him. Harry whistled politely and the old man lit a dog end with a blinding match and then pointed at the fly leaf.

'There, that's me, George Jowett.' Harry could make out the Cyrillic for George but the rest was all crazy mirror writing, except, penned in waning ink: 'Nikita Kruschev,

Tbilisi,'57', in Roman script. George took the book back and stowed it carefully in a side pocket.

'Oh aye, I were a big Labour man myself. General Secretary o't Sorters' for five year. I were on't General Council with George Woodcock. Almost got on NEC o't Party, but I were too left.' He puffed out a stream of smoke and scratched his belly through his frayed pullover.

'Anyhow, you're well out of it all now lad. All them women's libbers.' He nodded at the door and the departed women.

Harry's right forefinger rose to correct him but he let it pass. None of it was his problem any more. The old man could say what he pleased and Harry could smile and nod and drink his tea as he had done before all this had started. Anyhow Harry's mind was on something else. Something his brother Charlie had said to him thirty years ago, when George had been shaking hands with Kruschev.

They had been sitting in a little cabin then. It was Charlie's desperado shack on Canvey Island when he was working as a pipe fitter at the refinery. Charlie had got him his first job as his labourer. An easy start in life that had been, working for his big brother. Charlie had shown him the ropes, although he had never really grasped them properly. He was not cut out for a pipe fitter. When he met Peggy and she put him through a chemistry degree, he found things much easier to grasp. He was a theory man, really. Charlie had said:

'Theories don't leak like fucking pipes do, do they?

How wrong he had been. But it was the memory of something else Charlie had said that was drawing Harry back. They had been drinking Carnationed tea then and sharing a last Senior Service. Charlie was sitting on the top bunk, swinging his legs and Harry was lying on the old, horse hair sofa that could not be moved because its legs had gone through the floorboards into the sand beneath the shack. Charlie had the cigarette which also gave him the floor. He spoke words of wisdom about women.

'No wonder you don't get anywhere with the birds Harry. They want a bit of fun man. Get your hand up their skirt. They don't want to talk about fucking politics.'

Charlie had handed over the advice with the dog end and then laid back and blown perfect smoke rings; something else Harry could never do. But it had been politics. Politics every minute of the last thirty years. General committees, regional committees, national committees. And now it was over. A sheaf of old agenda papers, once more important than anything in the world, blowing away like winter leaves.

'Aye, them lot'll have your balls off, lad, and then you'll be use nor ornament to any bugger. Now then!'

The old man puffed a few times at his dying cigarette and dusted its ash from his lapel. Harry rose to his feet to rebuke him but instead wandered out of the hut into the sunshine. He wanted no more of any of this. No more theorizing. Putting one foot cautiously on the gravel and craning his neck out to peer round the bushes, he checked to see that the two women had gone. The old man came out to join him, conscious of having said the wrong thing, looking anxious to be forgiven. Harry knew he ought to defend Jo, at least. By rights she should have been the candidate: if her youngest hadn't been doing his GCSEs, if there had been any rights. But instead he just said,

'Times have changed, George.'

'Aye, maybe you're right. It's just that...' Instead of going on the old man took out his baccy tin, stuck a paper on his lower lip and teased out a palmful of tobacco.

'Roll?' he offered. Harry declined.

'Its just that when I think of...' but his thoughts became clouds of smoke that drifted out over the canal and up through the pale underbellies of the young ash leaves. Something in the movement of the smoke was leading Harry back to the roots of that morning's sedition.

The rustle of leaves and the songs of early birds had drifted in through his open bedroom window and woken him at first light. Before he could drift back to sleep the excitement of polling day had seeped into his head and roused all the demons there to a new day's fury: he knew he would have to get up. Meeting times and speeches and the whereabouts of canvass cards began to clatter around his brain. He reached across for Peggy and although he remembered immediately that she was not due home from America for another two weeks, he was still shocked. The same shock ran through him now, standing on the canal bank with his hands in his pockets. According to his watch, he should be hammering home Labour's plans for pensions to a meeting that Jo had organized in the YMCA. What would Peggy say when she came home and found out? She had offered to cancel her trip to be with him on election day, to support him, see him through. A slap of guilt knocked his head forward. He felt like a banker, fleeing with his investors' life savings. A cat, prowling through the shadows on the opposite bank, stopped and looked at him reproachfully.

In truth, he had been glad to decline her offer since the fear of failure had always hovered around his optimism. He had a brief losing speech as well as a long victory one folded in his inside pocket. But he would rather not have delivered it in front of Peggy. This was to have been the first real thing he had ever done on his own. The first thing Peggy could not have done better herself in a lunch hour or two. He had planned to be established in London by the time she returned: a couple of flats lined up for her to choose from, theatre dates booked, restaurants sussed out. He had planned to impress her.

'She'll be impressed alright,' he thought, and giggled out loud so that the old man began to giggle with him.

'Aye, it's a laugh right enough,' said the old man.

Harry nodded and watched himself with almost

objective curiosity as he shelved the whole question of facing Peggy so that he could get back to the events of the morning and sift through them.

He had lain in bed staring at the ceiling, watching one of his demons pasting up tomorrow's local headlines. 'Beamish Bounces In,' seemed about right; but it toyed with one or two others: 'Beamish Blasts Tories.' 'Hurricane Harry Roars Home.' He had begun a friendly dispute with the demon over this, "Breezes Home,' surely,' he had suggested, but the demon knew best. 'No, no! hurricanes do not breeze, breezes breeze.' Harry had deferred modestly and the demon went on: 'Labour Landslide,' the hope that had sustained them all through the dark years. Then, very speculative: 'Beamish to Head Department of Technology' and 'Harry Heads for Number Ten.' He lost himself in a semi-erotic, self-satisfied doze of success, but it was interrupted by his most persistent demon: the little scientist, who appeared in a lab coat and did Harry's rapid estimations for him. He was welcome enough when Harry was teaching, feeding him with quick information to astound his students, but he had been bursting in uninvited recently and producing unasked for estimates. He appeared now and scribbled Harry's monthly sex average on the ceiling. It was very small. The demon went on to compare this with the average quoted in a recent survey Harry had read in the *Observer*, which was hardly fair. He began to argue. He had been busy, Peggy had been busy, they were busy people dedicated to a Labour victory. They were not juvenile dilettantes. Anyway, after the election they had promised themselves their first ever holiday alone, and, although they would probably spend it reading the *International Guardian* and disparaging the leadership, it was a start. Just this one last push.

What was doubly unfair about the demon's barging in with this humiliating statistic now, just when he needed confidence, was that he had appeared the last time they had been making love. Peggy had been very complicatedly on top, and his demon had insisted on trying to work out the elasticity of her oscillating breasts. All tied up with age and the tautness of their bodies. The effect had been ruinous.

The cat on the opposite bank had some poor rodent pinned to the ground and was expertly angling its jaws for the death-blow. Harry had considered seeing a psychiatrist about it all but he couldn't think of a way round his local GP, who, although he was a good enough bloke, Harry knew to be an active Tory. A biology teacher at school had told him that it was the male menopause: an obsession with lost opportunities, with things past. That certainly squared with the ghosts he had been seeing recently: turning round the ends of aisles in supermarkets, passing in the street, sitting at the backs of meetings, shaking their heads in doubt. And he had been playing his Bogey videos over and over again, late at night, after campaigning. Drinking wine and trudging through the Sierra Madre or rolling on the Caribbean out of Port Au Prince.

The demon began another calculation so Harry rolled out of bed and padded to the bathroom, reproaching himself for bourgeois egoism. He was a worker and a socialist. He had begun as a pipe fitter and his ideas were real things, welded together at the joints into an iron philosophy, not half baked, dilettante constructions. He peed out a thin, constricted stream and felt better.

As he peed, worrying slightly at the thinness of the stream - the operation not far off - the sun came up and poured over him through the frosted glass. It anointed his bald head and trickled kindly over his naked body. He looked down at his little pot belly, round like a Bhuddist idol's. He began to rub it consolingly with an open hand. As if it had been a war wound, which, in a way, it was; so much of the struggle recently having been accompanied by wine. This rubbing action splashed his stream against the edge of the bowl, sending a cool mist onto his feet; a sort of blessing.

The demon was back on the wall, in front of him, going on about the periodicity of the Earth's orbit, drawing a graph of the length of days against days of the year and showing how the curve was almost symmetrical about a line through the solstice. Harry nodded with approval. This was more like it: he even considered working it as an analogy into the Great Speech he wrote and revised constantly in his head; something about seizing the hour. Then the demon wrote a line of poetry and rubbed it off immediately with his cuff, as if it had been somehow shameful. But Harry had already read it. It said:

'Oh come to my arms, my Beamish boy.'

What was he up to? Harry could not make head nor tail of it but it sent a little shudder through the iron welds of his philosophy.

Beside him the old man gave up sucking on his dog-end and flicked it into the canal.

'When I led that delegation to Tbilisi in Russia.'

Harry's finger twitched to point out that Tbilisi was in Georgia but he let it go. He was getting used to letting things go.

'I was sure we'd never be beat. Never! But...'

He waved one hand and a frayed cuff in the air, groping for the invisible enemy that had defeated them.

'...But there y'are.

After a pause he went on again.

'Of course, it was that last bloody Callaghan Government that did the damage. One bloody cut after another. Always think they can do the job better than the Tories can. Never bloody learn. Still...'

He sloshed the grouts from his mug onto the path.

'...Still, there y'are.'

They stood, nodding agreement as a little blue cabin cruiser gurgled past, heading south. Its helmsman fidgeted as they stared and nodded absently at him.

Harry looked at his watch. He should be leaving the pensioners' meeting about now and going up to the polling stations in the north wards. There had been that dirty Tory allegation about Labour supporters impersonating absent voters during the Council elections up there. Filthy lies, of course. His blood warmed momentarily with the old fire but it passed. Something, quite beyond his reason was drawing him away.

'You can stay here, if you like.'

The old man, his hands in his pockets, was indicating the hut with the toe of his shoe. Harry smiled.

'I won't thanks, George. I'd better be getting on.'

'Oh well, suit yourself.'

They shook hands and the old man said,

'I suppose you'll be going to London.'

Harry supposed he would be and nodded.

'Well it's that way.'

The old man pointed in the direction of the little cruiser and Harry set off after it. A few steps on and the old man called him back.

'Here!'

He took something black out of his pocket and skimmed it through the air. It was a black, bargee's cap and it fitted perfectly.

Chapter 2

So he was Bogey as Harry Morgan in *To Have and Have Not* rolling nonchalantly along the tow path, his jacket over his shoulder. Crunching the green elm seeds under his thin leather shoes. Shaded, by his new cap, from the tropical sun overhead.

He became mesmerized by the left-right flicking of his shoes in and out of view. They seemed to flash on and off in new, pristine colours, as if his optic nerve had a loose connection somewhere. He had become so accustomed to the uniform greys of middle age that the new, youthful colours shocked him. A sweet shock. He strode on, wondering where he had last seen his feet in those colours.

Suddenly he recalled the occasion with a clarity that stopped him in his tracks. It was a Sunday afternoon in the fifties. It was Autumn and he was walking down Conker Alley with his father, kicking up dead leaves, looking for conkers. Harry had wanted to leave the grammar school and go labouring for big money with his brother. They were trying to discuss it. His father had fought Hitler for his grammar school place and he was almost in tears with sorrows that he could not express. He kept clearing his throat in false starts, then looking at Harry, blond and bright in his Sunday best, and choking up.

'Don't do it mate,' he managed after an effort and they walked on a mile or so, chewing toffees as the dingy afternoon closed in.

'My father told me,' his father had said quietly, looking at his own feet like the boy he must have been when his father had told him. 'Never take your coat off to work mate, or you'll never put it on again. And I wish I'd listened to him. I do.' And then with workers' hands he gently cupped Harry's neck, drew him aside and kissed him on the head.

'Don't do it mate.'

A little sorrow shivered down Harry's breast as he thought of his grandfather who had been born in Spitalfields workhouse and given the name Beamish by the clerk there after his mother died. He had found her name in the workhouse records during a frenzy of genealogical activity the previous year: 'Liza and then a squiggle', Flemish jute weaver,' in the entry for deaths 1852. It was the only trace of her he could find. Presumably she had been posthumously anglicized from Flemish to Beamish by the clerk and Harry's family name was born. He had been both proud and ashamed of his name's origin. And to think her great-grandson had almost become an MP in Westminster. He fancied he heard a little groan from his ancestors as he let them back down a notch into the pit. An uncomplaining but woeful moan. But that was not why he had revisited the scene or why it had revisited him: it was something he had shared with his father in that rare kiss, he was sure.

Harry stopped in the middle of the tow path and stared down at his feet. The little cabin cruiser he had seen earlier was struggling at the lock gates just ahead and he knew he would have to lend a hand. But first he had to get to the bottom of this without distraction: to think it out.

His father and grandfather stood beside him, both staring at his feet that had come so far, scratching their heads for the meaning in it all. His own sons joined him and they all looked at one another, puzzled. Not like fathers and sons at all but like mates. Was that it? Was that all there was to it? Had he been dragged half out of his wits to be told that his forefathers could make no more of it all than he could? Surely not.

He strode on, hitching up his trousers by the waistband, Bogey fashion, angry at the very suggestion.

At the lock, the driver of the little cruiser was getting into a terrible state. His legs quivered like a stage comedian's as he tried to open the great elm gates and his badly tethered boat had strayed away from the bank like a disobedient dog on a long lead. He tried to call it back.

'Come here, you fucker!' he cried, almost weeping. 'Come here!'

Harry put his shoulder to the lock gate and it sped open in tiny whirlpools of duckweed. The thin man, gasping for breath, shook a head of grey hair at him and whistled out his thanks. He seemed lost, the effort of opening locks beyond him, and he looked hopefully at Harry's cap. Harry, soft Harry, said:

'You jump in.'

The thin man hauled in his boat and fell into it over the sides, scraping his shins on the gunwales but determined to press on. Once at the helm he peered at Harry through the doghouse window, his knuckles white on the wheel, his face screwed into a prune of anxiety, and gave a little nod to proceed.

Harry dragged the cruiser into the lock and thudded the gates shut behind it. The man was now white with terror and trembling. Harry shouted down to him.

'Are you alright?'

He nodded, so Harry tethered the boat for and aft to the lock's iron capstans and cranked in the water from the upper reach. It burst through in amber sheets, roaring and kicking up a storm of spray, heady with a stagnant fragrance. It raced past the cruiser's bows until it was impossible to tell which was really moving. His scientist demon was going on about Einstein, wagging his finger and saying:

'In the absence of a fixed point, all motion is relative.'

But Harry was holding the cruiser against the side with his foot on a capstan and the spray in his face. He was Charlie Allnutt in *The African Queen*, raging down the Ulanga, his heart pounding under his notebook full of appointments.

'Bollocks to Einstein!'

The storm subsided and the boat rose the last few inches in serene calm. The thin man still puffed and blew anxiously even after Harry had towed him out of the lock and onto the still upper reach.

'OK? That's the last up lock. They're all down from now on. OK?'

But the thin man made no attempt to hide his distress. He stood at the helm doing an incontinent dance on the floorboards. Harry tried to reassure him.

'You'll be alright. It's all downhill now.'

'Come with me,' he blurted out, and then trying to retrieve some dignity. 'If you can. Just to the marina. If you're going that way. I'm not really up to this yet.'

It suddenly occurred to Harry that if Jo had instituted a search for him along the canal bank, then the boat might be the safest place for him. He smiled at the thin man and at his own cunning, then stepped aboard and shoved off in one smooth movement: Lord Jim, racing to provision a trader in the Malacca straights. The howler monkeys screamed their applause.

Once they were under way, the thin man stopped his nervous gambolling and calmed a little. He still gripped the wheel with white knuckles, peering occasionally over his shoulder to Harry, blowing out sorry little puffs of breath and smiling excruciatingly, but never speaking.

Harry sat in the stern well, trailing his hand in the cool water. The tropical sun beginning to burn his cheeks. He studied the back of the thin man who jerked the wheel inexpertly from side to side and thought of asking him why he tortured himself like this. But something was distracting him. His mind was going back to the morning again.

He had left the bathroom and gone back into the bedroom and begun to dress, listening to the news on the radio alarm. He smiled at the increased unemployment figures and then shook his head gravely in the mirror and practised:

'I take no comfort in these disastrous figures.'

He would have to work that into his speech in the YMCA. The local paper wouldn't take a press release, Tory bastards that they were, but he could get it in through his speech.

The cruiser ploughed through a weeping willow. Its branches rattled over the superstructure and trailed through the stern well where the thin man grappled with them like serpents.

'Go on! Fuck off! Go on!'

Harry watched him trying to shoo them out of the boat and then drifted back to the morning.

Peggy had laid out his polling day clothes before going to America. There was a new Party tie in red silk and two dazzling white shirts, one for changing into before the count, folded neatly on the dressing table. He dressed carefully in the mirror, practising fragments of speeches.

'I am convinced that Britain will reject the selfish philosophy of Toryism.'

Or should that be Tory philosophy? More direct.

'Labour means business!'

Jo had drummed it into him that he had to finish off with the national slogan at every opportunity, whether it was appropriate or not.

'Labour means business!'

He tried it with an aggressive thump on the dressing table and tried to look like Mussolini, but it was not really his style.

'It would be rash of me to promise...'

A cunning prefix that. Peggy had translated it as,

'We haven't a fucking clue what will happen.'

'It would be rash of me to promise,' the radio said.

It was the Party leader in pre-recorded discussion with a Government minister. Harry felt a little thrill of exaltation, which, mixed with the solvent fumes that gasped from the plastic bag of his freshly dry-cleaned suit, made him quite dizzy. He nodded and nodded his approbation of the leader's speech. How homogeneous they had become at the Party-electorate interface. Hermetic.

'What you mean,' interrupted the Tory, 'is you haven't a clue what the effects of your policies would be...'

Harry smiled and nodded and then hurriedly frowned and shook his head into the mirror.

'No, no, no! Not at all. The structural damage done to Britain's manufacturing base by this Government will not be easy to...'

'...Repair,' the leader finished off. 'But we are confident that the electorate will endorse our realistic programme of industrial regeneration. They know that Labour means business.'

Harry swelled with pride and optimism, although his euphoria was marred by the nagging fear that whilst he was quite as clever as the leader, the leader was no cleverer than him. Not that that mattered, at all. They were going to win, and that was all that mattered.

Trying to avoid another willow, the thin man ran the cruiser aground on a shingle bank and Harry had to pull himself out of his remembering to shove them off with the boat hook. The thin man did a little dance of thanks on the boards and Harry went back to the morning.

He had finished dressing and then struggled to fix a red rose into his lapel. It seemed to resist him consciously. In the distraction of trying to coax it in he drifted into objectivity as he listened to the rest of the debate. The leader seemed to be getting into one blind alley after another, resorting to saying, 'Labour means business,' at every impasse. A sharp young PR man at a regional seminar in Leeds had told Harry that every time the slogan was used on prime time TV, five thousand votes went in the can. He wondered, now, if the leader's strategy was simply to repeat the slogan, regardless of context. In lieu of a straight answer that might have committed him to something. His demon, of course, had already estimated the rate of vote generation as sixty-two per second on slogan repeating alone and was announcing the running total as the debate progressed. Harry nodded to himself, impressed. He continued to struggle with the rose, sneering, tutting or smiling at the contributions. At the end of the piece he had managed to get the rose into his lapel but found himself nodding along with the Tory. He switched off the radio and shuddered. It was not the first time recently that things like this had happened. He had been enjoying the *Daily Telegraph*, for instance. Not that these little dissents need be debilitating. They could be a strengthening experience if put into perspective. According to the PR man in Leeds.

The day had soon got into full flow. There were answerphone messages of good luck from Peggy and one each from both their sons. There was a long letter from his daughter and three identical death threats from a Russian émigré, new to fax machines. He had breakfasted in high spirits.

They were motoring easily now down the middle of the canal and the thin man took the opportunity to lean against the side of the cabin and wipe the sweat off his face with a rag.

'Hot enough for yer then? Buggered if I can remember when it were so hot.'

Harry could remember. It was a scorching Bank Holiday Monday on the Lea at Broxbourne, just after Suez. He was rowing a girlfriend under willows then. What was her name? Without any warning a cold hand in the water grasped his and almost pulled him out of the cruiser. He sprang forward onto his knees, cradling his hand in his lap, afraid to look at it, gasping for air. The blood drained from his face and he breathed quickly in an attempt to stave off fainting.

The thin man looked back at him in distress and gave a little squeak. Harry laid back in the seat and closed his eyes. Insanity loomed up in front of him, wailing like a ghost-train ghoul. His legs turned to jelly. He felt faint again. Or was it not the ghost of the past but the touch itself? In its instant it had been cool and sensual. It had brought the taste of her, but not her name, back to his tongue like a kiss. The terror that had shaken the welds of his philosophy at dawn returned. Ideas were breaking out of their cells in his brain. Anarchic thoughts ran everywhere, storming the Bastille of his reason. No, surely that was an unsuitable metaphor for a socialist. He groaned out loud.

They were passing under an iron bridge that marked the end his constituency. He ran an eye over it for traces of the fly-posters that had caused so much trouble earlier in the campaign, anxious to anchor his mind on the banal. Then he noticed Legrand whom Jo had posted on the bridge to look for him. Legrand was lounging on the rail, reading a rolled up novel and smoking instead. Harry had talked with him the previous day. He was an enigmatic man: an ex coal miner from Barnsley with an unexplained French name. Now a brilliant but cynical academic researching into obscure labour history in Bradford. He had told Harry:

'Before you go down to Westminster Harry, you and Peggy go for a drive in the Dales, or wherever you fancy retiring, and pick out a nice little cottage there. Let that be your goal, otherwise you'll be terribly disappointed in Parliament.'

Harry had smiled at such cynicism with his legendary fortitude. Legrand had been proud of him. Now it seemed a hundred years ago.

On the tow path a couple of Young Socialists with their earnest Trotskyist secretary were poking about in the bushes and shouting 'Not here!' to one another. So Harry slipped down onto the boards with the oily ropes and looked at the sky passing. He felt the latticed shade of the iron bridge trickle over his cheeks and saw Legrand from the soles of his feet as he gave a glance down the canal between turning pages. But he knew he was safe where he was: they would never think of checking a passing boat. He was struck by the aptness of the metaphor. They were poking about the towpath of history. He almost called it out to the young Trotskyist who would have appreciated the joke, but instead he noted it for use in the Great Speech.

The thin man's feet shuffled a few steps but he said nothing. Harry lay still in the bottom of the boat until they had passed under the dripping arch of a railway viaduct and then he sat up again, smiling because he realized they would never follow him out of the constituency. Never. No wonder they had been beaten so easily for so long. The thin man looked at him and let out a moaning whistle.

'T'in't a police job, is it?'

'No, no, no!'

Harry assured him, too eagerly perhaps, with three shakings of his smiling head.

'No, nothing like that.'

He looked Harry up and down with frank but kindly suspicion and leaked out a final, sigh of resignation. Harry felt he deserved a fuller explanation, although he knew nothing could ever allay his perennial fears.

'I just need a bit of time, that's all. '

The thin man hitched up his trousers by the crotch and said,

'We can stop for a pint at the Collier's, if you like. I owe you a pint. For all your help, like. We'll see if Harold's there, eh?'

'Yes, why not?'

Harry lay back against the transom. The little outboard massaged him between the shoulders as they chugged to the next lock. He almost put his hand back in the water but thought better of it.

The next lock was down and easy. Just a gentle curtsey onto the lower southbound straight. Then a quiet butting through spangled water to the Collier's Arms where they tied up with other cruisers at a wooden jetty.

Ashore, the thin man gained confidence and led Harry along the boards into a beer garden, sweltering in the afternoon sun. He pointed out an empty table to him.

'There, you get that table there, in the shade, and I'll get the beer. Pint, is it?'

Harry put a thumb up to the suggestion and then sat at the table trying to make a cooling bellows of his shirt. He listened to the dronings of late lunchers and the sugar-tipsy wasps, drunk on spilled lemonade. The droning enticed him into another beer garden. It was a Sunday lunchtime long ago. He was feeling guilty about something. What was it? Something to do with boats. It was coming through clearly now: he was with his father again, and there was his brother Charlie and their mad Uncle Jack. Harry was trying to suck Tizer out of a thick glass bottle through a punctured straw and everyone was laughing. But what were they doing there? He stopped pumping his shirt-bellows and stared through the garden's hedge at the cruisers nodding in the sunlight. They had all been sailing on the gravel pits at Cheshunt. That was it. His uncle had whisked them from the boredom of Sunday morning to the wide breezes of the high seas; sailing in a leaky dinghy he had bought for a tenner in one of his wild extravagances, and now they were all drinking grog and laughing like pirates. All except Harry. They had left the women in the house to cook the lunch and he was feeling guilty about it. And about missing Sunday school, which he had begun to take seriously. A kind of prep school for the angst of the Labour Party, really, looking back. He could even taste in the Tizer the worry that God may have punctured his straw in a kind of perverse, Methodist punishment. Early steps on a slippery slope; all tied up with drinking. The image went suddenly but the guilt remained. He had let Jo down badly. Left her to cope. Women were always left to cope.

To pick up the pieces of tantrums, lay out the corpses of silly warriors, weep for bombed out homes. It was their history. He shuffled uncomfortably on the bench. What madness had resurrected the memory of that Sunday, as fresh as the day it was painted, just to cue feeling guilty? How long would these thoughts be on the loose before they were locked up securely in their cells again?

Jo had had to cope the time the Council leader cracked up and locked himself in his office in the Town Hall for three days. She had convinced the press that he was working on a secret policy strategy for the district elections. Really he was playing *High Noon* over and over again on the video. She had sweetened the night porter, who turned out to be a Labour man anyway, to sneak in food and messages, although no answers came out. She had written the policy document that finally emerged with the red-eyed leader onto the front pages. They had done well in the district elections that year. A triumph for the Council leader who become an MEP shortly after. Jo would cope.

The thin man came back with the beer and with another man. At first glance he looked remarkably like Harry. This man, who must have been drinking inside, winced and blinked in the sunlight, shading his eyes with one hand and groping with the other for Harry's as the thin man made the introductions.

'This is Harold. Er, what's your name?'

'Harry,' he said with automatic honesty and they all shook hands and sat down and sucked the tops off their lukewarm beer.

As Harold grew accustomed to the sunlight he lowered his shielding hand and slowly, hesitantly, recognition dawned on him.

'Harry Beamish? The Labour bloke?'

He seemed to be preparing to tell the whole beer garden. Harry nodded and tried to dampen Harold's voice with little patting gestures near the table top.

'Shhh!'

'Put it there lad. I was out first thing to vote for you myself. I hope you give them a right arseing, lad. I do.'

'Harry Beamish? The Labour bloke in the election?'

The thin man blew a series of soft whistles as he looked from Harold to Harry and back again. He pecked at his beer and then blew more whistles. He was determined to keep the secret but it just burst out of his thin breast.

'He's running away Harold. Buggering off!'

Harry couldn't deny it so he just shrugged and threw himself on their mercy. They drank for a while in a silence that teetered on the brink of hostility. Harry began to sketch out plans for a second flight, although it would be a very public one this time. Then Harold said, simply:

'Had enough then?'

It was said with such sympathy that Harry's throat went dry and he had to moisten it with a swig of beer. They sat in silence again. Harold prepared to speak by unwrapping a new pack of cigarettes and sparking one up with his disposable lighter. He arranged the lighter on the pack and then moved the two carefully into a pre-determined position on the table top, as if he were making a thoughtful chess move.

'Last November,' he began,' six months after I was made redundant, I locked myself in the garage, didn't I, Ernest?'

Ernest closed his eyes and shook his head slowly in remembrance.

'Didn't just lock the door neither, did I Ernest?'

'No you didn't, you daft bugger.'

Harold leaned forward on one elbow and lowered his voice.

'No, I nailed the bastard up with six inch nails. Couldn't face anyone. Bent fucking ends over with my club hammer. I spent about a week in there, didn't I Ernest?'

'Ten days,' the thin man corrected and then, as if at some secret signal, they both began a duet of smokers' cackles that ended with them wheezing desperately, like punctured accordions. Harold had to dry his eyes with a napkin from an uncleared plate and drink half a pint of beer before he could go on.

'I had a pile of old magazines and papers in there and I read them all, although the cat had pissed on them. Aught, you understand, so long as I had something to read and didn't have to think.'

The thin man took their empty glasses and fled inside for more beer. Harold settled on his elbows and stared through the trees at the canal. Harry took the opportunity to look him over. He wondered if anyone of their generation was sane any more and tried desperately not to notice their uncanny resemblance. His demon, however had no intention of passing up such an opportunity. He was pointing out not only their height and build, but their identical baldnesses. And other, subtle similarities, like their shrugs which Harry claimed was Gallic and Peggy insisted was Semitic to bait his prejudices. Even their large front teeth that protruded when they smiled and the green tint to their eyes. The demon made no suggestions, just observations.

'I'm alright now,' Harold said, clenching his fist and biceps in a strong man pose. 'Bit too much of this, I suppose.' He swirled the suds of his beer in the bottom of the glass and held it up to the sunlight.

'But there y'are. I can't complain.'

He stared into the space between him and Harry and went on.

'It's funny really, you and me being here like this. Ironical. I mean we're alike in a lot of ways, aren't we?' He shuffled forward and spread out his hands to make himself clearer.

'I mean we must be about the same age and we're both Labour men, if you see what I mean.'

'Yes, I see what you mean.'

Harold began to develop his theme of irony.

'And here's you with an exciting career opening up and a chance to give them one back and you can't face it, and here's me, well, finished! I'd give my right arm to be in your shoes, I bloody well would.'

He looked Harry in the eye.

'Would you?' Harry asked.

'Too bloody right I would.'

Harold didn't hesitate.

'I'd give the sods down there some stick, so I would. Them toffee-nosed bastards in their red braces.'

He jerked an invisible rope tight between his hands.

'I'd hang them in their braces, if I had my way.'

Harry couldn't stop himself from laughing. He knew it must have seemed rude, but he was stuck by the idea that hanging Yuppies on elastic might be a fitting compromise on capital punishment. Given the Party's current ideological flexibility.

'I'm not bloody joking. Look at me! Fifty year old engineer: finished! There's no other word for it. Finished! On yer bike! Down the road! Don't call us, we'll call you! Your country doesn't need you! Fuckoffski!'

He had dried his throat with passion and now tried to drain the suds from the bottom of his glass but they wouldn't move.

'Investment! That's the problem with this country. Always has been. We tooled up for the Industrial Revolution and we've done anything but re-tool ever since. Now then!'

He put a thumb in his waistband and swirled his empty beer glass.

'And us.' Waving a forefinger between himself and Harry. 'English workers. We're the daftest bastards in the world, so we are. Still think we're a cut above everyone else. Workshop of the world!'

His argument began to disintegrate into slogans.

'Bloody sweatshop of the world would be nearer the mark. Live in shit! Eat shit! Rotten with class and privilege! No wonder they won't have the Social Chapter. Why should they? Trained us to live on shit, they don't need to give us bread even, let alone cake.'

He stopped, aware of encroaching incoherence, and peered into his glass again.

'Even the bloody Spaniards are better off than we are.'

They both nodded sadly at the grass. What more could be said? Even the bloody Spaniards. The words were potent with tribal pride and fears: images of stealthy galleons gathering in the Channel. Loaded with Jesuits, tightening their thumb screws; England undone. Harry was moved with admiration for Harold's oratory. There might even have been a good slogan for the Great Speech in there somewhere had Spain not had a socialist government and England a reactionary one. Not that any of it was his problem any more. But he took a pleasure in Harold's eloquence. Objectively, of course.

The thin man returned, balancing a tray of spilled beers, biting his tongue with concentration. When they were laid safely on the table he let out a long sigh of relief.

'Cheers!'

He plunged his nose into his glass, looking all the time between the other two with terrified eyes. As if he knew exactly what was about to happen.

Harry had never made up his mind on the philosophy that says we cannot think outside our vocabulary. Because, so often, ideas marshalled themselves, on the quiet. Behind the arras of consciousness, before leaping out fully formed. The thin man must have sensed that this was happening now even before Harry did. As Harry leaned forward to speak to Harold he plunged his nose back into his glass, his eyes wild with anxiety.

'You can take my place, if you like,' Harry heard himself saying. He was not really surprised.

'We're almost identical. You said so yourself.'

The thin man exploded. A tempest of beer and foam bursting from his nostrils into the glass. He surfaced and began to cough and gasp desperately into a large grey handkerchief. When he had calmed, Harold turned to Harry and looked him steadily in the eye, a faint smile on his lips fishing for confirmation that it was a joke. Harry stared him out without smiling. Harold began to chuckle softly at the proposition and the thin man, recovered, added his own laughter to the ridicule of the idea. Harry began to smile too.

'Can you do a Cockney accent? Not too strong.'

Harold laughed and slapped the top of his thigh.

'Cawkney accent? Gawd blimey, leave it out mate.'

They all laughed.

'Perfect,' said Harry and shook Harold heartily by the hand. 'You've got the job, congratulations.'

Harold shook with laughter but the thin man just looked from one to the other and breathed in little gulps of air. His face turned waxy yellow under his stubble.

Despite his laughter Harold followed Harry's hand as it reached inside his jacket and took out a flattened cylinder of paper.

'Here's my victory speech. It's word-processed, so you'll be able to read it alright. Not too heavy on the Cockney though, just the vowels. The diphthongs really.'

He was becoming pedantic now and he tried to erase the last words with a waving of his hand.

'Anyhow.'

He slid the speech across the table top. Harold looked at the thin man and roared with laughter until he began to sob. But he read the victory speech anyway with shrewd, tearful, eyes.

'Oh dear me,' he sobbed quietly. 'I only came out for a packet of fags.'

He writhed and cackled in an ecstasy of irony.

Harry looked, smiling approval on Harold's attitude, then took out his pen and began to write on the back of a 'Sorry you were out' leaflet.

'I'll give you this,' he said, just like a doctor writing

out a prescription. Suddenly he felt sure of himself again. He had not felt so sure since he was a boy. Not, ironically, on a day of ironies, since he had joined the Party and begun to take everything with such paralysing seriousness.

He wrote, 'Dear Jo.' Then he paused. He almost wrote, 'I'm sorry,' but it wouldn't have been true so he simply wrote:

'This is Harold, he'll stand in for me. He's a good man, don't take it out on him. Good luck. Love Harry.' He toyed with the idea of reminding her that she had once said all men were the same. But they had been drunk then and rowing and it would have been pretentious, so he let it go. One word was much like another anyway. Simplest was best. Yeas and nays. He folded the leaflet into a taper and wrote 'Jo' in the margin of the printed side.

'Take this note to the Labour Rooms in Union Street. Ask for Jo and give it to her.'

He waved it like a small and threatening stick.

'Only to her. That's important, you understand? Only to her. No-one else must see the note. If you change your mind, destroy it. You understand?'

Harold held one piece of paper in each hand and shook his head slowly between them, a residual chuckle still shaking his belly under his tee shirt. Harry continued, confident all opposition had been overcome.

'Of course, we'd have to swap clothes, but that's no problem, we're about the same size, aren't we?'

He placed his shoulder alongside Harold's to convince him. 'There! We could change now, in the bog.'

He held out an open palm. What could be more reasonable?

Harold made a small pile of the two papers and laid his soft hands flat on the table top, pressing them down hard like a sceptic at a seance, trying to look serious. Twitches of smiles flickered at the corners of his lips.

Suddenly he raised his palms off the table and held them a foot above it. He held them there for a full minute, his face curving into a big grin. Then he brought them down with a crash.

'You're on!'

And he held out his hand for shaking again.

'Good man!' said Harry.

The thin man sat motionless, his wrinkled head rising and turning stiffly as a marionette's from one conspirator to the other. He puffed like a steam engine.

'You'll end up in gaol, the pair of you: daft buggers. The bloody gaol! D'you hear! Members of Parliament! It's probably treason. The bloody Tower you'll end up in!'

They left him at the table with all the guilt and anxiety of the situation crushing the breath out of him in little whimpers and found the one lockable cubicle in the gents' toilets. It was a tight squeeze and neither of them were agile. Taking off their trousers they had to resort to supporting one another with arms across the shoulders while they hopped around the basin on one bare leg each in a sort of lewd Bavarian jig. Their white, hairy flesh was ghastly. Several times they crashed against the door, grunting and puffing. A prim youth was driven to hammer ferociously on the door and shout 'Perverts!' over the top. Harold said,

'So intolerant, young people today.' And they both nodded.

They emerged back into the sunlight. One parliamentary candidate, suitably briefed, complete with red rosette, and, Harry was wounded to see, false smile. One man in jeans and black tee shirt and a handsome bargee's cap; Harry Morgan as ever was. They presented themselves proudly to the thin man who took up one of his jigs beside the table and wailed like a stage spectre.

'Oooo! You'll get done, the pair of you. Why can't you do things properly?' He stopped jigging and looked accusingly at Harold in a last attempt to shame him to his senses.

'I'm surprised at you Harold. He's an MP.'

He paddled the air towards Harry with deprecating fingers.

'But you're an engineer.'

It was no good. Harold had the bit between his teeth now. Harry's suit had transformed him. He was smoothing out the pleats in his rosette with an engineer's precision and saying loudly, as if a latent and now unrestrainable music hall artist had been awakened in him:

'Well it's been nice meeting you chaps and thanks for your support.'

He shook hands limply with them and beamed falsely at the lingering lunchers who had turned on their elbows to look at him. They seemed ready to vote for him just for breaking the sweltering monotony of the day.

'Must go now, more babies to kiss. Ha, ha!'

And aside to Harry, quite seriously,

'You haven't forgotten to vote?'

What a wag! The whole beer garden was laughing with him. He would make a wonderful MP. Harry and the thin man followed him to the car park and waved him off in a rusty Morris. Someone shouted,

'Good luck 'arry!' with great warmth and Harry felt a small pang of regret at being out of it all. But on the heels of regret trod the feeling of relief that he had discharged his obligations to Jo. Harold was the sound Labour man of their myths. What more could they want?

Harry turned to the thin man who was shrinking from the burden of it all, tightening his belt as if he had actually lost weight in the ordeal. He put his arm round him and said, plaintively,

'Please don't worry. It's not your fault, and anyhow it doesn't matter.'

'Not to you, I can see that. But it matters to me.'

He swilled down the last of his beer with a grimace and took a step back towards the jetty. Then he stopped and turned to Harry. He was holding up three stiff fingers which he folded down, one at a time.

'I vote Labour. My parents voted Labour. And, fuck me, their parents voted Labour. Now then!'

'But they're all the same, Ernest!'

Harry stunned himself with the words and stood looking into his hands. As if the argument he had been in a tug of war with all his life had finally let go and left him holding the incontestable truth. The thin man was looking at him with contempt. Harry lashed out guiltily.

'Don't look at me like that. I've given my bloody life to the movement, I have. And I've had it up to here. Let Harold do his bit instead of talking about it. He's a Labour man too, you know. So are you for that matter.'

The thin man groaned; he had gone too far. He had heaped another worry on a man made of them.

'I'm sorry.'

The thin man looked at him with wet eyes. Harry began to waffle to stem the flood of tears that were threatening.

'Think of it as doing jury service. Yes, like jury service.'

He began to ad lib a great constitutional amendment as they both walked slowly back to the boat.

'All members of the House of Commons could be called up off the electoral roll like jurors'

He nudged the thin man's elbow, trying to include him in the argument, cheer him up.

'It's an idea Ernest, isn't it? Couldn't be any worse, could it? What do you think?'

The idea was beginning to appeal to Harry and he half expected a serious answer.

'You daft bugger,' said the thin man, nodding towards his little cruiser.

'Come on, I can take you as far as the marina. I'm tying up there but you can walk or get a bus to Sheffield. I suppose you're going to London.'

The thin man seemed calmer after the lunchtime drink, despite all the traumas that had attended it. He still puffed out little gaps of breath and peered anxiously at the canal ahead but he had stopped his jigging. The land was flatter and they cruised along quite serenely, unbothered by locks. The outboard hummed steadily and the sun stirred clouds of insects over the water.

So he was going back to London. He looked down at his new clothes: a crumpled black tee shirt, faded denims and incongruous dress shoes. Hardly the triumphant return. But then they were all gone who had waved him off. There was no-one there to notice even.

A wave of self pity rushed over him. He tried to struggle against it but it settled on his clothes: he began to lament the passing of his suit. It was the first decent suit he had bought in thirty years. God knows he had bought few enough clothes. All the jumble sale clothes of his life danced before his eyes in a macabre, clothes-line jig. Tears welled up. He had never been smart or fashionable. He had always dressed in end-of-line separates from sales. So that sometimes his bottom half and sometimes his top half, but never all of him, was in fashion. Early in the campaign the Tories had crudely lampooned him in a leaflet as a stumbling scarecrow. Very low, that had been and not helped by Jo framing one of them and hanging it in her office. But he would have the last laugh on the bastards. Their chief executive would have to announce his victory tonight with bitter pomp and ceremony. And all the time he would be strolling along a canal bank in the cool summer night, free as a scarecrow. Nevertheless, the passing of his suit rankled.

He would have to buy new clothes. To return to the ghosts of his boyhood not an MP was no dishonour. But to return a tramp, that was another matter. He reached for his credit card holder, which, of course, was now in Harold's back pocket. True to his bargain, however, Harold had left all his money in the pocket of his denims.

It came to ten pounds fifty-seven pence. Ten pound eleven and six in old money. That was less than he had left London with thirty years earlier. Nothing had really changed. Change; there it was again.

'Change,' his demon said, 'is a figment of reality. Your soul is a rock in a river of time, washed by its passing but essentially unchanged.'

No, that was bollocks. He had read it somewhere when very drunk and it had taken advantage of his memory's defencelessness to insinuate itself. Harry was a scientist, he was not confused about the nature of time. He had once sat cross legged on a laboratory bench and asked a bright new set of sixth form chemists,

'Does time define change or change define time?'

He could remember grinning donnishly and waiting for an answer. An ambitious smart alec had pointed out that they only had two years to cover the course and suggested that they start straight away. The kid had gone to Oxford. He found himself gazing back on the scene with a soppy grin, wondering whether he would ever teach chemistry to young people again. Whether he would ever again scrape little magnetic discs around the board, passing them off as atoms. The sadness of things past crowded in on him like faces at a window. With no warning, the face of a girl he had once met in France appeared at the window. She was smiling with the coyness of a past age. It was a memory of unbearable innocence from a time when he had wandered through France without a care, the girls whistling after him as he walked through their villages. The memory had been safely locked up for thirty-five years, but now it was out on the loose, untarnished. He had simply stood with her under a big tree, sheltering from a summer storm, shyly exchanging cigarettes. And here she was again still wearing the perfume of rain and road dust as fresh as... Harry held his head in his hands and, for the first time since the Coronation, he cried.

'Too bloody late for tears lad. You've done it now. That Harold's a mad bastard. He'll go through with it.'

The thin man looked at him and raised a forefinger in warning. 'He's not daft, neither. Reads bloody books all the time. He's been to the Open University. Oh aye.'

He shook his head with gleeful doom and to emphasize the danger, he repeated, like a death knell, the one word:

'Books!'

Harry wiped his eyes on his tee-shirt and composed himself with deep breaths. The crying seemed to have flushed out the sadness, leaving him with an a taste of optimism. A medicinal taste: not well but on the mend. He even put his hand back in the canal and rubbed his arms and head in cooling water.

They could see the marina now at the end of a long straight. The thin man relaxed his grasp on the wheel and sat on the side, steering with one hand and looking out along the side of the boat. The breeze of their moving rustled his grey hair. He seemed almost peaceful.

'Why do you do this?' Harry asked.

The thin man looked at him puzzled. Harry immediately regretted the question. He wanted to know why he tortured himself with the task of sailing. But he should have left him in his brief peace. He tried to modify the question.

'I mean, you've got a job on sailing this single handed. Those locks are a two-man job, really.'

The thin man wasn't fooled.

'I know. I make a prat of myself, but I'll get the hang of it.'

He squinted into the breeze like an old salt. After a minute or two he went on.

'My Elsie was the sailor. Knew all about boats.'

He nodded at the jumble on the boards.

'Kept it Bristol fashion when she was alive, Elsie. She came from Hull y'see. Died in January. Made me promise to get the boat out in Spring and sail it.'

He stood up at the wheel again and turned his back on Harry to save them both embarrassment.

'We've had some times on this boat.'

They said no more until the boat was moored securely at its berth on the new Enterprise Quay. The quay had been opened by the Prince of Wales and local civic toadies, including the Tory candidate, just before the election had been called. Suspicious, that had been. The old anger began to smoulder in him. The thin man disconnected the petrol tank from the outboard and locked it in the cabin.

'Some thieving sods round here.'

He said the words apologetically from inside the little cabin, as if Harry had been a visitor from some sheltered neighbourhood. 'Here, take this.'

He squeezed back out of the cabin and handed Harry a blue nylon bundle which uncurled in his arms like a waking cat. It was an old coat, sprouting white filling from the cuffs and arm pits. 'I know it's hot now but it'll be cold tonight. You could be glad of that.'

They stood quietly in the sunshine, looking at the dazzling boats tugging at their mooring ropes along the quay. Harry still fumed inwardly over the name. A few yards of chippings, a badly fitting coat of paint smeared on by unemployed kids doing a stretch on some work scheme. Enterprise Quay in six foot high letters and then photo after photo of the Tory candidate and the Prince of Wales beside it. All over his election literature, they had been. Bloody good photos too. Not that it was Harry's constituency, nor his problem any more: it was just the inertia of the campaign, running on.

'Enterprise, bloody, Quay!' Harry snorted.

The thin man was rolling his shirt sleeves down and buttoning up the grubby cuffs. He nodded at each of the boats individually.

'Most of these were bought with redundancy money when Helliwell's went. Quay Giro, Harold calls it.'

He unbuckled his belt and began to repack his shirt tail into his trousers.

'*Key Largo*, see? Harold's a big Bogey fan.'

He turned away from Harry and began to work on a cramp in his arm, whirling it around like an aeroplane's propeller.

'I'm going for a bit of tea now. You... if you like...'

'No, no, no. Thanks.'

Harry was very definite and the thin man looked relieved and offered him his hand.

'Well good luck Harry. It's been er. You're a daft bastard.'

'Thanks Ernest.'

They crunched off in opposite directions on the tow path's new chippings, the thin man shaking his head.

There was a good long straight now, leading south into mining country. Harry began to step it out briskly, almost trotting in his anxiety to flee the election.

'You cannot flee the election,' his demon was saying. 'It is a general election. It is all around you. You are part of it.'

But he was in no mood to argue and broke into a shambling run, elbowing the demon off his back, blindly determined to get on.

A mile into the country, he slowed to a strolling pace and regained his breath. He was feeling more secure now, ready to take on his demon.

'You are quite wrong,' he began. 'I simply quit. I quit because...'

But the sun stirred up the fetid aroma of maggots from an angler's bait box and he was suddenly back with his brother Charlie, fishing in Epping Forest. They were squatting at the margins of a dried-up pond, trying to avoid the putrid mud, sharing a tiny dog-end Charlie had impaled on a thorn. Carefree. There had been an election on then too. It must have been the fifty-five one because Harry's mother had made them both do a bit of leafleting for their local candidate. That was the last year Charlie had been at home. Their mother had introduced them to the candidate at the committee rooms in the Co-op: a big man in pin striped trousers and a black jacket. He had a very posh accent and an upper lip stained orange with snuff. And a twenty thousand majority. After he explained about his majority they stuffed most of his leaflets down a manhole and went fishing. Nevertheless he had managed to win. He even went on to become a minister for something very boring in the sixties. They had been the days to be a Labour MP. Just the occasional hand-shake with awestruck Party workers, women contentedly making the tea, ethnic minorities uninvented. Away on the horizon thunder rumbled and he began to feel guilty about the comfort of the memory. But he was jogged out of his memories by the arrival of an old man and his dog. The pair of them seemed to rise out of the dock leaves by the tow path. The man ran to catch Harry and skipped into step beside him.

'Bugger me, eh! I said, bugger me!'

He mopped his forehead with a handkerchief and then tromboned into it down his bulbous, broccoli coloured nose.

'Jip!'

The dog gasped onto the tow path, its tongue hanging out in the heat.

'Bugger me, it's hot.'

Harry smiled what he hoped was a thin and discouraging grin in reply. Encouraged, the man moved closer and synchronized their steps.

'Hot! I don't think I've known it this hot since I were in Egypt. Now that were hot, lad.'

He cleared his throat and gobbed into the brambles.

'I worked there. Over there! '

He swept his stick up across Harry's chest and pointed at a mill with bricked-up windows and elderberries growing in its gutters.

'Thirty-four year I did there. From being demobbed in forty-five while that cow came to power in seventy-nine. That's thirty-four year, innit?' Retired just before the redundancies came round. Got fuck all.'

He spiked a passing carrier bag with his stick and tossed it over his shoulder.

'Have you been to vote yet?'

Harry toyed with the idea of simply ignoring the old man and striding on, but he could not bring himself to do it. Instead he slowed down so that he could catch up.

'Yes, first thing this morning.'

The man's eyes were full of tears and he was holding the whole of his chest in a hand's span, gasping for breath as he shuffled along.

'Well I hope you voted Labour,' he gasped. ' Get these bastards out.'

Harry nodded silently to him and he slew a few wild raspberry canes with his stick in a sort of muted triumph. They walked on quietly for a while, the dog loping behind, nosing in tin cans and peeing up tree trunks.

'The Labour bloke where I vote's a southerner.'

He jerked a thumb over his shoulder, back along the canal to Harry's constituency.

'Oh aye?' said Harry, in his best Yorkshire accent.

'Aye. Teacher or something. Knows nowt, of course. But what else can you do? There in't a lot between them all I don't expect.'

'No, I don't suppose there is.'

Harry agreed and the spring seemed to go out of their steps. They trudged along like a retreating proletarian army, grimly held by the ghost of a lost cause. Suddenly the old man confided in him.

'I'll tell you the trouble with this world, shall I? This world, nowadays.'

He indicated which world by drawing an arc over it with his stick.

'There's t'many...'

He fiddled the air with wriggling fingers for the word, '...t'many...Things! Now then!'

They marched on in step, chewing on this philosophy.

'When we were wed in thirty-eight lad, we had a bed, a table and four chairs and that were it. Now then.'

He looked at Harry who was on the verge of telling him that when he and Peggy were married in the sixties, they had rather less, but he let it go in the interests of making progress.

'Aye, that were it. Apart from that we had nowt. Look!' He put his stick under his arm, and making a begging bowl of his broken hands he nodded desperately into its emptiness.

'There lad, there. We had nowt. Wed in thirty-eight. Now then, listen, because you'll not believe this. You don't know. Wed in thirty-eight, right? Forty while forty-five in forces. Now listen.'

He held Harry by the forearm with gentle fingers as they slowed to a standstill.

'There'd been a Labour Government in two year before we got a bit of carpet for the front room. Now then! Bloody nigh ten year for a bit of carpet. And look there!'

A bridge carried a track over the canal to a domestic tip where a huge red Axminster was spread over a jumble of televisions and tumble driers.

'There y'are, look! Now that can't be right, can it lad? Cheerio!'

And aware that he would never make a clearer point, the old man started over the bridge, waving his stick in the air without turning around.

'Jip!'

The dog limped after him. An American politician had once said something about 'things' being in the saddle of history. He had read it in a book.

'Too many fucking books, you read.'

Charlie was putting right a bit of Harry's bad pipework: undoing a jammed nut.

'Karl Marx and you can't screw a fucking nut on without cross-threading the bastard. Go and make the fucking tea.' Harry had suspected, even then, that Marx would have had no use for a worker who couldn't screw nuts on straight. But he had stirred up the tea with visions of his people in power. Always vague visions. Not like Russia, of course, far too cold, but then not like anywhere else. Like...well that was the problem.

The sun hammered down, fanning the dust over his shoes and jeans. He was Fred C Dobbs in *Sierra Madre*, staggering down to Derango, wild with gold fever. He looked up at the Tory-blue sky and wondered how Harold was getting on.

Chapter 3

Harold found the Labour Rooms in Union Street easily enough, emblazoned, as they were, with Harry's posters and buzzing like a beehive with the coming and going of Party workers. He went in gingerly through the open door against a tide of number-takers and runners who all waved long thin strips of coloured paper at him and smiled at his red tie. Nobody asked what he wanted. He wandered from room to room looking for someone who might be Jo. Spotting a sign for 'Agent' pointing up some stairs, he found her alone at her desk in a quiet office.

She took the folded note he handed her and read it in silence, without expression. Then she got up and closed the office door quietly on them both. She looked at Harold and a smile rippled at the corner of her mouth. He responded with a beam of his own.

'Men!'

She roared and brought her fist down so hard on the desk that the telephone leapt off and hung, strangled by its cord. The answer-phone began to play her own tranquil voice, mocking her.

'Hello, this is the Labour Hotline. I'm afraid there's no-one in the office at present but...'

She smashed the machine to cogs and broken pieces with her fist.

'Men! Men! Men!'

Harold began to back towards the door. He had rashly thought that he was doing the Party a favour, like putting up a garden poster: they had always been so grateful for that.

'Stand still!'

She walked round him slowly, eyeing him up and down.

'Pull your shoulders back, he doesn't stoop that badly. What am I saying? Get out! How dare you!' And then.

'Stand still!'

She stopped behind him and Harold grew suddenly cold as he felt her heavy breathing, transmitted through the floorboards to the soles of his feet.

'I'll kill him! I might kill you! You wanted to take his place.'

She turned and punched the door so hard that it sprang open and quivered on its hinges. It seemed to vent her anger. When she continued it was in a business-like voice.

'Say, "I would like to thank the returning officer and his staff".'

Harold cleared his throat.

'I would like to thank the returning officer and his staff.'

'Oh for Christ's sake!'

Hearing footsteps on the stairs she tried to slam the door shut but her punch had broken the catch and it hung ajar.

'Are you fucking serious about this, or what?'

A circle of weasel faces stared in through the gap in the door but no-one dared go in. She walked round him and her desk in a wide ellipse, grunting.

'Hmm!'

After a few orbits she stopped by the desk, opened a drawer and handed Harold a pair of sunglasses.

'Put these on. OK, now say in a husky voice, "I would like to thank the returning officer and his staff".'

'I would like to thank...'

'OK, OK.'

She made a few more orbits and then stopped in front of him.

'Listen,' she said, waving a paper knife. 'This is what you do.'

Chapter 4

Harry made good time after he left the old man and his dog. By eight he had left the Pennines and was walking eastward into flat mining country with the sun on his back. It was a dreary place with hardships showing through the threadbare soil in gashes of coal slag. It was the heart of Labour's power. Once it had been their fist, but no more. On a picket line, during the great strike, a miner had asked Harry if he was a miner himself. Harry had laughed and held his soft, teacher's hands out before him.

'Do they look like miners' hands?' he asked.

'Do they?'

The miner showed him his own hands, soft with a year's idleness, the doom of their tribe in them.

Near a village of grey council houses, he found himself standing on an aqueduct, high over a road that ran under the canal in a tunnel. Somewhere in the distance a loudspeaker was forlornly urging people to vote Conservative. Below a group of Labour Party workers were flapping around their own loudspeaker van, fumbling with the wrong bits of paper, accusing each other of incompetence as the minutes ticked away. Harry leaned on the rusty guard rail and watched the show from the gods. He glanced at his watch: eight ten, one hour and fifty minutes to the close of polls. He knew this time well. Knowing it was part of him. It was the time Labour Governments were lost to soap operas on the telly. In this time a young woman for whom he had offered to baby-sit while she went to vote had stood in her doorway, nodded at the screaming kids and asked him, unexpectedly:

'Is this what you mean by getting more women involved in politics?'

She had voted, of course. For some toe rag who joined the Democrats, as it happened. He could feel the shame coming back into his cheeks. Below, an open row had developed.

'Fuck the lists man, just knock 'em out. They're all ours anyway...'

'Oh, right. Just knock 'em out. Why not abandon canvassing altogether?'

'Right! Right! That's a good idea.'

'Shit!'

A fight seemed likely to break out but from under the bridge. A big, simple lad, whom Harry could tell from ancient instinct had been sent on an errand to get him out of some committee rooms, shuffled up on heavy boots and said, breathlessly,

'Quick, back to the committee rooms.'

They all crammed into the van and disappeared into the tunnel beneath his feet. The row continued, unwittingly amplified for the whole polling district.

'Agent! Agent! You couldn't organize a fuck in a whorehouse!'

'Bollocks!'

'Your candidate's a wanker, anyway.'

'Wanker, is he?'

'Aaagh!'

The van rocked with internal violence as it passed a handsome middle aged couple, strolling, hand in hand, back from the polls. They shook their heads in pious despair. Harry pressed on, shaking his head too. He had never understood miners.

As he left the village behind him the canal began to turn southwards in a wide arc. The thunderstorm that had been grumbling all day in the distance loomed like an angry sack over the fields. It let out chilly gasps of air, flecked with raindrops. He took up shelter in the doorway of a derelict lock-keeper's cottage that had an iron map of the canal system as far south as the Thames bolted to its wall. Hard to make out under the mud and flakes of rust, but he got it into his head that if he didn't dawdle, he could make it to the outskirts of Doncaster before the pubs shut. Nottingham the next day and the Grand Union the next. He might make it to within a mile or so of Charlie's place in Tottenham. Although this was not quite clear, a trek across a bit of Hertfordshire might be needed.

A clear plan seemed to be forming in his sub-conscious. It was urging him to get a move on. He looked out anxiously at the cloud which was hanging about a hundred yards away, blackening the canal. Now that he could see it close up, it seemed to boil with purple rage. The idea flashed in Harry's brain that it contained the wrath of God. Waiting to fall on the Sodom and Gomorrah, Tory-voting South while the Labour North basked in its innocent sunshine. It would have made a great political picture, very symbolic, a nice little target leaflet for the Methodist vote.

Harry dithered in the doorway trying to decide whether or not to make a run for it. The rain was light and refreshing but the cloud looked angry. He was physically frightened by it. What he needed to know was how big it was. He tried to conjure up his estimating demon to do some calculations for him, comparing the light intensity of the shadows and the sunshine. Something like that; but it refused to get involved. All his good sense told him to shelter until it had blown over but the urge to get on shoved him out into the shower. Pulling his cap down tight, Harry made a run for it.

He got about half a mile through the chilly air when the storm exploded around him. He was drenched to the underpants in seconds. Soaked beyond caring, he had decided to enjoy the anarchy of it all. To slosh through the puddles. But a barrage of painful hailstones drove him under an elder bush for shelter. He crouched there, with Ernest's jacket pulled over his head and watched the lightning while his calves knotted slowly with cramps. There was so much symbolism in storms. Probably just his own Methodist upbringing, of course, but he could definitely see a symbol of human society there. Blocking out the sun and then compensating with its own faulty lighting. Just like politics, that was. Just like a politician to notice it. He noted it all for the Great Speech. Tidy it up later.

Chapter 5

By half past nine most of the canvassers, knockers-up, number-takers, runners, poster pasters, drivers and spies had called it a day and made their way back to the Rooms in Union Street. A few socialist zealots were still out, running it to the line, but the old hands who wanted the first pints off the celebration barrels and a good view of the television were already round the bar swapping stories and prophesying a historic victory. The consensus was good. They had won the seat back, no doubt about that. Whether the millstone South would drag them down again remained to be seen from the telly. But they had done their bit alright. Won their bit of the line. And with a bloody good MP. The People's Choice, as Jo had succeeded in labelling him. Whatever the South did, they'd have Harry to give them some stick in Westminster. Good old Harry, who never flagged or doubted.

'Where is Harry?' someone asked.

Upstairs, in the agent's office, Jo had called the Party officers together for a briefing. The leader of the Council Group, already drunk, turned up with a bottle of whisky and waved it around in a general invitation. She toyed with the idea of throwing him out but settled instead for telling him, very quietly, to close the door. They all knew that something was wrong, but no-one dreamed... Jo came straight to the point.

'Harry's run away...'

A vice-chair began to laugh. She let him laugh it out into silence so that no-one would be in any doubt.

'...But he's left us this look-alike.'

Everyone stared in horror at the imperfect pseudo-Harry, simpering nervously beside her. Jo half hoped that somebody, perhaps the limply upright chairman, would put his foot down and insist on the truth being told at once. But he didn't. Everyone waited for her to take the initiative.

'This is what I have decided to do.'

She looked from face to face of the children whose party it had fallen to her to spoil and then she went on quickly.

'First, I'm judging that I can get Harry back. Second, it's going to be close. Close locally and very, very close nationally. Third, we couldn't face the kind of by-election a fuck-up like this would produce. So...'

She sighed and laid her hands flat on the desk.

'...We're going to run Harold here until I can find Harry and bring him back. The story is that Harry's gone down with hay fever. Nice green angle there, could develop into ME, I suppose, if we're pushed.'

She began to drift off into a tactical trance but pulled herself back to the nightmare of reality.

'He can only appear in dark glasses and croak a few words of a victory speech. I'll handle that. He cannot see anyone. Anyone, understand! The Party outside this room must not know. I expect discipline on this.'

She waved her paper knife at everyone in turn until they nodded their oath.

'Heather, you take Harold to your place and keep him there until I pick him up for the count. OK, clear everyone?'

Nobody made a move or sound.

'Are you fucking politicos, or am I on my own here?'

Big nods all round.

'OK, go and put the word out.'

Chapter 6

By half past ten, with the polls well and truly closed, Harry was suddenly gripped with a voyeur's lust to watch the whole thing on the telly. The idea of sitting in a comfortable pub and watching events unfold from a safe and anonymous distance grew until it throbbed. Like a sexual desire. He even felt a petulant anger that there was no pub immediately at hand and began to regret those he had passed so casually. The beautiful evening, with the sun setting over Doncaster and the aroma of wild garlic in the hedges by the tow path, suddenly became tiresome to him. He felt exhausted by so much fresh air and oppressed by the emptiness. His wet clothes began to chill him and he longed to sit down in a brightly lit pub. He began a heavy jog, exaggerating the dragging of his feet in self pity. After a couple of hundred yards he grew bored by the rhythm of his jogging and began to practise dragging one foot like Lon Chaney as the Frankenstein monster. Then, swinging his right arm so his knuckles almost scraped the ground he did Charles Lawton as Quasimodo. He even stuck his tongue to his palate and hooted, to add verisimilitude:

'The bells! The bells!'

Quite reprehensibly disablist, of course, but he carried on until he almost ran into a young couple kissing in the shadows of a bridge. The lovers fled, white faced, with a snapping of elastic and a zipping of zips. Harry had no option but to jog on chanting,

'The bells!'

No explanation even began to suggest itself to him.

Mercifully, a copse of tall trees and a bend in the canal obscured him from the lovers. After a short walk he came to the Fullers' Arms. He stood on the cinders of the pub's car park and breathed deeply to cool his embarrassment. It was a quiet little inn with a few expensive cars outside. From its open windows Harry could hear a *Newsnight* presenter saying something about a close, a very, very close finish. It seemed ideal for his purpose. He went in.

In the saloon bar everyone's attention was riveted to a big television on the wall. Harry crept in and stood at the bar like a latecomer to a meeting. He pointed to the bitter tap and was quietly hissed a pint , half of which he drank straight off before leaning on the bar to watch the television beside a plump and gently swaying woman wearing too much jewellery.

The news presenter, shiny with expectation, was bouncing a sheaf of papers on his desk and listening to an earphone as the cameras panned in on him. A fanfare of brass. He put down the papers and rubbed his hands with the relish of a biblical scholar about to unroll the Dead Sea Scrolls.

'Well! with the polls now closed and counting already begun in some urban constituencies, *Newsnight's* exit poll is forecasting the closest finish in a general election since the war, with the possibility, and I must stress that the exit poll is conducted on a limited sample of voters as they leave the polls, the possibility of an unprecedented dead heat between the Tories and Labour. Exciting stuff...'

The prognosis, with all its implications, caused Harry to give a little start and slop some of his beer on the tiles with a loud smack. The woman beside him turned and leaned her head back into several chins to try to focus him. She looked him up and down slowly with either lust or contempt. He could not quite decide.

'The excitement.'

He simpered apologetically. She ignored him and lifted another gin from the bar.

Closing time came and went without ceremony. Excitement mounted as the city seats raced to be the first to declare. Harry gave another little start when he saw his own constituency lit up as a possible Labour gain.

Lady Thatcher came on, said to be tired, but really drunk, Harry fancied. She drawled on patronizingly about the will of the people. The woman became animated at the sight of her and turned, in lieu of anyone else, to Harry. She gestured at the screen with her glass and Harry could see her own resemblance to Thatcher: the thin, sadistic lips, the mousey prettiness. Magically attractive. He had once said, when drunk, admittedly, that she owed her popular success more to sado-masochism than to monetarism, but no-one had taken him seriously.

'Maggie Thatcher, said the woman. 'A shit!'

Harry raised his glass to the toast. She went on.

'This new bloke. A shit!'

Harry smiled and nodded. She finished her gin and started another with a further toast.

'The Labour bloke. A shit!'

Harry tried to look disapproving.

'And that what's-his-fucking-name. A shit! The lot of them,' she added, ecumenically. 'Shits!'

Then she added as an afterthought, as if she had been too harsh. 'Mind you I don't suppose they're all shits. He's got a nice arse, for instance.'

They were looking at Harry that morning: very sensible and confident, speaking into a microphone. He was saying:

'...No, I am confident that the electors will reject the narrow, selfish philosophy of this Government and vote to be part of a caring community with Labour...'

'Well, Harry Beamish there, in West Yorkshire, confident of victory. We'll be able to go back to his constituency later and see if his confidence was justified.'

A ghost of regret passed over him: to be in there, amongst it all, on St Crispin's Day. But the woman was speaking to him again, leering with a sort of stage lechery.

'He could fill my ballot paper in, any time.'

'Who?'

'Him, Breamish.'

'Beamish.'

Harry had long forgotten, if he ever knew, how to flirt with women, so with some trepidation, he said,
'Bit like me really, don't you think?'
'Who?'
'Beamish.'
'Who's like Beamish?' she asked, obtusely.
'Me.'
'You!'
The idea took some time to sink in and when it did she seemed about to burst into laughter which Harry pre-empted. 'Yes, me. More bloody well like him, than you can imagine.'
'You?'
She sniggered openly.
'You, like him? He's an MP. You're a fucking tramp, man!'
She snorted out the last word in a hoot of derision and then,
'Ha! ha! ha!'
She fog-horned all round the bar, turning heads and setting the brandy glasses humming in sympathy. Harry flashed an angry look at himself in the bar mirror. His cap was plastered low on his brow like an imbecile, his coat was sprouting tufts of filling everywhere. Grey whiskers spiked his sun-red face. He turned his anger at the dilapidation on the laughing woman.
' Tramp am I? You pissy bitch!'
Her laughter shut off in a glottal-stop and she fixed him with sober eyes. Trouble.
'What did you call me?'
She looked more like an implacable Thatcher than ever.
'Do you know who I am? Maurice!' she bawled.
The landlord, mercifully not Maurice, took Harry by the upper arm and whispered,
'You'd better shove off a bit sharpish lad or you'll end up in the fucking canal.'
'Tramp! Tramp!'

She spat at Harry which seemed to calm her: the last word.

'Come on,' said the landlord. 'This is all I need, this is. I'll lose my licence; put the fucking tin lid on today, that would. Go on, on yer bike.'

But Harry dug his heels in obstinately.

'I want to watch the results too.'

'Well watch them somewhere else.'

'Where?'

The landlord was as soft as Harry and as fatally vulnerable to reason. He saw the woman beginning to work herself up again and clasped his own bald head in a trembling hand and whispered, 'Alright, go out and then come in the front, into the public. There's a telly there too. But,' he finished off, crescendo. 'Sod off now!'

Harry went.

'Alright Mrs Tucker. I've sent him packing.'

The landlord tried to sooth her. She turned to him and began to pout, with a wounded air.

'Pissy, he called me. Pissy! Gin please, Derek.'

Harry crept into the public bar, cautiously ordered another pint from the barmaid and sat in huddled contrition to watch the results from the end of a table of young students. They were arguing about the election with flamboyant hand gestures and loud, immodest language. Harry kept his own hands clasped between his knees and tried to watch the television but a beautiful young girl was kindly trying to include him in their discussion.

'What do you think?'

She nodded at him like a senile grandparent to be humoured at Christmas and then lip-mimed her question for him with slow nods of her head.

'Do you think Labour will win?'

Harry was struck dumb by her beauty. He stared at her blond hair and perfect, honey-coloured skin. He was mesmerized by her dimpled smile and the tiny drops of burnished gold that trembled on her ear lobes as she nodded her head to coax an answer.

'The general election. Today. You know.'

He disintegrated. He took off his cap, panicked at the revelation of his shameful baldness, thought of replacing it and ended up wringing its brim between his knees, blushing crimson, stammering.

'I, I, I, I...'

'Ask him if he thinks it will make any difference if they do win,' said a young man, with an ugly hint of cunning in his voice. Everyone laughed and the argument restarted with renewed vigour.

Harry was transported back to a committee room he had visited that morning in the front room of a woman's council house. She must have been about the same age as this girl. But she was a thin, sparrow legged woman, covered in bruises, surrounded by kids all the colours of the human spectrum, threadbare with poverty. There had not been a crumb of the comforts of wealth anywhere in the room. Not one. Not a trace of human frivolity. The poverty had oppressed and revolted him so much that he fled from it at the first opportunity, gasping for air as soon as he was out of her door. She caught him in her front garden as he made his way on tip-toe through the dog turds to his car. She said:

'I'm sorry about the dog shit.'

Then summoning up the courage to put the question she had followed him out to ask.

'When you get down there, will you try and put the Child Benefit up?'

He had nodded silently and shaken her hand.

'They'll put Child Benefit up.'

He threw the suggestion onto the table. The argument jolted to a halt as if he had thrown one of the dog turds onto the table. They all turned frowns on him, even the beautiful young girl. At once he felt guilty of intrusion. A rancorous, vulgar old bugger. He reprieved himself by slopping a little beer over his chin, skirring it off his whiskers with a shaking hand. Then he settled to watch the television. There was Harold, wearing dark glasses, beaming and coughing into a huge handkerchief, his right hand, clamped in Jo's, punching the air victoriously. The crowd took up a chant.

'Harr-y! Harr-y!'

They sang as, invisible to them, a red 'Labour gain', flashed in time, beneath them. The chanting grew louder and on the rostrum Jo and Harold and the falsely beaming returning officer exchanged small, stiff, nodded signals.

Harold raised his palms to the crowd for quiet. They gave a great roar and subsided into near silence. He stepped forward to the edge of the rostrum and surveyed the multitude with a slow sweep of little nods. Then in beautiful anticlimax he gave a loud croak. The crowd erupted in laughter and Jo stepped forward to deliver his speech for him. They had pulled it off. Even the returning officer was laughing. Everyone would love him.

'Politician's throat,' Jo announced.

More laughter. The cameras panned the hall: laughter and red rosettes everywhere. Huge rosettes on people Harry hardly knew. The biggest rosette of all on a plump businessman he had never seen before. Even the television commentator was laughing. Harold would be fine. Harry felt both relieved and jealous. Jo had quelled the crowd.

'Yes, Harry's suffering from politician's throat,' she repeated, singing the words into the microphone like a pop star. A residual titter rippled over the crowd.

'And why not? We've had to suffer it for the past month.' More roars.

'Harr-y! Harr-y!' raged again.

She patted the storm down with both her palms.

'But don't worry, he'll have plenty to say when he gets to Westminster as part of the new Labour Government.'

Frenzied roars forced her back from the microphone to take a deep breath before going on.

'But first I would like to thank... I would like to thank...' she blustered against the roars and whistles, 'the returning officer and his staff...'

Protocol. The old rituals, linking past and present. Nothing too serious in this change: first eleven out, second eleven in, as they had said as Young Socialists.

Jo did the thanks to the returning officer bit with tears of relief in her eyes. The crowd were chanting again.

'Harr-y! Harr-y!'

Then, for some reason:

'Maurice! Maurice!

'Maurice! Maurice! There he is. That's the tramp who insulted me Maurice. Hit him.'

There was the drunken woman again, dreadfully tenacious. And there too was Maurice, blocking out the television with his sail of a shirt, looking round for Harry.

In the slow-motion sequence that followed, Harry took in Maurice's every feature. He was a classic rugby man run to fat: in no shape for rugby any more but perfect shape for hitting small tramps. Not unlike the baddy in Chaplin's films. He towered over Harry and stared down at him: grey whiskered face to clean shaven jowly face: man to man. For a moment Harry could have sworn it was the same man who had stopped him in the street that morning to call him ' a silly little man,' so casually. As if he had nothing more pressing on his mind, Harry decided that he probably had a complex about size and he made a mental note to analyze it scientifically, later. Maurice turned with menace to the landlord.

'I hold you responsible for this, Derek,' he said.

In that moment, for the second time that day, Harry was out the door and into the fresh night air, pounding down the tow path with a small drunken posse in pursuit.

He was already beginning to establish a lead when one of the posse fell in the canal and the rest gave up the chase to fish him out. All except Maurice. He plodded on with heavy, regular strides.

After half a mile, as he approached a deep and complicated lock, Harry estimated he had no more than fifty yards lead. His demon, substituting this in a simple uniform motion equation, told him that Maurice would be upon him in about two and a half minutes. He had better try to hide in the bushes around the lock.

The tow path ran steeply up to the lock. Harry's feet began to slip on its dry gravel. He had to haul himself up on an oak spike that a landlubber had forgotten to remove from a sluice crank. The spike came out in his hand and Harry took it with him into the little copse which turned out not to be a copse at all but a thin hedge around a concrete pumping station. There was no option but to stand and make a fight of it. He had the high ground, for once. And he was armed with what reminded him of a pick-axe handle. He practised a few swings with it and felt the thrill of its destructive power run up his arms and into his shoulder muscles. He settled his feet firmly in the dust. It was a pose he fancied he had once seen in a Home Guard recruiting poster. But he had no time to pursue the idea: Maurice had arrived at the foot of the slope. Harry whispered:

'Right, come on! Let's have you,' but moved back into the bushes anyway, as an added precaution. No point looking for trouble.

Maurice took one stride up the slope and then stopped dead as the danger of his position dawned on him. Slowly, he stepped back down onto the level tow path and milled about in the gravel, trying to get his breath back. Harry became convinced that he was the businessman he had met earlier that morning, although the coincidence was fantastic. He began to wonder if he was not a spectre of his own imagining, a sort of pursuing Fury of guilt. But as soon as Maurice ballooned out his cheeks to contain the flatulence of his shaken beer Harry recognized him beyond doubt. He had belched in exactly the same way as he got out of his Jaguar that very morning outside the

Labour Rooms, when he had looked Harry straight in the eye and said,

'You silly, little man.'

It had pierced Harry to the heart: a sudden and unsuspected thrust, right on target. Normally, Harry would have seen him off effortlessly but this time he simply retired to Jo's office and stared through the window at his own reflected ghost. Deep inside him the fear had stirred that the Tories were the more honest of the two parties: gross in their privileges, unconcealed in their greed. The turning over of the idea had rattled foundations like a small earthquake. A weaker echo of the tremor returned now.

Although it was some small hour of Friday morning it was not dark. The West still had a rosy glow about it and the sky was a pale violet colour with only the brightest stars managing to shine through. In this pale light he watched Maurice pace back and forth at the foot of the little mound, peering into the bushes. Harry's demon began to pace beside him, eyeing him up and down like a tailor measuring a customer for a suit. Maurice stood still and peered hard into the bushes towards Harry. The demon stood beside him and indicated a point in the middle of his forehead.

'There,' he suggested to Harry. 'If you hit him there, it will achieve maximum leverage on his neck. It will, of course, involve a high probability of inaccuracy. Here, however...' he lowered his hand to Maurice's chest but shook his head doubtfully at the prospects, '...success is most likely but the damage inflicted would be minimal.'

He walked around Maurice and then pointed to the top of his head and smiled.

'I would strongly recommend a vertical blow to the top of the head. Just about here.'

Harry raised the spike, rustling the leaves above his head. Maurice immediately turned towards him and their eyes met through a lattice of moon shadows.

'We don't have to go through with this,' their eyes agreed. Maurice looked away quickly. After a few face saving prods in the lower bushes with his shoe, he turned and started back along the tow path, making up a story for his wife and friends. He was only a little disappointed that he had not been able to beat Harry; slap him about a little, throw him in the canal perhaps, nothing drastic. Harry lowered the spike and began to tremble as the adrenalin wore off. He had struck a blow, metaphorically, for all the silly little men everywhere. The Philistine was in retreat before his arms. The idea exhausted him and he was overwhelmed with the need to find somewhere to sleep. He tossed the spike into the bushes and continued his weary jog southwards: the Knight of the Woeful Figure, scourge of robbers and giants, defender of silly little men. It was all very exhausting.

Chapter 7

Shortly after three, with the first grey light of Friday out on the streets, a rearguard of crapulous revellers in the Labour Rooms sat behind drawn curtains and watched the last results come in. Only a handful of safe seats remained, there were no surprises left. Labour had won with a working majority of one and the exhaustion of a post-natal trauma lay over everyone.

The wild abandon of the night had gone: the chants and songs, the hugs of comrades, the laughter and tears and the sly kissing of extra-marital tongues; speeches, eulogies, fiery promises, magnanimous consolations and sentimental weepings, had all been trodden into the carpet along with cigarette ends and shells of the pork pies whose ordering had led to such bitter accusations of racism on the Social Committee only the previous day. A few quiet groups sat around the room now leaning on three legged tables, drawing and redrawing maps of the New Europe in puddles of beer.

As soon as victory had been clinched a fight had broken out amongst a branch of hard-nuts from the big housing estate over the precise nature of state capitalism in Stalin's Russia. The combatants, with clots of black blood congealed in their eyebrows, were now growling at one another about the ramifications of the treaty of Brest-Litovsk.

'Fucking Trotsky,' a councillor was saying, 'was simply recognizing the de facto victory of German arms, that's all.'

Jo cast an eye in their direction and they lowered their voices to whispers. She was sitting with Harold and Heather watching a television that kept blinking on and off as if trying to sleep. Her eyes did not blink but stared blindly at the screen. She was rolling her head gently from side to side, grunting occasionally as an idea worked its way through her brain.

A small boy who worked the computers interrupted her with a message on a torn piece of paper. It was from London. Jo folded it absently and drummed on the table with it as she went back to her ideas. The boy had to interrupt her again.

'They want a reply now.'

She stared at him until he was forced to look to Heather for help. Heather nudged her arm.

'Yes, yes,' she waved. 'Confirm. He'll be there.'

The boy went back to his office of chattering printers shaking his head. A light began to dawn on Jo's face.

'Of course! Of course!'

She sighed the words out and thumped the table so hard that the floor shook and the television stopped blinking.

'Of course he will.'

And then, rapturously, to the whole, uncomprehending room,

'He'll be there! How could he stay away?'

She turned to Harold who seemed to be on the verge of taking off his sunglasses and calling it a day, and kneaded his shoulder almost tenderly in celebration.

'It won't be long now,' she said enigmatically.

She had a plan and its optimism radiated from her face. She began to take command again. Waving the piece of paper in Harold's face she said, 'Extraordinary PLP meeting, in view of the blah, blah, blah: Sunday, Central Hall Westminster.'

She folded the paper into a taper and used it to conduct what she said next, emphasizing Heather's or Harold's role with a prodding of it.

'Heather, you take him down. Use what's left on the sly roll, there should be plenty there to keep you going until he starts drawing.'

She turned the taper on Harold.

'You'd better learn Harry's signature before you start drawing from the Fees Office. Shouldn't take you long.

Then we can set up a local bank account and you can relax a bit, no-one knows him from Adam down there.'

Heather began to muse aloud on a pedantic detail.

'Why does he need to imitate Harry's signature? Why not just write Harry Beamish in his own hand? After all it's not as if they're going to have Harry's to compare it to. I mean...'

Jo froze her with a stare and changed the subject.

'He can stay with Lawrence and Jean in Islington, they're reliable. I'll telephone them to say you're coming.'

She turned the taper back on Harold and prodded home her instructions.

'Tell your wife you've got a job in London. It's true really, isn't it?'

She made him nod his assent to this bizarre crumb of truth in the whole cake of deceit.

'I'll give you a telephone number for emergencies and some money. Tell your wife it's an advance on wages, that should allay suspicions. Harry didn't know many MPs that well. Anyway,' she added as a bitter aside, 'the bastards never look outside of themselves long enough to notice anyone else, so you should be safe enough. That's about it really, we'll play the rest by ear. Oh, I nearly forgot, you change back to Harold on the train up every Thursday. I'll have to sell Harry as an absentee MP. Probably secure him against deselection, usually does.'

She was babbling. It made her look angrily at Harold, standing, blissfully ignorant of the dangers she was fending off with her infinite pains. He made the mistake of smiling and her hands twitched for his throat. She toyed with the idea of shaking him by the neck, banging his head against the wall. Until he was aware of every one of the traps that gaped around him. But her infinite pains extended into the future so she turned her wrath on the neighbouring table instead. The councillor for the housing estate was on his feet, leaning on one fist and banging with the other on the table top, shouting.

'Don't be such a prick!' How could they fight on? What were they going to use for ammunition...?'

Jo cast him a terrible glance and he sat down quickly and concluded, in a whisper.

'...fucking beetroots?'

'I'm going to try to find Harry,' she said. 'I think he's heading for London. He's got a brother there: Tottenham or Walthamstow, somewhere around there, and if I know Harry...'

She never finished the sentence but nodded with angry satisfaction.

'You just get Harold away from here as soon as possible. Our only dangers are here at present. Get him to London this afternoon if you can. Any problems with that?'

The other two shook their heads in unison.

'Don't you call me a prick. I don't care if you are a fucking councillor.'

They left together as the first blows fell in the Brest-Litovsk debate. No-one noticed them go.

Chapter 8

Harry plodded on. He had to put as much distance as he could between himself and Maurice before he could think about sleeping. He was delirious with exhaustion and fancied he saw the Aurora Borealis shimmering over Mexborough.

As dawn was breaking, he found an abandoned car nestled between two overhanging hawthorns. He slumped onto the back seat the springs were still like new. 'Japanese', he thought sadly, and fell asleep.

Before, or it might have been just after he fell asleep he found himself standing beside a young Peggy. She was writing abstracts for a pharmaceutical journal at a kitchen table. She was writing quickly in her clever, illegible hand, trying to earn enough money to get them out of the freezing flat they were in. He was standing beside her in his welder's overalls, looking down onto her hair, still chestnut brown. She had stopped writing to show him a college course that she had biroed round in a prospectus. She was trying to persuade him to apply for it. He saw himself being painful about it.

Very easy it had been then, under Wilson's Government; scrapping aircraft carriers to create college places for workers. He had let Peggy down badly. Wilson too, for that matter.

Sleep blotted out everything but the taste of being young again, which ran and ran through his dreams.

He woke up bathed in sweat and suffocating from the heat and from the disappointment of awaking to middle age.

The morning sun had already turned the car into an airless oven and the quilted coat he was wearing stuck to him like a poultice. His mouth was arid.

He fumbled to open the door and burst out, peeling off the coat and gasping for breath. As he stretched his hands up to the sky the cool morning air wafted under his tee-shirt so that he sighed aloud with relief and a minute later he was swimming, naked, in the middle of the canal.

From the middle, Harry could see both ways along the water, past the overhanging trees. About half a mile ahead was a little marina where there seemed to be some sort of fuss going on and behind, not ten feet from the car he had slept in, he could see Hari Krishna Seth who had pursued him out of the Labour Rooms the previous day. He was sitting beside the canal, calmly floating a matchbox boat with a lilac leaf sail.

He smiled at Harry and said, quietly, so as not to disturb the morning calm,

'Good morning Hari.'

Harry was so shocked that he sank momentarily. On the way down, he earmarked this phenomenon for later scientific investigation: a functional relationship between neurological trauma and body density? A PhD in there somewhere, perhaps. He soon recovered himself.

'Hi, HK!'

He waved a few sunny diamonds his way, trying to look nonchalant. Immediate panic was postponed as he remembered that HK was a Hindu and might, hopefully, see him in a kinder light: a sort of pilgrim or something. Harry struck out for the bank but HK raised a pale palm.

'No Hari, do not let me disturb your morning swim. I have not come to interrupt your journey, only to bring you some breakfast.'

He unwrapped a fastidiously white napkin, releasing the aroma of fresh coriander and cumin which floated across to ravenous Harry who had to tread water and pretend to be as serene as HK. Harry watched him carefully.

'Jo's not with you, is she?'

'No, Hari. I am on my own.'

That was true. HK's role in the Party was a mystery. He owned a string of chemist's shops and was rolling in money. He always wore silk shirts and a navy blue blazer with some kind of regimental badge on the breast pocket and had a bristling, military moustache. He also spoke with the affected nonchalance of someone trying to get a part in a Noel Coward play. To all appearances he belonged in the old Tory Party, with Macmillan and all the decent chaps.

Yet he was the most assiduous of Party members. He gave money without stint and never asked any favours in return. Also, and this bemused Harry most, but probably made him the model member of the near future, he never once mentioned politics. He revelled in confusion. Once, in HK's house, Harry had picked up an old photograph of some ancient men from the mantlepiece, and by way of conversation, asked,

'Relatives of yours, HK?'

'No, they are gods, Hari.'

Harry had almost dropped the picture in non-conformist horror. He had never been sure whether or not HK was taking the piss, but he had always treated his responses with great caution afterwards. He was looking very concerned now.

'If you would rather be alone, Hari...'

'No, no. I'm getting out now, anyway. Just a quick dip.'

He hobbled up the gravelly bank and drew on his clothes over wet limbs. He was starving.

'Come and eat something! A samosa! Some potato and cauliflower and a chapati. Drink some tea, Hari!'

'Thanks, but I'll just have a pee first, if you'll excuse me - the cold water.'

Harry hid himself with decorum in a bush and peed musically into the canal.

'How did you find me?'

But HK wanted to make a meal of the answer to that question so he patted the soft grass beside him and called, 'Come and have some breakfast Hari and I will tell you. I think you should eat some breakfast.'

Harry nodded, turning his piss' parabola into a wave that clapped agreement on the water.

'Yes, yes, I'm coming.'

HK was sitting cross legged before the spread napkin, pouring tea from a flask and pointing out the various delicacies.

'These samosas are delicious, Hari. I made them myself, this morning.'

He handed Harry a paper bag of samosas, blatantly labelled with their local take away's logo. Harry smiled and sat cross legged beside him. A cosy little sixties' tableau: guru and disciple. When they had finished the samosas, HK brushed some flakes of pastry from his silk tie and squeezed Harry's knee, anxious for him to ask again how he had found him.

'How did you find me?'

He smiled serenely and rolled his head from side to side in an ecstasy of theatrical delight.

'Jo told me she had lost you on the canal bank. And I know you must follow the canal back to London. It is a path you must follow if you are to find yourself, Hari.'

They both chuckled and HK slapped Harry's knee.

'I'll have to find another path now, of course.'

HK held up two palms in negation.

'No, no, no! I would not hinder your journey Hari.'

Harry believed him.

'I came to see if you were all right. You have plunged into deep water Hari.'

He threw a pebbled into the water and they both nodded as the ripples spread along the canal.

'If there is anything I can do for you.'

He handed Harry one of his elegant business cards.

'You must promise to call me.'

Harry promised.

'One other thing I must tell you Hari, because I cannot bear to see you like this.'

'What?'

HK placed his hands, palms up, in his lap, like a yogi, and nodded into them, earnestly. A ripple of apprehension ran up Harry's spine.

'You should get a bicycle, Hari.'

Harry laughed out loud with relief and complete bewilderment. But HK was serious.

'It would be quicker and much more dignified for a man in your position.'

He joined in the laughter and began to shake Harry's knee, playfully.

'It will put some muscles on your skinny legs, Hari. Ha! Ha! Ha!'

He massaged Harry's knee heartily, laughing all the time so that his own fat frame shook like a jelly. He had thought of something hilarious and was struggling for the breath to get it out.

'You have legs like Pinocchio, Hari! Ha! Ha! Ha!'

Harry let him laugh this one out alone: he was not proud, but he had some sensibilities.

'Ho, ho, Hari. Pinocchio would not make a very successful politician though, I'm afraid. His nose.'

He began to wobble into hysteria.

'Westminster Palace would not be big enough to contain it. Ha, ha, ha!'

Harry was impressed by this knowledge of European folk tales but sorry that he did not know of a jelly Buddha or something in Indian literature so that he might return the observation. He fed himself a consoling chapati full of aromatic cauliflower and watched a kingfisher streak low over the water while he waited for HK to subside.

'I am sorry, Hari. You have lovely legs.'

He stifled a new wave of laughter into a whimper and then lumbered heavily to his feet, giggling gently. He shook the napkin's crumbs onto the surface of the water and then waited patiently until small fish rose to peck them from the surface.

'Jo is very upset by all this, Hari.'

He blushed at the insensitivity of coming directly to a point and immediately tried to deflect his words.

'Women, Hari! They have no time for romance. Work! Work! Work! Ah well!'

He clapped the gravel from his buttocks with loud smacks and gathered up the breakfast things.

'This weather reminds me of when I was a boy.'

The words were no sooner out of his mouth than he began to weep softly. Too much laughter, of course. Harry's mother had always warned him that too much laughter ended in tears. Harry knew he should have hugged him, but it was out of the question.

'Thanks for coming HK. And the breakfast.'

'Be careful, Hari. And if you need help, any time, you must call me. Reverse the charges.'

He lost his struggle with the tears and bundling the breakfast things quickly in the napkin, waddled off down the canal bank, stiff from all the cross-legged sitting, waving over his shoulder.

Harry sat by the water, slowly winding a piece of abandoned fishing line onto a cigarette packet until he caught a glimpse of HK's red Mercedes through the trees opposite as it lumbered back onto the road. He watched until he lost sight of the car and then he got up and set off, wondering where to stash the fishing line.

A couple of hundred yards into his new day's journey, Harry spotted the rubber arc of a bicycle tyre, humping out of the water a few feet from the bank. He tried to pretend he hadn't noticed it; tried to shove the image off his field of vision, but that only made things worse. He got a stick from the hedge and gave the wheel a prod, hoping, but knowing that it would not be, just a floating tyre. He hooked the stick under the wheel and pulled. A bright yellow racer rose out of the water. He propped it against the hedge and admired it as it dripped dry, sparkling in the sun. It had the cryptic words, 'team banana' printed on its tubing and, even to Harry's eye, it had the look of a serious machine. Of course, he would have to hand it in to the police. He had said something only the other day about whole sections of the community being abandoned to lawlessness. Having their videos nicked with impunity. And here he was, born out by fact. He nodded piously.

All the same, it would be difficult, under the circumstances, to return the bike just yet. Perhaps he could leave it at a lock-keeper's with an anonymous note. Yes, of course, he'd do that. He mounted and pedalled off, full of the thrill of spokes and sparkling wheels.

The bike was so unlike the boneshakers of his memory, so taut and efficient in its operations that Harry began to eulogize, as if he were delivering his maiden speech on the theme of the British bicycle industry.

'Modern advances in material technology offer this liberating mode of environmentally sustainable transport to all.'

He turned the little sound-bite over on his tongue. It would take a long time to come off the drug of constructing them out of every new idea. It was probably a defence mechanism against being overwhelmed by the new, he decided, a sort of mental displacement activity.

'Sound-bites are the gendarmes of radical thought.'

There, that was about right.

Sooner than estimated, he came to the little marina he had seen from the middle of the canal. An animated group were gathered on the bank, pointing out something to an uninterested policeman with his hands in his pockets.

Harry stopped at the back of the little group and peered, like them, into the water.

A wooden cruiser lay on its side, sunk to its gunwales with two gaping rents in its foredeck.

'Sheer bloody vandalism! Senseless bloody hooliganism!'

A beautiful, mature woman wearing a very tight track suit bottom was pointing out the wreckage to a row of precariously leaning women, arms under their breasts, tutting. The men stood back, watching her buttocks quiver with rage under the tight black fabric. She said,

'They should have their arses flogged!'

A low moan, covered quickly by a cough, escaped one of the men. Most of the backs of heads nodded.

'What's the Labour Government going to do about this? Eh?'

She stamped angrily on the mooring rope, sending ripples down the canal and up her thigh.

'Flogging's too good for them.' Harry suggested, summing up, with politician's acumen. The Will of the People. All the head backs nodded. He still had the touch. He went on, riskily,

'They want hanging from the yard arm.'

Some huge nods. Then someone said,

'Bastards pinched my bike, too.'

Grateful to modern advances in polymer technology, Harry whispered off on quiet tyres.

Chapter 9

Jo struggled to get the kids to school. They demanded pocket-money. She paid it from the election fund- probably an offence in itself- and they went off, grumbling. When the house was quiet she made herself a cup of coffee and sat at the kitchen table. The phone rang.

It was her cousin Russell, a freelance journalist in London. He was after an interview with Harry and when she told him that was not possible, her voice faltering only slightly when she imagined the consequences of telling him why, he began to angle for something else.

'Jo darling...'

She shifted the receiver to her other ear to suppress her exasperation.

'...Are you coming down for the PLP meeting on Sunday?'

'Yes, I am. Why?'

She heard him shift his own receiver.

'I wondered if you'd like to come round for dinner. Been a long time since we. You know... chewed the fat.'

She let him bumble on until he was forced to come to the point.

'Point is, Jo, I'm in the running for a big job. Scripting an election analysis for Granada. They have grand plans, Jo. I think they're hoping it'll run till the Government falls. Ha, ha!'

Even in jest, the thought of going through it all again in a month or so, sickened her.

'And you want me to tell you what's been happening on Planet Earth, is that it?'

'Well, West Yorkshire, anyway.'

The idea of any kind of break seduced her and she nodded complaisantly into the phone.

'Jo? Jo?'

'Yes, alright, Saturday tea-time.'

'Great! Mmmmm!'

He smacked an exuberant kiss down the phone in celebration of getting what he wanted and Jo smiled in the warmth of his satisfaction.

'Have to go now, darling. Lots and lots to talk about on Saturday though. Love to Jack and the kids. Mmmm! Oh, congrats. by the way. Who's a clever girl!'

Glowing reluctantly in his congratulations she drank one mouthful of coffee, then put her head on the kitchen table and slept.

The Saturday train down from Wakefield was packed with Labour Party people. They all congratulated one another with lots of laughter and long handshakes. The train rang with their confident, assertive voices and shone with their happy faces. Jo, having won a Tory seat with a new candidate, was the focus of special congratulations. She was back-slapped all the way to her reserved seat.

When she had got herself comfortable, just as the train was about to set off, two regional MPs and their secretaries scrambled aboard. They flung themselves into seats at Jo's table, gasping for breath. Jo knew them both.

One of the MPs slid his briefcase onto the table, pushing her paper into her lap. He flipped open the lid and took out a sheet of House of Commons notepaper.

'Congratulations, Jo. Brilliant job.'

'Congratulations yourself.'

He brushed aside the congratulations.

'No, no. Mine was a piece of cake. Seventeen thousand!'

He beat a tattoo on his stomach to indicate the solidity of his majority.

'But yours is a new scalp. Well done!'

Jo blushed. One of the secretaries was sent to the buffet car for coffee and rolls. When she returned, having no seat, Jo had to squash against the window so that the three women could face the two MPs and listen to their parliamentary gossip.

She found herself remembering her mother, who had died the year Thatcher came to power. Bitter year, that had been. She had always meant to dedicate her share of this long-awaited victory to her memory. Harry's treachery had robbed her of even that.

She could see her mother now. They were sitting in her front room in Leeds, just before she died. They were talking about politics. Her mother was trying to console her.

'T'int so bad for you really, love. Not nowadays. When I were your age we were bloody grateful to work for half a man's wage. And we had no help with house. Not like now. Woman in number ten. Bitch, mind you. But you can't have it all at once, I don't suppose.'

Jo looked at the two MPs, settling themselves comfortably into their seats. The one with the sheet of paper had put on his reading glasses and was saying:

'Lex's got Chief Whip.'

They all congratulated Lex in his absence.

'Sound man, Lex. Mind you, he'll need to be a bloody magician with a majority of one.'

No-one said anything. The MP went on.

'And I'm Whip for the Region.'

Jo congratulated him. His secretary blushed for him. He put the paper down and looked over his glasses at Jo.

'Where's Harry, by the way?'

Jo felt the sweat break out on her forehead. The Regional Whip went on.

'Not run away, has he?'

Everyone roared with laughter and Jo felt faint.

'No, no, no, no! Ha, ha, ha, ha!'

She thought she might vomit at any moment.

'No, he's gone down to see his old dad in London. Run away!'

Another round of laughs.

'There's word that Lex has fixed up a PPS for him in Education. Have you heard anything?'

Jo said she hadn't.

'Well he's a lucky bastard, tell him that from us.'

He included the other MP who nodded his agreement and added.

'Four years, I've done, and one minor committee place. That's all I've had. He'll be a minister in no time if he keeps his nose clean. I can see him going up like a rocket, can't you?'

She watched the flat fields of Lincolnshire speed by. The heat-wavehad scorched them yellow at the edges, giving the scenery an alien look.

When she arrived at Russell's bachelor flat in the Fulham Road with her overnight suitcase she found his own suitcase blocking her progress through the narrow hall.

'Going somewhere Russ?'

'No, no, not for a couple of hours.'

'You wanted to see me. Chew the fat.'

'I do, I do, darling. It's just the most marvellous opportunity for me. You'll be thrilled.'

He stood back, spread out his arms as wide as he could in the little passage, and beamed at her.

'Jo, I've got the job. I travel up to Manchester tonight.'

He nodded and nodded so enthusiastically that his joy seemed to induce an involuntary resonance in her. She smiled and shook her head at the same time.

'I'm so pleased for you.'

The sarcasm was not lost on him and he put his arm around her huge shoulders and squeezed as hard as he could.

'Jo! I've only just got the phone call. You know the media. Rush rush...'

He began to get carried away by the rush but checked himself.

'I've got the dinner ready and everything. Come and have an aperitif. Relax!'

Sipping milky Pernod from a tumbler tinkling with ice cubes, Jo was shown over Russell's apartment. He showed her a new Hockney he had taken in lieu of payment for a big job with an advertising agency, now rocking on the brink of bankruptcy: which she was to keep to herself; and a real Aztec brooch of gorgeous silver. She felt herself drooling over it like a Conquistador and it flitted through her mind that she could take it away from him, as she had taken his toys when they were children.

'You'll have to control that girl of yours, Elsie. She's hit our Russell again and took his cap gun.'

Their mothers, who were sisters, had worried about Jo when they thought she couldn't hear them.

'She's built like a brick shithouse, Elsie, but it in't as if she were a lad, is it? I mean.'

'I know, but she'll grow out of it.'

They had thought about this dubiously for a while and then Jo's mother had sighed.

'Ee, but your Russell'd have made a lovely lass.'

Jo touched the scar on her cheek. She had got the scars when they had fallen through the garage roof together. Russell had fallen on his feet.

'Do you think I'd suit a pony tail, Jo?'

He was holding his thick, blond hair back in a bun and turning his face from side to side in a tall mirror. She was spared answering because the microwave oven pinged and Russell shepherded her into his diner-kitchen.

'Boeuf Bourguinonne! Your favourite. So don't say I'm not good to you. And a nice Burgundy. Harrods!'

He served from a rustic casserole and filled their glasses.

'Here's to us all, Jo: to you and me, to the cause and to the future, oh, and to Harry, of course. What a pity Harry's not here.'

'Yes, it is a pity, isn't it? To us all, then.'

The wine went straight to her neck and shoulders and she rolled her head in a wide circle and sighed.

'Oh God, that's good.'

'So!'

Russell ran a handful of fingers through his hair and held out some thoughts for Jo to look at.

'Everything hinges, as I see it, on what we can offer the Lib Dems and who gets what in the Cabinet. By the way, a birdie whispered to me the other day that Harry could go straight in as a PPS in Education. Heady days, Jo!'

She had half hoped that he would talk about his new job

or his holidays in Mexico, anything but politics or Harry. She wanted to change the subject but that would arouse his suspicion and she had to be careful. Even so she could only manage an ambiguous grunt in reply. He waved his fork at her, in case she hadn't read the implications.

'Be a very nice job for you there. PA to a minister soon, Jo. Lots of...'

He didn't finish the sentence but pretended to manipulate the reins of a horse and winked at her. A flush of anger ran through her.

'I can't just leave the kids and come down to work in London, Russ. Not just like that. It's not as if I were a lad after all, is it?'

He recoiled in mock surprise and held up his hands to field her wrath.

'Sorry! Sorry!'

In her head, Jo ran over the scenario that would follow her saying, 'Anyhow, he's buggered off and we're running an imposter in his place. Ring that through to your editor,' and a small, pre-hysteria giggle broke out.

'That's better.'

He refilled her glass.

'Tell me what's been happening up in the old country. What were the issues on the doorstep?'

She felt dull and leaden, doomed to disappoint him.

'Oh, same as all over: unemployment, the VAT thing, crime...'

'Immigration? Was that an issue?'

Jo shook her head.

'Not really.'

He seemed disappointed. She knew what he really wanted was anecdotes for articles and she raked around in her brainful of election junk for something that might be useful to him.

'I can tell you a funny story. True, too.'

She oiled her throat with a long draught of wine and Russell hurriedly refilled her glass.

'Harry's brother Charlie, he's a plumber in Tottenham, I think, took to wearing a balaclava and shooting Rottweillers with a bow and arrow in his local park. Called himself the Masked Avenger. Made a big story in his local paper. Anyhow, our Tories got it wired up from Central Office and they tried to run it in our local rag. I got wind of it from one of the journalists there. '

Russell began to titter and Jo joined him.

'Not funny, Russ. Ours is a daily. Saturation coverage. Could have made him a laughing stock. They had him targeted as ridiculous. Did a wickedly funny A5 of him as a scarecrow.'

They both burst into laughter.

'But, as luck would have it, Harry was meeting a delegations of nuns over the abortion issue, when one of their councillors storms in, pissed as a newt and waving a bloody penknife around. I managed to trade them. "The Lord moves in mysterious ways," Harry said.'

Jo laughed herself to tears with relief. Russell removed their plates and put a bowl of fruit on the table. He looked at his watch.

'I'm sorry about this Jo but I'll have to go soon. Make yourself at home though.'

He clattered some keys down beside her.

'Here are my spare keys, just pop them through the letter box when you leave. There's lots of wine and a bottle of brandy and there's microwave meals in the fridge, so just relax and enjoy yourself, you must be exhausted. And give my regards to Harry when you see him tomorrow. Now: keys, money...'

He stood in front of her and went through the annoying ritual of patting his pockets and intoning the names of things he must not forget. He seemed so fresh and bright and pretty in his white silk shirt and Italian trousers as he searched for something in a drawer, growing angry. She was reminded of another time he had been angry. He had been drinking with her and Harry after the miners' strike. He had suddenly burst out:

'One bloody paperback, I got out of it. Shit sales too! Didn't even cover expenses. It was a photographer's strike, of course. Sundays couldn't get enough pickies.'

In the row that followed, in a frenzy of jealous exasperation, Harry had accused him of having too much hair for a man of his age. They had all three roared with laughter but she just managed to glimpse what he had meant now before the vision bolted from her mind.

'Did you do much in the election, Russ?'

He was becoming quite frantic in his search of the drawer.

'What?'

Jo knew that he had heard her so she just sat back and waited. He pretended to be preoccupied and waved a hand vaguely in the air.

'Oh, you know.'

'No, I don't.'

He found what he was looking for in the drawer and slipped it furtively into his back pocket; then he came back to Jo's question.

'Do! Oh don't ask! Telephone, telephone; fix this, write that. You know.'

He looked at his watch and smiled apologetically.

'Must go, Jo.'

He leaned down to kiss her but she grabbed his arm and sat him down. The wine had flushed her face.

'Jo, I have to go.'

'I'll tell you why we won, shall I?'

He folded his arms and sighed theatrically and she couldn't find the heart to spoil his delight. She quoted some figures that came into her mind.

'There are seventeen thousand pensioners in our constituency. That's twenty-two per cent of the votes.'

Russell instinctively jotted down the figures on a scrap of paper.

'Two thousand of them were organized in a local association against this fuel tax.'

He stowed the piece of paper and looked at his watch in agony. She became angry again.

'They'd had enough of being pissed on, Russ! Tell them that at Granada. And they picked up the nearest weapon and hit the bastards: which happened to be us, God help us. Fucking spineless shambles that we are.'

She waved him away indulgently. He kissed her on the head after all and fled.

'Cheers, Jo! I'll ring.'

For some minutes the flat echoed with Russell's manic spirit and Jo sat in it like a sailor marooned on a desert island. Then, when silence had settled, she admitted to herself that she was glad to be alone at last.

She made her first cup of unhurried coffee in two months and stood drinking it by the kitchen window.

Across Bishop's Park a dredger was working off Putney Pier and she listened to the faint, delayed braying of its rusty chains. If Harry had been there he would have been estimating its distance using the speed of sound in summer air or something and telling her all about it. Why had he forsaken her?

A teenage thrill creaked along some disused nerve in her stomach and she filled the half empty coffee cup to the brim with brandy. They had been comrades, after all.

She remembered the first time she had ever seen him. He was making a speech at a Militant meeting. It was in a pub long since pulled down to make way for Sainsbury's.

Did they all meet up now over the shopping trollies full of wine by coincidence then, or to commune with the spirits of their youth? That was a question.

He had begun with the words, 'When the Roman Empire fell, in the sixth century,' but soon got down to lambasting the Labour leader, Wilson, it had been at the time; rolling them in the aisles with his Cockney wit, innocently calling for revolution.

They had had such plans. Harry would make the speeches and she would organize the victory. She would write the manifesto of the revolution and keep the waverers on the straight and narrow in the long march. She would make history in the cryptic minutes of secret meetings and, she realized, as the brandy reached her loins, she would make love to the men who made history. There was no denying it; that had been the plan. No-one had found the courage to admit it but it was true.

She caught a glimpse of herself in the window and a rage began to blossom as she regretted cropping her blond hair. It was all right for the others, they were younger than her, girls, most of them. They didn't have scars like duelling wounds running across their cheeks. Harry had once quipped, pissed at the time, that she looked more like Hindenburg's second at a duel than a Labour agent. Everyone laughed and she laughed with them but it had been another wound, another scar.

She turned her face from side to side. Her eyes were still as blue as ever but they were besieged by lines now. Lines that could not be ironed out even when she opened her eyes candy-box wide and dragged her cheeks down with her fingers. She began to feel remorse for abusing her carcass. Hadn't Saint Francis asked forgiveness for ill-treating his brother donkey of a body?

She had been ill-treated, all right. She began to slide into self-pity. Saint Francis had founded a great order.

What had she accomplished, really, when you came right down to it? A good honours in history, and then what? Grimly lectured dull apprentices at the college. Foisted a handful of drunken councillors on an undeserving public. Helped Russell write his thin and insincere paperbacks. Slaved to bring Harry to a sweet success he had thrown in her face, treacherous bastard that he was.

It didn't add up to a life. A half-life perhaps. Harry had introduced her to the term in some scientific, metaphorical way to describe the rate of decay of support for a government but the expression's literal meaning had haunted her ever since. A half-life.

'I am living my life,' she said to the Thames across the park, 'like a prison sentence. Crossing off the days against some great release.'

The melodrama in the image made her laugh at herself in the window. She was not a child. Someone had to keep the Labour Government in office. There was work to be done. They couldn't all run away.

She found a C. Beamish, plumber in the Yellow Pages and rang. A recorded message said:

'This is the Masked Avenger. Dah, dah, dah! Dah, dah, dah! Speak! Prrp!'

She had become expert at leaving telephone messages.

'Hi! This is Jo Firsby, Harry's agent. Harry and me have got ourselves separated in London. Bumpkins eh!'

She tried a little laugh and instantly wished she could wipe it off the tape. She brought the message to a more business-like end.

'Ask Harry to ring me on this number, will you?'

The dredger off Putney Pier had stopped working for the night. 'Its crew will be at home or in the pub by now,' she thought. 'They've done their day's work. They can enjoy themselves.'

The Fulham Road was beginning to stir with young people, strolling towards the West End for the night. Their voices carried up through the still, hot air and in the open windows of the flat. The anti-climax to the last three days fell on her like lead. She had done her job. Won her corner of the field. By rights, if there were such things, she should be feasting at the victory table. Reliving the battle. Being slapped on the back. Planning the future. With Harry.

Instead she was marooned in Russell's flat. Alone. In a hot and alien city.

She drank another cup of brandy in gloomy anger and decided to go out. Perhaps she would go up to the West End and find a ticket for the new *Macbeth*. Very appropriate that would be. A play dripping with betrayal. Or perhaps she would just get drunk in a wine bar somewhere. Frighten some Yuppies. But outside, in the stifling evening heat, her energy evaporated. All she could manage was to walk as far as the Putney Bridge and lean on its balustrade, breathing the cooler air over the river until the light faded to a violet glow in the West.

The job was not over yet. She had to find Harry and bring him back. First she had to get Harold to the PLP meeting. Somehow explain his dark glasses, his inability to speak.

A fine rain began to fall, stirring the scent of stocks in the park. The effect was delicious and refreshing. The air in London seemed foul, exhausted. An idea turned in her mind. She would go up front on the disguise. Work in a smog mask with the dark glasses. Something ecological. She strolled back to the flat mentally drafting a press release. A new allergy. It would need a name.

Chapter 10

As HK had foretold, finding the bike changed everything.

For the first two hours Harry whispered over the gravel of the tow path like a morning tide, driven by the sheer ecstasy of his mobility.

Between two milestones of dubious accuracy, he estimated his average speed as eleven point four miles per hour. He had never dreamed he could propel himself so fast. Even the surreal possibility of making London before nightfall bowled across his mind. He was intoxicated.

This would definitely go into the Great Speech: the cycling road to socialism. He breathed in lungsful of morning air. It had everything. He could hear Jo sketching out a press release: 'Environmentally friendly with a big F, this is Harry, and health, health, health,' although Harry had never been happy with the health cult: Nietzschean, he had always suspected. It led to the Hitler Youth and leather shorts; anathema to Cockneys. His mother had held the leather shorts against the Nazis more than anything and she'd been bombed out twice. Which road was he cycling? That was the question.

He decided just to enjoy the cool breeze on his cheeks, which, he suspected, were getting badly sunburned.

By mid-afternoon he was in Nottinghamshire and dehydrated. The cool breeze had deluded him. He had taken off his cap and stuck it in his back pocket and now, sitting under a tree near a lock, his scalp throbbed to the cloudless sky and his face creaked when he smiled. Luckily he could see a canal-side pub from where he sat. It was lively with lunchtime trade. He got up stiffly and hobbled into the beer garden on seized joints, trickling the bike beside him on its lovely, sunstruck spokes.

At the bar, he caught a glimpse of himself so terrifying that he actually looked over his shoulder for the tomato-red apparition that grinned at him from the mirror behind the barman. He tried looking dignified but it only made him more conspicuous. His dehydration verged on delirium. Perhaps some avenging agency, he thought, was branding him red like a medieval malefactor so that decent folk would know he was a runaway Labour MP.

'Excuse me sir, but have you seen a runaway Labour MP passing through?'

'Bright red, was he?'

'That's the one.'

'Yes, he bought a pint of Perrier water and a ploughman's about two o'clock.'

He took himself to the remotest corner of the garden and ate his lunch.

After a second pint of mineral water his paranoia subsided and he began to rough out the rest of the journey. He had at least seven hours before nightfall and that should see him into Bedfordshire or even Hertfordshire. He could sleep by the canal tonight and make London by Saturday afternoon. That would be a good time to arrive. Saturday afternoon had always been his favourite time of the week in the days when he had finished work at Saturday lunchtime. The weekend beginning, full of optimism. He caught a whiff of Brylcreem, tempting him back to the fifties but he shook himself back to the present with a shudder. There had been enough of that, for the time being. He would ring Charlie as soon as he arrived. Charlie would put him up for now. Give him time to think. He was not ready to think yet. He was still passing through the anaesthetic phase of flight. And the weather was so nice. He decided to shove off again.

A nearby table of businessmen, motor traders or something, were predicting the consequences of the election in the anxious gloom of Birmingham accents.

'If they reflate, things'll be alright. Before the inflation bites, at least.'

'If they can keep a tight rein on wages...'

'A tight rein! There'll be fucking chaos from day one.'

They ignored their ploughman's lunches and chewed their fingernails instead.

Harry watched them leave the table and glide away in Jaguars, their food and drink, hardly touched.

After leaving the grammar school, Harry had only worked with his brother for a few weeks before setting off to hitch hike around Europe. In Switzerland he had met a Frenchman called Louis from Vesoul, and he had shown him how to live by gleaning the table tops of cafes in the town centres. He had become good at it too. Not as good as Louis, who could pose as a waiter and remove still warm courses from bewildered diners, but pretty good, for an Englishman.

A faint pride in his old skill glowed inside him and then flared up into a passion. He went over to the table and calmly made a parcel of all the lunches in an abandoned *Financial Times*, stacking the plates neatly and laying the knives and forks, less one set, which he trousered deftly. Then he bundled everything, including several books of matches advertising a Birmingham ball bearing company, into Ernest's old blue coat and knotted the arms firmly over it all. With the bundle hooked neatly onto the handlebar stock, Harry set off south again.

He pedalled through the rest of the scorching afternoon and into the cool early evening. The names on the milestones turned back to the whimsical Anglo-Saxon of bank holidays out with his mad Uncle Jack and near Nether Heyford, on the Grand Union, he decide to look for somewhere to sleep for the night.

A signpost said that Watford was fifty miles down river and he fancied that he was now in comfortable striking distance of London. It was as if part of a great task had been completed and he allowed himself to give way to hunger and thirst and the need to stretch his back.

The countryside was all prosperous farms and neat hedges now. Groups of tall thoroughbreds walked through the lanes, glistening in the heat. The roads were gold-leafed with horse-shit. 'Not many Labour voters,' he thought, automatically; dogmatically, perhaps. Even a neat rubbish tip, corralled in wattle fencing by the tow path, looked prosperous. He dismounted and wandered into it, turning over carpet tiles and broken floorboards with his toe. He rescued a good sized tarpaulin, with securing ropes, for a bivouac, a hub cap, for a frying pan and some floorboards for a fire. He also found a wire basket. With a little bending it mounted on the handlebars as a perfect carrier, although it disfigured the gorgeous lines of the machine horribly. There wasn't much else he could make use of, except a toasting fork which he waved over the tip like a diviner's rod scouring the minutiae. A length of plastic-coated washing line turned up and a rusty screw driver, and that was it.

He bundled the wood in the tarpaulin, balanced it between the saddle and the handlebars and set off to look for a place to camp.

At an exclusive marina he took advantage of the clubhouse toilets to have a leisurely crap and to wash his socks and pants in a hand basin. A man in a white shirt and cravat came in and peed at the trough. He watched Harry plunging his socks in and out of the shallow grey water with mounting anger. When he had finished, shaken himself dry and zipped up, he asked:

'What on earth do you think you're doing?'

'I'm washing my socks.'

Harry had had many a caning at school for telling simple truths like this. He could smell that old familiar storm of incomprehensible wrath brewing around this man. He tried to propitiate him by sharing more of his plans. Peggy often accused him of being secretive.

'And my underpants.'

The man put his hands on his hips and swelled as if preparing a great shout but instead he turned and nodded to an invisible friend.

'They've only been in for a day and they're washing their bloody socks in the club's hand basins.'

He addressed the invisible friend as if he was the last man on the planet who shared his civilized standards.

'They'll be billeting half a dozen Blacks on my cruiser next, I suppose.'

'Oh, you read that too, did you?'

Harry had learned this technique canvassing intransigent racists and it seldom failed, although it had got him a black eye once in Bradford.

The man turned and stormed out of the door, the shout coming out now, loud and lusty.

'Arthur! Arthur!'

Harry heard his heels digging into the gravel as he goose-stepped off in search of Arthur. He had almost finished anyway. When his pants were clean he used their abrasive elastic waistband to clean his teeth, not very satisfactorily, and left. The man was coming back over a footbridge with Arthur who not only wore a cravat with his shirt but a double breasted blazer with gold buttons. Harry spread his damp underwear on the top of his bundle to dry and pushed off along the tow path. He wondered who Arthur might be. Did they have commodores on the inland waterways? He doubted if they did. The commodore and the irate man hurried their ill-cared-for frames over the bridge at a wobble and darted into the toilet building, to check, presumably, whether he had stolen any of the fittings. When they came out they seemed disappointed that he hadn't. This failure to fulfil their expectations of him seemed to anger them more than his trespassing.

'Go on, shove off!'

The commodore shouted, nautically, at least. The other man added, coarsely, 'Piss off! And don't come back!'

Harry had noted before how failure to comply with stereotypes invoked hatred: it would go in the Great Speech.

About a mile on he found the perfect spot to camp, in the lee of half the vaulting arch of a disused viaduct. The span over the river had been pulled down but on either side it still rose up like two brick ramps with elders growing in its stumps. He quickly tore down a sapling, quite out of line with conference decisions on the environment, and made a bivouac of the tarpaulin. Then he lit a small smokeless fire of tinder-dry sticks near the entrance and sat by it to unwrap his bundle. There was plenty of bread and cheese, although Branston pickle had got everywhere in the hasty parcelling and there was some wilting lettuce and sections of squashed tomato. He spread it all out on the innards of the *Financial Times*, setting the front page aside for reading, and began to plan a sandwich.

At this point the finding of the toasting fork revealed itself as providential. By poking the prongs through both bread and cheese he could make a passable Welsh rarebit. Also, by taking the rate at which the cheese bubbled as proportional to the heat falling on it and by varying the distance from the fire in units of one metal bottle top, he could roughly verify the inverse square law of something or other.

He opened a bottle of cider he had prudently stuffed into the arm of Ernest's coat at one of his watering stops and was content. Amidst the ruin of his career and God knew what consequences for the cause and for his marriage, he was content. He had only known the feeling a few times before. It was the conscious knowledge that the moment was good and self sufficient. There was no screen of metaphor between him and the fire, no meaning in the indigo sky beyond the one shared with the late swallows and the early bats. One day he would be dead, but now he was sitting under the fading sky by a good dry fire with food and drink, and it was glorious. If only he could play the mouth organ it would be pure *Sierra Madre*.

This realization broke the spell of contentment. He was no longer Fred C Dobbs but the whiskery old guy, which put a different complexion on things. He picked up the paper and held it at arm's length to read in the fading light.

The PM was promising a fresh start for Britain in the world. Investment in the infrastructure. A healing of wounds. A regeneration of spirits. A nation once again. It was good stuff and Harry took a big swig of cider to drown his sorrow at not being there with him.

Buried on the inside page was news of the extraordinary meeting of the Parliamentary Labour Party on Sunday, in the Central Hall, the Commons being closed on the Sabbath and Labour equivocal on Sunday opening anyway. Harry turned over a page and there was Lex Latham, an old comrade from Militant days, smiling from the centre of an in depth article on the new Chief Whip. How, the article asked, would he steer the Government's business through the House with a working majority of just one?

'I know every MP on the Government benches and I know their determination to make this parliament work....'

Harry never read what else Lex had to say because his eye had been drawn further on to the beacon of his own name in print. 'I'm particularly looking forward to seeing my old colleague,' it had been comrade in the old days, 'Harry Beamish. He was my agent when I was first elected in seventy-four. MPs of Harry's calibre wouldn't let a Labour Government down.'

Clearly the finding of the toasting fork was part of a bigger providential package altogether.

He finished off the cider and heaved the bottle into the canal with a splash that sent roosting birds screaming for safety. The cider and the fatigue of the day soon had Harry stretched out under the tarpaulin and asleep. Nothing could quite erase his faith that Jo would sort it all out.

His plan to arrive in London on Saturday afternoon proved too optimistic. At Luton he picked up the River Lea, which he knew from childhood would take him to the Tottenham marshes, not a stone's throw from Charlie's place. As the river wound through Hertfordshire he dawdled in little anglers' cafes that seemed to have been preserved for him like cheesecakes under a glass dome. By the time he reached Hoddesdon it was already getting dark. At the Cook's Ferry in Edmonton he bought a pint and phoned Charlie.

Charlie had read the exact meaning of Jo's regretted laugh and now Harry got a different recorded message.

'Harry, Jo rang. She wants you to get in touch. Don't come here, I'm working away for the next couple of days.'

The last part of the message sounded unconvincing and it alarmed him. It went on.

'Go to Nogger's place. He'll see you alright. Alright?'

He took his beer down to the canal side and sat with the soles of his shoes just touching the water. Most of the furniture factories had gone now but the air was still faintly redolent with the fragrance of cellulose thinners.

When he had sat there with Charlie, fishing for gudgeon, still tiny, even through the magnifying glass of nostalgia, the atmosphere had induced hallucinations. Or perhaps it had been Charlie's stories, told in short chapters between getting up to let the barges through. Great stories, they had been. Stories about blags and ghosts and bum-bandits on the marshes. Stories about the factory: about Big Lil who got the apprentices' trousers off if she caught them alone in the lift. About oral sex behind the thinners drums. And, of course, about great strikes where the bosses were always vanquished. Innocent stories. Then Charlie had been called up and sent to the Middle East where nothing was innocent and when he came back the gift of story telling had gone. Afterwards he could only manage the second rate craft of telling true stories.

What had he meant by , 'Don't come here.'?

In the Middle East, so Charlie had said when he came back, politicos shot each other over unimaginably tiny trifles. Harry began to look suspiciously on the crowds of drinkers outside the pub and decided it was time to get on.

It took him a mile or so before he recalled Nogger to mind with any clarity. Harry had last seen him in the early sixties when he kept a filthy old junk shop in Limehouse, somewhere off the East India Dock Road. Surely he couldn't still be there. He had seemed old to Harry in the sixties. And wasn't the place all Docklands now? Yuppie flats and tower blocks. Perhaps he had misheard the message.

In the middle of Tottenham Marshes someone took a pot shot at him with an air rifle. He heard the pellet trill past his ear with an urgent whisper.

'Get a move on.'

He knew from old memory that if he followed the Lea all the way to the Thames he would come out in Silvertown or thereabouts. Not far from Limehouse, anyway. He pedalled as hard as he could, although it was becoming dangerous to go too fast now. In the country the surrounding darkness had illuminated the sky with an indigo wash but as the city's lights crowded in on him it turned jet black and starless. He only managed to navigate by the pale ivory of the canal and the ghosts of moonstruck pylons by the tow path. There was an irony here: the lights of the city turning the sky darker rather than lighter: a metaphor for the Great Speech, for certain.

'We must be careful that the very glow from our industry does not blind us to the stars of our destiny.'

Three centuries too late, or course, but not bad. Jo would edit it into a sound bite for him.

'Destiny's archaic, Harry. Future's the word you're looking for, And...'

But he had to break off suddenly from his speech-writing because he had ridden into a tunnel under

Stratford High Street and he was temporarily blinded. He got off and began to push the bike gingerly in front of him, feeling for the iron edging to the canal with the front wheel. Ahead were faint noises of feet scuffling in the gravel. He stopped and struck a match and it shone like a stage spotlight on a young couple copulating vigorously against the brick wall which crumbled and pattered to the ground in tiny pieces with each of the man's pelvic thrusts. The man seemed to be maintaining his rhythm admirably, keeping his end up, as it were, but the woman's pleasure was ruined. She stared angrily at Harry over her lover's heaving shoulders.

'Gaw'n fuck awf, you old git!'

Harry tossed the match into the canal and hid gratefully in the darkness. He clattered past the couple and went on his way. There had been no need to be quite so rude: ageist, really.

The Thames loomed up suddenly. There was a void in the street lights ahead, a complex of locks and then the huge river of his childhood, swollen in the moonlight off Blackwall Point. He let the bike fall and scrambled down to a tiny beach of muddy stones.

Squatting at the water's edge, he washed his face and arms in the Thames and breathed deeply.

Now what?

The tide was beginning to ebb. Flotsam from Southend, rounding Bugsby's Reach rose and fell on the boiling water. The constant note of the rushing water was changing to a murmur. Its skin swelled to bursting point.

He had come home and the tide was turning for him.

'No, no,' his demon was pointing out. 'This is merely a phenomenon caused by the moon's gravity.'

'Shut up!'

The demon went off with the hump. Harry had had enough of knowing or investigating the mechanisms of the world, he wanted to taste its essence, before it was too late.

He sat and watched the river until the flotsam began the return journey to Southend and then the fatigue of the past three days came over him.

He toyed with the idea of finding Nogger's place and knocking him out of bed but thought better of it. He would have to avoid any disturbances. What if he were arrested for vagrancy and held until he could be identified?

He began to doze lightly and dreamed a sketch where a big, dim policeman was leafing ponderously through a bound copy of 'The Representation of the People Act', turning over one leaf at a time.

'Don't say nothing here about MPs what run away. You're not allowed to be one. You'll have to go back.'

He jerked awake with a shudder and got up stiffly. Then he made his way, via some slippery wooden steps, to the East India Dock Road and pedalled westwards towards the City.

Compared to the canal bank the tarmac of the road was like silk and he glided effortlessly round the Isle of Dogs, where there had been all the trouble about the far-right councillor getting elected. It had been a big issue for a couple of days but soon gave way to harder copy. His contribution to the deluge of invective that had gushed had been to say, on his local radio, that he could think of no punishment more fitting for a fascist than to be put on the council with a Tory Government in office. He was accused of levity and even of racism by someone who said, curiously, that all white Cockneys were racists: in their blood, or somewhere. Jo had warned him to watch his step around deep water and stick to the core issues.

He was so tired by now that he found himself jerking awake from tiny naps, even as he pedalled. He kept remembering how, a couple of years earlier, he had slipped off the icy canal tow path whilst cycling to school during a cold snap. It was the day after he had watched the bombing of Baghdad on the TV, during the Gulf War and he had always wondered if it had been a subconscious attempt at suicide because he'd enjoyed the drama so much. Right through the ice he had gone and when he came up his bike was nowhere, only his cloth cap afloat, upside-down like a coracle. The memory was fading in and out of dream, the chilly memory of the ice bringing out goose pimples under his tee shirt. He would have to find somewhere to sleep soon.

A tiled pedestrian tunnel under the river appeared unexpectedly beside him and he stopped at its entrance and peered in. It was terribly eerie, lined with tiles the colour of nicotine and lit with weak electric bulbs. It might have been a set for a Jack the Ripper film. The impression put him right off the idea of sleeping there but he pedalled through it anyway, past a couple of winos who snored heartily in a common pool of piss and out past the Blackwall Gasworks.

There was a definite hint of daylight in the sky now and he knew he would have to find somewhere to sleep quickly if he was to be fit for anything tomorrow.

He pedalled down King William Walk, past the Cutty Sark with the half moon in her rigging, then westward down Jamaica Road and Southwark Street and Stamford Street and still nowhere to sleep. A mild panic threatened but subsided when he saw a bridge of dark arches carrying a train southwards out of Waterloo. He cycled under the bridge and dismounted. He would doss down here for a few hours and then call on Nogger when the hour was more reasonable.

It was very dark under the arch and it took some time for his eyes to accustom themselves to it. There seemed to be some quiet activity going on, like the polite murmuring of a concert audience before the conductor arrived.

A line of brick alcoves ran off the road into the tunnel supports and Harry turned into the first of these to bed down, delirious with the prospect of sleep. It was completely filled with people.

Most of them were very young; younger than his youngest son: skinny-wristed kids, wrapped in newspaper, stretched out on flattened cardboard boxes, on wooden pallets or on the bare stones. A couple of older men talked quietly, sharing a bottle of cider. An old lady, wrapped in a dozen coats, turned painfully in her sleep and called out, 'Don't you come near me!'

One of the cider drinkers caught Harry's eye and gestured towards the other end of the tunnel with the bottle.

'There's room farther down.'

And since Harry just stood there with his lower lip trembling, he added, kindly,

'You'll be alright, mate.'

The two men went back to their conversation, whispering out of consideration for the sleepers and Harry pushed on past the alcoves.

Each one showed almost the same scene. Towards the middle of the tunnel the berths were more substantial, some with partitions made of wooden pallets and some of whole packing cases with sacks hung over the entrances. In one, a blue gas flame hissed under a kettle. In another, two debilitated old tramps fought bitterly, without the strength to hurt each other, sobbing in their frustration.

'It's not yours, it's mine.'

'Bastard! You bastard!'

Harry carried on towards the end of the tunnel, which now seemed very bright by comparison to this inner darkness. It would soon be light. A dawn choir of birds roosting in the bridge supports began to tune up for the next performance.

As he walked, he recalled, quite vividly, a speech he had made to the students' union at his local college the previous week.

'What an unwelcoming place this Government has made society for young people.'

And he had gone on to list unwelcoming features to growing applause. The crescendo had been when he said,

'Our young people abandoned to sleep under bridges in cardboard boxes.'

The shame of using that image so ignorantly choked him now. He had never dreamed. Never dreamed. In his guilt he said aloud, ridiculously,

'Why wasn't I told?'

As if he was important: a minister or an MP or something.

He found a spot in an alcove and laid his tarpaulin in it. One end of the bit of clothes line he had found in prosperous Bedfordshire he tied to his wrist and the other end to the bike frame. A very young sob echoed from deep inside his dormitory and he fell asleep.

Things did not look so bad next morning, at least not through the one eye Harry opened when someone trod lightly on his ankle and then apologized.

'Sorry.'

It was a young man returning to his own futon of pallets with an *Observer* magazine. He sat on the end of his bed and began to roll a thin cigarette. He looked at Harry who quickly closed his eye, not yet ready to make eye contact. Instead he curled into a last comfortable position and tried to estimate the time of day from the sounds he heard.

A majestic church bell, probably Southwark Cathedral's, was ringing nearby, but there were no clues there for heathen Harry. There wasn't much traffic. But then it was Sunday. It was cool. But then he was deep in the shade of the bridge. He was beginning to enjoy the game when a car bumped up the curb and stopped on its ratchety handbrake. The driver's door opened and slammed and then a rear door squeaked open. It was a van then. A half-hearted stampede shuffled out of the alcove.

The young man with the *Observer* magazine was shaking him by the foot so Harry rose onto his elbow and blinked at him.

'Soup wagon.'

He nodded to a small white van standing nearby with its back doors wide open. From the van two tough-looking Salvation Army men were doling out soup and a generous handful of rolls to an ungrateful queue. Harry joined the queue behind the young man who tucked his roll-up behind his ear after sucking it to make sure it was out.

'Plenty of rolls on Sunday.'

Harry went back to his own nest and sat cross legged on the edge of the tarpaulin. The soup was too-hot minestrone in a polystyrene cup and he put it on the ground in front of him and looked at his watch as if plotting a cooling curve for it. It was only nine o'clock. This was not so bad really. It might have been the Oso Negro. All it wanted was an old man saying there was a gold mine 'not ten days from here.'

Instead a woman was saying, in a desperately restrained voice,

'No, no, please. Two more nights. Then I'll be gone, honest. Please.'

It was a tall, skinny young woman with a headful of brown rat tails. She was balancing three beakers of soup on a cardboard tray and pleading with one of the Salvation Army men, a sergeant by his stripes, whose face was racked on some painful dilemma.

'You can't keep kids here, can you? I mean, be reasonable.'

She shook and shook her rat tails.

'No. no, no! Of course not. But I need two more days to get the money. That's all.'

The sergeant plodded on with his own line of argument.

'Social Services will put you up in bed and breakfast. Better than this.'

He nodded towards Harry.

'No!'

'Why not?'

She lowered her voice to a whisper and spoke close to the sergeant's ear.

'I've told you. If I go to Social Services, he'll find us.'

The sergeant had begun to shake his head in disbelief but she went on, convincingly.

'Oh yes he will.'

'We'll take you to another borough. He can't find you then, can he?'

He smiled at her and she lowered her head and turned it so that Harry could see her face for the first time. He could read in it that she knew a hundred danger signals unknown to him. She foresaw with her deep brown eyes the danger in thwarting the sergeant's well meant plan. She touched his stripes with her fingertips.

'He'll find us. Believe me. Please. I know.'

'But you can't keep kids here.'

He started again at the beginning of his argument, then added.

'It's dangerous. They're not safe.'

'This is the only place they're safe.'

The sergeant gritted his teeth and nodded lots of angry nods at the litter on the floor.

'What are you going to do then?'

The woman brightened at the scent of success.

'I need two hundred pounds. Then I can get away to a safe place and start again. I'll have the money in two days, then I'll be gone. Promise.'

Harry noticed that she spoke with a northern accent. It had been overlaid with estuary but the vowel sounds were still there, solid, under the veneer. Curiously, it made him feel at home. As she said the words she rearranged the cups on her cardboard tray with confidence, as if they were chess pieces and she a grand master, but neither she nor the sergeant nor Harry believed her for a moment.

'OK. Two more days.'

The sergeant held up a vee of fingers to emphasize the length of the reprieve and then drew two big oranges and some chocolate bars from his pocket. He balanced them on the woman's tray like old fashioned Christmas presents. She smiled as if the world had done her a great favour.

Back at the van he was approached by a crapulous toff in soiled evening dress, holding out a beaker.

'Any chance of a refill sergeant?'

'No! Bugger off!'

He slammed the van doors and squealed off on smoking tyres.

'I'll report you to your, er...'

But no-one was listening and the toff was unsure of the ranking system in the Salvation Army, so he sloped off westwards, shaking with what looked like the DTs.

Harry watched the woman walk back to her cubicle. She sat in the doorway on the edge of a pallet and put the soup and rolls on the stones. A girl and a boy both about five years old crept out and took the food back into their lair. She lit a small cigarette and smiled a tired, smoky grin at them.

Harry balanced the rolls across the rim of the beaker and strolled over to her. This was none of his business. He would not get involved. He had to get to the Central Hall for midday. Just a neighbourly visit.

'Hello.'

She looked at him warily. The kids were cross legged inside, dunking rolls in each other's soup.

'I couldn't help overhearing your conversation with the Sally Army man.'

The formality of his address shocked her to her feet. She moved him gently sideways by the elbow, instinctively hiding her children from him.

'What do you want?'

He had not really considered this question.

'I, er, wondered if I could help you.'

For a while they both considered whether he could. She looked him up and down and he saw himself reflected in her face.

'Oh this.'

He stood up straight with his hands by his sides, palms outwards to show his innocence.

'This is just temporary.'

She smiled, then waved a hand over her cubicle.

'So is this.'

'Quite! Quite!'

They both surveyed the general shambles without speaking. Then she went on, cautiously.

'How did you think you could help me?'

'You said you needed two hundred pounds.'

'Have you got two hundred pounds?'

He could see where this was leading, of course, but he could only say the inevitable.

'No, but I can get it for you.'

She shook her head slowly from side to side, her eyes closed, laughing in her throat. When she had finished laughing she fixed him with a stare of complete contempt. He tried to return the stare. After all he had nothing to feel guilty about. But his eyes could not face hers. He looked her up and down instead. She had clearly fallen suddenly from a recent prosperity. Like a prosperous refugee forced to flee with whatever they stood up in. Her expensive jeans, greasy and bagged from sleeping rough. Her fashionable woollen jacket creased and flecked with crumbs. Her well-cut hair all twisted into rat tails. They all seemed to accuse him. As if he had made a bargain with her and not kept his end.

'Do you know how many men have told me that?'

He held up both his hands to accept the charge.

'I know, I know, I know.'

Peggy had been involved in their local women's refuge: he had been jealous of its call on her time and never quite convinced that it wasn't all a bit of a game. He shuffled uneasily at the memory.

'Why don't you try a women's refuge?'

She seemed to relax and smiled. He wasn't sure whether the smile was one of pity for a silly old bugger doing his inadequate best; knowing a couple of words of jargon, or for a little kindness.

'I have. He finds us.'

'How?'

She sucked the last smoke from her cigarette and ground the butt under her sole.

'He does. He's a big man in the clubs. He's got friends.'

The words clanked out like ice cubes and chilled him. He could feel the menace of the man in the shadow of the bridge.

'And two hundred pounds will get you away?'

He had not meant to ask the question because he had already placed her South Lancashire accent and now he felt like a hound nosing at her last cover. He blundered into another question in a clumsy attempt to extricate himself.

'How are you going to get the money in two days? I mean, here?'

He asked it with idiot jollity, as if it were a question in a parlour game.

'How do you think?'

He stopped himself from blundering any farther by rummaging in his pocket and taking out his last grubby fiver, snapping it tight between his hands to uncrease it. As if to acknowledge its inadequacy he said,

'I can remember when these were as big as a *Daily Mirror.*

She looked puzzled.

'Fivers.'

She still didn't understand. A week ago he had scattered the things like confetti. Now one of them seemed dangerously large.

'Take it. Please. I'll bring you the rest, here, tomorrow, as soon as the banks open.'

His decisiveness seemed to convince her of his seriousness and alarm her at the same time. She dithered.

'No, you keep it, really. We'll manage. Honest.'

But Harry knew what he had to do. He pointed at a spot on the floor between them.

'Here, tomorrow, noon, two hundred pounds.'

Back at his place a threadbare yellow dog was just finishing off the last of his soup. It looked at him expecting a kicking but continued to lick the remains of the soup from his beaker anyway. The beaker beat an elliptical retreat across the floor from its rasping tongue. Harry patted it on its flinching withers and it immediately took advantage of his softness by occupying his tarpaulin and curling up to sleep.

Harry tucked his jeans into his socks and began to untie the washing line from the bike's frame.

'Here! It was nice of you, but we'll get along.'

The young woman was beside him offering him his fiver back. She trembled with alarm. Harry waved it away with nonchalant largesse.

'I'm just going to a meeting of the Parliamentary Party,' he said, taking his teeth to the clothes-line knot and completely oblivious of the spectacle he presented.

'But I'll be back here at noon tomorrow with the money.'

He mounted the bike and set off. But after a few yards he returned and wobbled a couple of circuits in front of the young woman.

'After all, there's a Labour Government in now. We can't have this sort of thing.'

He would just sort out this one case and then get on to Nogger's place. Just one last job.

She watched him ride off towards the Albert Embankment and then checked the fiver to see if it was genuine.

Chapter 11

As he left the arches, Harry's retina was branded with the image of the dog, curled up in the tarpaulin. It suggested some grotesquely carnal French dish to him: tarte aux chiens, chiens en impermeable, something like that and this twisted his thoughts to violent death which filled him with foreboding. But bowling along the Albert Embankment with a fresh breeze off the Thames blowing all the fetid air of the arches away into nothing more sinister than an old Flannigan and Allen song they had sung when he was a small boy, he felt better. He would find Harold at the PLP meeting, get the woman's money, work out some way of eluding the Chief Whip and then he would get Nogger to ring Charlie for him. Things seemed to be getting complicated again in a familiar way.

Opposite Whitehall Stairs he turned around in the saddle to look for the cause of a rhythmic scratching sound that had been bothering him since he set off. It was the yellow dog, trotting effortlessly behind him in the gutter, its eyes peeled for food. He pedalled himself breathless until Westminster Bridge trying to lose it but the dog seemed to be attached to the bike by an invisible string. He abandoned hope of shaking it off and called it to him with a click of his tongue. It moved a stride closer and wagged its tail but it did not look up from the gutter. The feeling of foreboding returned. His mother had always told him to steer clear of the South Side.

Harry and the dog took a couple of hazardous turns around Parliament Square in the honking traffic and then settled on a bench at the edge of Westminster Abbey's gardens.

He was not exactly sure where the Central Hall was, but he knew it was not far. He would just relax for a few moments in the sun and then see about getting into the meeting. The dog might prove a problem, of course. If he had a piece of string, real not imaginary, he could tie it to the bike, kill two birds with one stone, that would. The incidence of bicycle theft in Tory Britain had become notorious.

Westminster Abbey clanged out half past eleven, frightening some pigeons into flapping a quick circuit of the gardens.

Harry surveyed the Mother of Parliaments, her filigreed stonework being slowly digested by the very acid of her greatness and he knew it was all hopeless. There was no parliamentary road. His people belonged in their workshops in the suburbs and provinces. Making things, wiping their hands in their overalls. All this belonged to a tall dark-haired tribe who exuded the exotic oils of centuries of confidence. The whole edifice intimidated him like a peasant at a banquet.

He began to sketch out a theory in which the Tories were the Norman conquerors and Labour the champion of the poor, industrious Saxons. It was a nice, simple theory in which all the Normans wore black wigs and all the Saxons blond ones. Not unlike a fifties film version of *Ivanhoe*, he had once seen. A bit rudimentary perhaps, need a bit of tidying up, but it could form a sub text in the Great Speech; sort of *obiter dictum*. He made a note of it.

Being Sunday there was not much happening outside the House of Commons. A couple of bobbies in shirtsleeves mimed to Japanese tourists that the House was shut today and a television crew prowled up and down outside the railings.

The leader of the crew, who wore a combined microphone and earpiece like an astronaut, stopped to talk to one of the policemen who laughed but shook his helmet at him resolutely. The television man moved on, talking urgently into his microphone and kicking at the pavement.

Harry felt hungry suddenly. And with the hunger came the unrefined regret that he was not sitting on the leather benches of the House. A week ago he had practised the nonchalant lounges he would give the television cameras.

He had just begun work on the image of himself as vagrant MP,

'My constituency is cardboard...' when there was a commotion on the pavement and the television crew sprang into action.

A famous left wing MP was leading a sizeable group of new back benchers around the Palace, pointing out Big Ben and Oliver Cromwell to them, with postures held carefully for the camera. He gave a long interview while the rest milled about awkwardly on the pavement.

One or two of the younger MPs, anxious to get on with the job of being firebrands, tried to engage passers-by in debate while they were waiting but met only smiles and polite Japanese bows in return. One was asked to take the photograph of a posing family who thanked him with many bows which he half returned.

The famous MP finished the interview and led his acolytes across Parliament Square, straight for Harry. They all milled around him and the famous MP gave him a consoling pat on the back and made a tittered-at quip about poverty in Tory Britain before they all swept on past Westminster Abbey, laughing.

A week earlier they had shared a platform at a big meeting in Bradford, but there was no recognition now.

Harry watched them shuffle off in the direction of St James' Park, jostling one another to be nearer the centre.

They stopped outside the Guildhall and were joined by another group of MPs coming down from the tube station. The two groups swelled, with boisterous back-slapping, into what was plainly an *ad hoc* left caucus and then quickly sub divided into smaller groups, each with its own agenda. The television crew reappeared and filmed the famous MP again who was now talking earnestly to a crumpled looking academic with cotton-white hair. Both men nodded sagely in profile.

The group began to swell with newcomers. Harry estimated there were about sixty MPs, some of them household names. One well known right winger who had done abysmally in his leadership challenge and two who had earlier failed to get into the shadow cabinet seemed to have undergone miraculous conversions and they joined the crowd tentatively, at the fringe. The television crew soon found them. Everyone settled into a bright noisy crowd which grew steadily louder as the sun baked it.

Suddenly, the hubbub died like an old gramophone with its spring unwound and everyone turned to look towards Westminster Bridge. Harry looked too, but whatever it was was obscured by the camera crew rushing to film it. He stood on the bench to see better and set the dog barking. One or two of the MPs looked at him.

When he had calmed the dog by picking it up and holding it so that it could see over the crowd like a child, Harry saw Jo walking across Parliament Square. She held Harold by the elbow as he walked painfully with the help of an aluminium walking stick to join the group. He still wore dark glasses but now he also wore what looked like a smog mask. Harry hid his face behind the dog which whined to be put down.

The camera crew broke off in mid interview and rushed up to Harold who spoke a few words into the microphone and then indicated his throat with a one-handed throttling action. The microphone was offered to Jo who made a brief statement to it and then handed a piece of A4 to the producer or whoever he was. The producer read the paper slowly and then rushed after Jo who was now in the van of the caucus as it made its way down to Central Hall, but she brushed him aside resolutely. He consoled himself by rereading the paper over the air to his controller.

Harry watched them shuffle off until only one MP remained who seemed to be looking rather oddly at him. He sat back on the bench and pulled his cap over his eyes, squinting out under the peak. The straggler began to wander tentatively towards him with one eye nervously on the rest of the party. Harry was pretty sure he had never met him although there was something familiar about him. The MP stopped in front of him.

'Here you are.'

He took a pound coin out of his pocket and pressed it into Harry's hand which had opened automatically to receive it. Harry looked up at him in bewildered relief.

He spat on the coin in imitation of his just remembered grandfather and touched his cap. He toyed with the idea of saying,

'Gawd bless yer guvnor.' But held back just in time. Mustn't overplay the part.

The MP seemed as relieved as Harry and stood in front of him, smiling. He seemed to be waiting for something and it flashed across Harry's mind with vivid absurdity that he might want a receipt.

'Thank you,' he said, without looking up.

The MP's feet shuffled on the piece of pavement that Harry could see under the peak of his cap and then ran off to join the others. Harry and the dog followed at a discreet distance.

By the time he reached Central Hall all the big names had gone inside but a few photographers and camera crews still hung around the entrance shooting mutes of the latecomers for regional news programmes to pass the time. He parked his bike and wandered up to the steps to try to see inside.

The Prime Minister flitted across his vision. He was smaller than Harry remembered. He had spoken in the constituency in the eighty-seven election, when Harry had been Chair of the local Party and he had been Shadow Chancellor. A sincere bloke really. They had had a brief drink together afterwards and Harry had taken to him at once. Now he was obscured by tall aides and jostling arse-lickers who tried not to trip over him as they half led, half followed him into the main hall. Harry found himself going up the steps to follow him himself but he was soon stopped by a pantomime sized policeman who took him firmly by the elbow and led him out into the street again.

'Go on, sod off!'

He said it quite kindly.

'There y'are flower.'

A sturdy old MP with a blue scared miner's neck gave him a handful of change and then limped up the steps with his hand on one knee.

'Get thisen a cup o' tea with that lad, it'll be all you get out of this lot.'

Harry looked down at one pound eighty-seven in change in his open palm.

When he looked up again he was surrounded by a group of latecomers all panting out beery breath and pressing money into his hand as if in penance for their lateness. The last of them, out of change, thrust in a vulgar tenner.

'Right, I've warned you!'

The policeman was outside now, enormous in the sunlight.

'Bloody begging now, is it? '

Harry offered him the money in an open palm and tried to disown it with a shrug of his shoulders.

'I wasn't begging. I merely...'

The cameras had turned on them both so the policeman simply shooed him and the money off with the backs of his hands.

'Move on now! If I catch you begging round here again, I'll run you in, understand?'

And aside to Harry, almost conspiratorially but with real venom, he said, 'Soft bastards, giving my taxes away already. Can't bloody wait, can they?'

Harry put the money in his jeans and stood beside the bike, trying to pretend he was an innocent cyclist and not a beggar at all. He would have to be more careful.

A small pandemonium broke out in the foyer and the policeman went back up the steps, grumbling something about maintenance payments probably going up again. He was passed by the dog coming down the steps with a whole salami in its mouth. It was followed by a man in caterers' check trousers, looking about himself theatrically.

Harry watched the scene with detached amusement. A life-sized Punch and Judy act really. It only needed Punch with a big slapstick saying, 'That's the way to do it,' to follow them all out of the Hall. Although it had always been a string of sausages made from old stockings when he had been a kid. The cameras seemed to have turned on him again for some reason.

'Right, that's it. That's bloody-well it!'

It was the policeman, thundering at someone.

When he saw the salami at his feet and the dog wagging its tail at him Harry felt overcome with self-pity at the injustice of it all. He thought of trying to disown the dog but realized immediately that the climate was wrong for any elaborate explanation. Instead he leapt onto the bike, which was in too high a gear, and standing on the pedals, praying the chain to hold, fled back across Parliament Square and over Westminster Bridge, the dog loping along comfortably behind with its salami.

He sprinted up the Albert Embankment and turned into the Jubilee Gardens where he sat at the parasoled table of a snack bar opposite two old ladies and muttered to himself between panting breaths.

'Christ! That was close! Must be more careful! Silly!'

The dog, underneath the table, began to tear at the skin of the salami.

The two old ladies stared at him in alarm and Harry tried to put them at their ease with a whiskery smile of uncleaned teeth.

From his beggings, he bought a tray of cheerless health-food and a bottle of mineral water for the dog and returned to the table.

The old ladies were eating sumptuous vanilla slices and his bitterness at not spotting them at the snack bar momentarily overwhelmed him.

'Where did you get those?'

He pointed accusingly at the cakes and the old ladies changed tables, carrying away their slices on buckling paper plates and muttering.

'Disgrace!'

'Police don't care.'

'Privacy? Ha!'

This was a disturbing trend. He would have to control himself. It was getting hotter and his eyes were feeling gritty. He moved further into the shade and struggled to suck orange juice from an airtight carton which gave him indigestion.

Soon he began to doze and then fell straight into a dyspeptic dream, etched vivid in stomach acid. It was a dream of heart-breaking sadness.

Peggy was sitting on one of their early settees. She had a gas bill in her hand and she was crying over it. Harry watched himself sit beside her and put his arm round her shoulder so that he could feel it plump and alive in his palm.

'We won't always be broke.'

He shook her playfully in a way that usually made her smile, but this time she looked at him with terrible anguish instead.

'We will.'

She said it with such authority that he began to cry too.

Harry tried to put his arms round both of them, to reassure them it was only a dream and that they would soon wake from it but they struggled. They struggled hard and he had to seize each of them by an arm and shake them. The ceiling began to fall on him. A woman, not Peggy, was screaming.

'Call the police!'

'He's having a fit.'

Harry was on his feet, the table and parasol capsized, his health-food scattered on the grass and the yellow dog holding the snack bar staff at bay with convincing snarls.

He still wanted to cry for the sadness in the dream but he had to deal with the nightmare he had woken into. He began to move towards the bike, the dog covering his retreat and his demon pointing out that the table was unstable because the parasol's long stem meant that its centre of gravity soon fell outside the narrow base of the legs: elementary really.

'I'm sorry about the table. Unstable design, really.'

'It's not my bloody tables that are unstable, mate.'

Harry raised himself up with aplomb and the dog barked furiously.

'You'll have to excuse me, I have an important meeting to attend.'

He tried his most patrician accent but it didn't cut any ice down here.

'I hope it's with a bleeding psychiatrist!'

He wheeled his bike towards the entrance with the rigid sanity of the insane and the dog followed with the gnawed remains of the salami held high.

Going back along the Albert Embankment, the dog now standing on Ernest's coat in the carrier and barking at the wind, Harry began to worry about going mad. St Thomas' Hospital loomed in front of him and he considered wheeling in for a check-up. Surely there was a Japanese machine he could be plugged into in there that would sort out all the syntax errors in his head. He only needed a little fine tuning really. But he recalled the desperate heroism in the woman's eyes under the bridge. All her anger locked up in them like a genie that could not be let out until the kids were safe.

He turned onto Westminster Bridge and proceeded with his own pragmatic caution. Of course, he was exploiting her really. It came to him as plain as day as he re-entered Parliament Square with the dog turning his cheeks ecstatically from side to side in the breeze. He was just using her plight in the ongoing displacement activity that he called his life.

'Life,' his demon had once told him, in a candid moment, 'is about four hundred and twenty haircuts. Not many, really, when you think about it.' But he was drawn back to his original idea. There was something for the Great Speech in it.

Somehow, the Labour Party distracted itself from its great mission, he wasn't quite sure what that was, with the urgent, anecdotal plights of the working class. Like getting haircuts. That was a bit dodgy perhaps, easily misunderstood.

He made a couple of circles of the Central Hall, passing uncomfortably close to New Scotland Yard on one of them, before installing himself in the doorway of a large building bleached white with pigeon shit. There was a good view of the main entrance to the Hall and the dog seemed happy to curl up in the shade. Harry settled for a long wait which he began by lecturing the dog.

'You! Yes you!'

The dog opened one eye to look at him.

'You stay here. Understand? Any more trouble from you and I'll...'

But it had fallen asleep and begun to snore. Harry began to doze too but retreated from sleep at the memory of the recent dream. Not a difficult dream to interpret, although if his mother had been there she would have found a thousand meanings in it, hidden from him. She had been a great interpreter of dreams. He was back at the breakfast table with Charlie and his sister Dot and their mother. He had absently let slip a detail of a dream he had had the previous night and none of them could leave the table until his mother had interpreted it properly. Charlie and Dot were looking daggers at him and his mother was interrogating him minutely.

'You're certain there was no fire in the dream. That's important. And clouds. Yes, but what sort of clouds? Storm clouds? White, fluffy clouds?'

He had not known any of the answers and his mother had been disappointed in him. Charlie always made up whatever answers he thought she wanted to hear but Harry never could. He shook himself out of the memory and took a short turn in front of the doorway. There was danger in a long wait in this heat. Sleep or a morbid decline into things done and dusted threatened all the time. He decided to estimate the volume of Westminster Abbey to keep his mind from mischief.

While he was musing distractedly on whether it was a canon of ecclesiastical architecture that the transepts in cruciform churches had to be the same size both sides of the nave or whatever it was, the MPs started to pour out.

Jo and Harold were amongst the last to leave with a small group who mimed concern and sympathy for Harold. One of them tried to shepherd him somewhere but Jo was being firm in her refusals and soon she and Harold were left alone. She gave him lots of instructions which she beat out with a forefinger into the palm of her hand. Harold nodded compliantly and then, after one false start, Jo left him and set off westward. Harold consulted a piece of paper which he turned through several angles and then set off himself, straight for Harry.

He stopped to consult the paper again when he was almost in Harry's doorway. Harry seized the moment and confronted him.

'Harold!'

Harold let out a yelp, muffled by his mask, and staggered backwards clasping his heart.

'You daft bastard! That's all I need today, bloody heart attack.'

He looked cautiously about and then moved into the shadow of the doorway with Harry, raising the mask and snapping it onto his forehead. The dog growled.

For some time he breathed in the unrestricted air gratefully, then he let out a long shuddering breath.

'I can't go on with this, lad. I mean, fuck me!'

He fumbled out a packet of cigarettes and tried to light one with a shaking match.

'What's all this, then?'

Harry waved a hand over the dark glasses and mask.

'This is fucking Eco-flu, lad.'

'What?'

'Eco-flu. Here.'

He handed Harry the paper he had been reading, turning it over first and stabbing a finger at it in explanation.

'Press Release. Harry Beamish MP. House of Commons. For immediate use.

Harry Beamish MP says he is determined to make his contribution to the new Labour Government despite suffering from the debilitating Eco-flu. Known medically as Srelbboç Syndrome after the Professor of Eco-toxicology at Prague University, the disorder is thought to be triggered by hypersensitivity to unfiltered uv light and non-metal oxide traces in the lower atmosphere. The symptoms: undulating flu-like attacks accompanied by loss of voice, come and go irregularly and without warning. His agent, Jo Firsby, believes the disorder has its origins in overwork during the election campaign but is confident of a speedy recovery.

'I may not be able to speak,' said Mr Beamish, but I'll go into the Government divisions if I have to be carried.'

Contact. Jo Firsby.

End.

Harry marvelled at the woman.

'I really can't go through with it, Harry.'

Harold had taken off his glasses and was pinching the bridge of his nose.

'To be absolutely honest with you, Harry. When I took this on I was sure we'd lose. You know, like we normally do. And well, no bugger'd care. Like they don't. I never dreamed we'd have a fucking majority of one and I'd be it.'

He handed Harry the glasses and mask, like a guard exchanging weapons.

'Here, we'll have to swap back.'

But Harry would not accept them. Instead he put a consoling arm on Harold's shoulder.

'I can't Harold. Not yet, anyway. I have a job to do first.'

Harold breathed slightly easier and took the disguise back, shuddering at the sight of it.

'When then?'

Looking at Harold, Harry knew he could not delay much longer. He had had three days out of the fray, for which he should be grateful, and yet the thought of re-immersing himself in it all filled him with apathy. He dithered.

'Oh, by the way, Peggy phoned. She thinks the tour may be finishing early. She says she'll go straight to Charlie's place, if that makes sense.'

Harry's mind was made up.

'Tomorrow, after twelve. I have to be somewhere at twelve, after that we can swap back, if you like.'

'That's too late. I've got to see the Chief Whip at nine thirty. And Jo tells me you were like that.'

He linked his little fingers and shook hands with himself.

'I can't possibly get away with it.'

'Of course you can. Get that clobber on. Grunt and cough. Few nods. You'll be fine. By the way, can I have my wallet back?'

Harry smiled like a crocodile.

'Jo's got it.'

'What!'

'Jo took your wallet.'

'But what about my credit cards?'

'That's why she wanted it.'

Harry marvelled again. He thought for a while and passed through several shades of anger.

'Oh well, it's no big problem. I've got to have two hundred and fifty pounds as soon as the banks open tomorrow.'

Harold was already shaking his head and pursing astringent lips. He smiled faintly with the satisfaction of a bureaucrat puncturing buoyant hopes.

'I don't know about that, Harry. Why do you want it?'

Harry thought of raging but decided instead that he owed him the truth.

'I met this young woman last night. She's got two kids and they're living in a cardboard box for want of two hundred quid. OK!'

'You said two hundred and fifty.'

'It's something extra for herself. What are you, Harold? The Chancellor of the fucking Exchequer all of a sudden.'

'Alright! Alright! I met him this morning.'

'Who?'

'The Chancellor. He said we had to show a firm hand from day one or we would be swamped with demands. Said we were a lifeboat for the women and children not fat-arsed spongers. Something like that.'

'Right, right.' Harry nodded, approvingly. 'That's dead right. That's exactly why I need the money. See Jo, tell her about our meeting and she'll get it for you.'

Harold still looked doubtful.

'Do this one last thing for me, Harold, and we'll swap back tomorrow afternoon.'

A policeman was wandering towards them, looking suspiciously at Harry and the dog. Harry picked up his bike and nodded to Harold to put his disguise back on. They began to walk towards Westminster Bridge.

'Where are you going?'

Gratifyingly in role, Harold croaked and handed Harry the same paper, only reversed again.

Biroed in Jo's heavy hand was an address in Islington.

'You can get a Tube from Westminster Bridge, change at Victoria, Victoria Line to Highbury and Islington. Or you could get the Northern Line to the Angel: I think it's somewhere between the two. You'll have to ask.'

He handed the paper back to Harold. When he had been a boy it was not a place to go alone. Now it was a select haunt of journalists and media people. Not really, he reflected ironically, the place for Harold to go alone.

They walked towards Westminster station, Harry trickling the bike beside him, catching his shins occasionally on the pedals. The dog nosed turds in the gutter.

Outside Westminster station Harry had the idea of taking some money back to the woman immediately. Just what Harold could let him have plus the remains of his beggings. A token of his sincerity, in which she had no reason at all to trust.

'How much money have you got on you Harold?'

'What?'

Harry began to fan the air towards him impatiently with his fingers.

'Money. Give me what you've got. I'll take it to the woman now, show our good intentions. Keep her spirits up till tomorrow. Stop her doing anything silly.'

While he was speaking Harold had begun the infuriating mime of a man discovering he has lost his wallet. Harry's face clouded in rage but Harold was oblivious of the warning signs. He was craning his neck, looking back down Victoria Street, as if Jo might be standing there waving money at him.

'She's forgotten to give me the fare. She promised to give me the fare.'

Harry gave him the last tenner of his beggings and pointed sternly at the paving stone he was standing on.

'Here! This fucking spot. Tomorrow, eleven o'clock. Two hundred and fifty pounds, or you keep the mask.'

A groan echoed from inside the mask as Harold took the tenner and set off gingerly down the station steps, fumbling the bannister rail in the sudden darkness.

Harry shoved off eastward along the Victoria Embankment for Limehouse.

Chapter 12

As he pedalled past Cleopatra's Needle, his rage at Harold's pennilessness condensed into a lump in his breast and the bitterness of his disappointment stirred up an old lesson his father had once taught him.

'They're all the same, mate. They'll give you anything but money. Anything.'

He had been talking about Jews at the time but it went for any rich bastard, MP or lah-di-da bloody official: they were all the same. It didn't matter that Harold was a Christian worker. The consolation lay in being right about the rottenness of life. That was the real opium of his people. He made a mental note of it for the Great Speech.

He left the river at Blackfriars Bridge and wound through the empty Sunday streets of the City with the dog sleeping contentedly in the carrier. They swept round St Paul's. Down Cannon Street and Eastcheap. Round the Tower and back down to the River at Wapping. Here, the Canary Wharf building, which had dominated the skyline all day, frightened him to a standstill. It was like a sun in a science fiction film. Looming on the horizon. About to collide with the Earth. His fright was so real that he stood in Wapping High Street and wondered seriously if there was any way past it. He desperately needed to sleep.

Despite all the changes, he found Nogger's filthy little hole of a shop easily enough in Noel Street. It was at the end of a short terrace of old East End houses, tucked under the railway line out of Fenchurch Street. He was quite sure it was the right place because it still had the ghost of a sign over the window.

'Jas. Howlett and Son.' Not specific about their trade, even then when Nogger's father had been the son, in the days of Fu Manchu.

For some time, Harry wheeled the dog up and down the opposite pavement, trying to pluck up the courage to knock.

Uncannily, nothing seemed to have changed since Charlie had first dragged him there forty years ago.

The same cock-eyed Players' Weights sign still said 'Sorry we're closed' and the self same junk seemed to barricade the door.

'Perhaps,' he thought, catching a glimpse of the Canary Wharf building over the roofs, 'it's a Cockney theme-park.' It seemed to be the only sense he could make of its survival in the hurricane of economic change that had raged around it. Or a film set. Once, in Yorkshire, he had driven onto a film set and Sir Lawrence Olivier himself had asked him if he would be kind enough to make a detour. It was possible.

A slight breeze caused a big plane tree beside the shop to tap gently at an upstairs window. Harry followed its example, knuckling the door with moderate restraint. At once, an upstairs window shot open with a bang in its loose sash and an old woman bawled at him.

'What d'you want? Eh? Eh? Go on, piss off!'

She sounded exactly like his mother's mother who had lived not far away in Spitalfields except that she would have added something colourful about getting her piss-pot over him. The accent seemed sadly doomed in the shadow of Canary Wharf. It should have got the boat to Australia with all the others.

'Well, what are you standing there for?'

'I'm looking for Nogger.'

'He ain't here.'

'Where is he?'

There was a silence. Harry tried to think up a strategy to deal with her. Aware that he was rudely demanding answers, he decided to try a bit of politicians' charm.

'I'm Charlie Beamish's brother, Harry.'

'Who? Never heard of you. Go on, sling your hook.'

Relieved, he tried another tack.

'Is Mr Howlett in?'

'No, he ain't.'

'Do you know where he is then?'

'He's gone.'

'Gone where?'

This seemed to tickle her and she began to bubble like a phlegmy cauldron.

'Not to fucking Heaven, that's for sure. Ha, ha, ha!'

Harry could not understand.

'I don't understand.'

She leaned out of the window and spoke slowly and clearly as if to an idiot.

'He's bleedin dead, ain't he?'

She slammed the window like the lid of a coffin.

While he was still looking up, reeling from the shock of the news, the door opened and Nogger, wearing white trainers and a *Jurassic Park* tee shirt, hissed furtively at him from the shadows of the doorway.

'Psst! Harry! Come in, quick.'

He pulled Harry in by the sleeve and shut the door behind him, catching the dog's tail. It yelped painfully but Nogger quickly calmed it with long, caressing strokes.

'Nogger, you're alive.'

'Alright, don't holler it up and down the street, eh.'

'But she said...'

'What, my old mum? She's a card, ain't she? Take no notice. Like that, your mum and her.'

For the second time that day Harry was shown two little fingers locked in friendship.

'But she said you were dead.'

Harry had been shocked by the old woman's lack of reverence for death: at her age, and Nogger's, for that matter. It was alarming.

'I am Harry. A bit. Tax purposes. Know what I mean?'

He shoved his way through a tangle of junk to a staircase at the back of the shop.

'Charlie's been on the blower. Give me the SP. You're alright here...'

He stopped in mid sentence and pointed back at the door.

'Better get that bike of yours off the street before some little bugger nicks it.'

Now that he felt secure, Harry could think only of sleep.

Nogger led the way up the stairs to a living room where his mother lay, propped up in a bed of grey sheets, carefully pouring a glass of Mackeson. She stopped pouring and looked suspiciously at Harry.

'It's alright Mum, it's Charlie Beamish's brother, Harry.'

She remained suspicious.

'Alice Crouch's boy.'

'Alright?'

She nodded and went on pouring her stout.

Nogger cleared one of two chairs at a table and waved a few crumbs onto the floor.

'Sit down, Harry. I'll put the kettle on.'

He watched Nogger put the kettle on an old enamel cooker and he was transported back to his grandmother's kitchen. She was fussing over him.

'You feeding this boy, Alice? He do look thin. Have a bit of grub, darling.'

'Have a bit of grub, Harry?'

'You feeding him, Norman? Give him some of that corned beef.'

Nogger turned his eyes to the ceiling in mock shame and held a tin of Arabic corned beef, like a wine waiter, for Harry's approval.

'Wog stuff, Harry, but it's kosher.'

He paused to consult the label and then corrected himself.

'Well, halal really, but it's alright. I can let you have a couple of cases if you don't flash it about.'

He made two hefty sandwiches and set the teapot to brew in the middle of the table.

Harry took off his cap and hung it on the back of his chair and Nogger's eyes flashed instantly to his bald head. He tried to avert them before Harry saw him. Nogger still had all his hair, Harry noted bitterly.

'You know Charlie got nicked for shooting them dogs in the park out in Edmonton?'

Harry shook his head despairingly.

'Nutter, your brother is.'

Smiling proudly, he poured the tea.

'I need a few favours, Nogger.'

He was beginning to feel delirious with fatigue and he wanted to get down to business before he fell asleep.

'If you could put me up for a bit. It'll only be a couple of nights.'

Nogger was waving aside any hint of objection and trying to begin a story of his own.

'Did I ever tell you about the time me and Charlie nicked an unexploded bomb off a site in Leman Street?'

'And if you could ring Charlie for me...'

'He got the explosive out with one of your mum's cooking spoons. Like lumpy marzipan, it was.'

He crumbled the imaginary marzipan between his forefingers.

'I could do with some clean clothes too, if that's alright...'

'We wrapped it in grease-proof paper and sold it to Sammy Bone to blow a strongroom door in Cable Street...'

Harry was shaking his head.

'True, Harry. On my life...'

'I met a woman with two kids today, Nogger. They're living in a packing case under Waterloo Bridge, on the run from her old man.'

'Charlie got your mum to tell him how to get the detonator out. What with her and my mum working up the Ordnance. They sat at this table and drew us a diagram. Right where you're sitting now. Charlie said he wanted it for school. I think they'd twigged though...'

'I have to take two hundred and fifty pounds to them when the banks open in the morning. She says she can get away for two hundred and fifty pounds.'

His eyes were beginning to close.

'Where you getting the money from?'

'A friend's getting it from the Labour Party.'

'Well, I've got plenty downstairs. Just in case, you understand.'

He waved both hands to rub out any suggestion of doubt that the money would turn up and went back to his story and Harry tried to pay attention to it.

'Well, he paid up.'

'Who did?'

'Sammy. Fiver apiece.'

Nogger drew his chair closer to the table and turtled his neck across to Harry.

'We had to go up to Walthamstow dogs to change them. Couldn't change a fiver round here in nineteen forty. There'd have been questions in the fucking House, Harry.'

He roared with laughter and then stopped short.

'No offence, Harry. Charlie told me you were having a bit of trouble in that line.'

'Just a temporary hitch, as it turns out, Nogger.'

Nogger stood up suddenly in case Harry elaborated on the temporary hitch.

'You look knackered, mate. I'll show you your bed.'

He led him into a little spare room stacked to the ceiling with boxes of Czechoslovakian shoes.

'Make sure you give him clean sheets, Norman. I know what a dirty toe-rag you are.'

They both laughed silently to each other.

'I have to be at Westminster Bridge by eleven o'clock tomorrow, Nogger. Don't let me sleep in, will you.'

'Here! Your brother and me...'

But Harry was fast asleep.

Chapter 13

At nine thirty Harold sat at Lex Latham's desk, sweating into his smog mask. Jo had written a note for him and the Chief Whip was reading it with a fading smile.

'Congratulations on your promotion Lex. I can't speak at the moment because of this Eco-flu, but I'm fit to struggle into the divisions, don't worry. The doctor says it could go at any moment. Peggy sends her regards.'

Lex folded the note and gave it back to Harold along with a pink copy of the week's Whip, all of which seemed to be underlined with three black lines. He looked at Harold and winced, coughing to clear his own throat in sympathy.

'Well, Harry, congratulations yourself.'

Harold inclined his head and smiled coyly.

'I hope you get rid of this bug or whatever it is.'

He looked suspiciously at Harold and then at his watch.

'Yes, right, down to business. We've got five minutes.'

They both looked at their copies of Lex's instructions.

'Obviously, things couldn't be tighter.'

Harold nodded and Lex sat back and began to expand on the general situation.

'We've told the Lib Dems to piss off. They wanted PR and a Cabinet place. So we're on our own. We're going to press on and let them bring us down. The sooner the better from our point of view, of course, which is the strongest card we have to play.'

Harold made a few ambiguous grunts and Lex leaned forward again running his pen down the list of the week's business.

'Now they won't try to defeat us on everything. They want to choose their issue. But here!'

He stopped his pen at the Thursday Finance Bill and redrew the three printed lines under his own instructions: 'your attendance is essential', making it a six line whip.

'This has the enabling powers to re-nationalize the railways and they'll have to have a go at us here. We'll be alright so long as there's no slackness.'

He embossed three full stops on the paper with his biro. Harold nodded and held up a thumb. He had a terrible feeling that things were going too well.

'You'll need to bring me a death certificate to get off this vote, Harry.'

His hand shot momentarily to his throat.

'God forbid, of course.'

Harold clutched his own throat and swooned theatrically.

'You dare!'

Lex put the paper aside and drew two more from a pile and pushed them across the desk to Harold.

'Your old school has won some sort of environmental prize. Greener Britain Award or some such bollocks. Jo's got all the info. High profile presentation at the Russell tonight. Here's your invitation and here's a speech for you to deliver.'

He looked painfully at Harold.

'If you're really not up to it, get Jo to do it. I've had it released, embargoed till tonight.'

He stood up and offered his hand to Harold, signifying that the interview was over.

'The PM's mentioned your name in connection with a PPS, Harry. This would be the perfect flying start for you. Make a big effort tonight. Anyhow, be a nice night out for you. Meet a few old colleagues. And you'll get a good dinner at the Russell. You look as if you could do with a relaxing evening. You've been overdoing it.'

He walked him to the door with an arm over his shoulder.

'Bit of a change from a curry at the Karachi, eh?'

Harold laughed too raucously for one with Eco-flu and immediately clutched his throat as if in pain. Lex went rigid with anxiety.

'Take care of yourself Harry. And give my regards to Peggy.'

He gave Harold's shoulder a parting squeeze.

'You've put on weight, Harry.'

Chapter 14

Next day both men turned up promptly on the appointed spot. Nogger had kitted Harry out in a *Jurassic Park* tee shirt, brilliant white plastic trainers and white cotton trousers that seemed to have been made for a stilt-walker. The right cuff was already black with chain-grease. In contrast Harold wore a smart, lightweight summer suit with a red silk tie. In his left hand he had a bright red plastic briefcase and under the same arm he carried a roulade of morning papers.

'Harry!'

He held out his right hand for shaking, breezy with the success of his recent interview with Lex. Harry noticed his eyes wandering up and down the concertinaed legs of his trousers.

'You're looking very smart, Harold.'

Harold blushed slightly and did a modest twirl.

'Nice, isn't it? Jo gave it me. Her cousin said I could have it. Good of him, eh?'

Harry looked at his watch.

'Have you got the money?'

'Let's get a cup of coffee, Harry.'

Harold walked resolutely to a mobile coffee stall. Harry picked up his bike and trotted to catch up with him.

'I said, have you got the money?'

'Sugar, Harry?'

Harry stared at him in dismay.

'Milk?'

'You haven't got it, have you?'

'Hold on, hold on!'

Harold raised a restraining hand to Harry's growing anger and reached into his pocket.

'Jo gave me fifty. For my own expenses. Here, you can have it.'

Harry took it with bitter disappointment.

'She says she's got the two fifty waiting for you in your

office any time you want to collect it. It's just round the corner.'

'No!'

'Harry! This has got to stop. I took the fucking oath for you today. I'll end up in Botany Bay if we get rumbled. Let's get off this while we can.'

He put his briefcase on the Embankment wall and opened it.

'There's this, too.'

He handed Harry the invitation to the Russell.

'It's your old school. Some of your teaching mates will be there. Kids you taught. And if you make this speech...'

He handed Harry a second piece of paper.

'...Lex says the PM's talking about a PPS. That's a Parliamentary Private Secretary.'

Harry scowled at him. He read the first few paragraphs of the vacuous drivel in the speech and checked his watch.

'You can tell Jo I'll do this.'

He flapped the gold-edged invitation at Harold and noticed, as he did so, that the awards were to be presented by an eminent duke. He looked more closely at the card with its rose and gilt edging and read, 'decorations may be worn' printed small, at the bottom. The germ of an idea twitched into life at the back of his mind.

'But until I've seen this woman and her kids alright, the mask stays on, Harold.'

He tucked his trouser cuffs into his lime green socks and mounted the bike. Harold gripped the handlebars. He seemed desperately disappointed at the easy collapse of his stratagem.

'Where will you get the money from?'

'From a friend.'

'You're being ridiculous, Harry.'

He kept his grip on the handlebars and used his free hand to wave in the air for a convincing argument.

'This Government is committed to start a million new homes in this Parliament, Harry.'

'Not by this evening, surely, Harold.'

'Don't you take the piss out of me! You're the one who got us all into this.'

'If you had brought me the money, you could have been on the tea-time train out of King's Cross.'

Harold let go the handlebars and looked crestfallen.

'One act of faith, is all they ask.'

'They?'

Harry covered his face with his hands and screwed up his eyes. He could see the woman's eyes like patient prisoners at their cell windows, silent and resigned. His encroaching madness knocked on his skull to be let in.

'People like her, Harold. Our people.'

He looked at his watch. It was almost noon.

'I've got to go.'

Harold made one last attempt at reasoning with him.

'Come to Jo's office, your office, with me Harry. It's just round the back here. The money's there.'

He pointed through a flock of angry seagulls squabbling over a bacon roll on the pavement.

'We'll get the money from Jo and take a taxi to this woman of yours.'

But Harry was already wobbling along the pavement through the lunchtime pedestrians.

'No more promises, comrade! Hard cash!'

'Fucking puddled! That's what you are lad. Fucking puddled!'

He had not meant to bawl this after him but the prospect of another day in the mask filled him with dread. He stood rooted to the paving stone and watched Harry's flying progress eastward along the Victoria Embankment with deepening gloom.

Cheapside and Cannon Street were treacherously clogged with traffic so Harry mounted the pavement and rumbled over it shouting 'ahoy!' in lieu of any bell or hooter.

At the junction of Mincing Lane he collided with a

business man in pin stripes and set the papers he was carrying free as doves in the wind. The man waved desperately to call them back.

'You bloody maniac!'

But Harry had no time to bandy words, he pressed on to Limehouse.

Nogger had given him a key to the back door and Harry let himself in with it. He stumbled over a pile of old paraffin stoves and called breathlessly for Nogger.

'That you, Harry?'

Nogger came down the stairs cleaning his upper dental plate with a grey handkerchief.

'Trouble with that corned beef is it gets under my fucking plates. You got your own teeth still, Harry?'

'Nogger, I need to borrow some money. I'll settle up...'

But he left the sentence unfinished.

Nogger put his teeth back in and castaneted a few trial bites at the air as he made his way towards an old safe, half buried under ancient typewriters.

'Two hundred and fifty, was it?'

Harry followed him, panting for breath and nodding at his back. He watched him open the safe with a long key and reveal its hoard of old brown envelopes and small cardboard boxes.

From one of the envelopes Nogger withdrew a neat slab of old white fivers, embalmed in a self-seal polythene bag. He handed them to Harry. Harry turned as white as the fivers.

'What's this?'

'Don't tell me you don't remember them, Harry. They're the Old Lady's. Monkey in fives. Pristine, they are, Harry. Pristine.'

To Harry's relief, Nogger had found a wad of the latest edition of ten pound notes and was counting them out, testing each one with a flick of his forefinger and thumb.

'I could get five grand for them, condition they're in.

He rolled the tens into a cylinder and snapped an

elastic band on them. The old fivers he held in his open palm and wiped clean of dust.

'Look at them.'

Harry looked at them with a strange sense of guilt. They were the promissory notes of gentlemen. They had been hard-nosed Tory bastards really, Harry knew. But even they had been unable to envisage this world of villainous photocopiers and the uttermost dishonesty to which their heirs had sunk. Conrad would find no empire builders in the City now. No pioneers to run the electric light of commerce into the heart of darkness. Only shifty swindlers. There was a sort of consolation in it.

Nogger and the old dog stood in the doorway and waved him off. The little roll of notes rubbed reassuringly against his thigh as he pedalled.

To avoid the traffic in the City he took the reckless decision to ride along the South side of the river and got hopelessly lost around Southwark Cathedral. He pedalled in a circular frenzy around the Borough Market and the Globe pub, getting more and more disoriented. Eventually, his head throbbing with blood and his demon estimating his pulse rate with a cautionary shaking of his head, Harry slumped into the shade of a big plane tree in the Cathedral gardens and listened to the organ inside playing Bach. The music reinstated his reason. He could not be far from Waterloo Bridge. All he needed was some straightforward directions.

He watched a group of Japanese tourists dithering in the entrance, wondering whether or not to take their shoes off. They were ushered in by a tall young parson or whatever he was, Harry had never been sure about the ranks of Anglican clergy. They inched inside with trepidation.

Before the parson could disappear Harry collared him for directions. He smiled at Harry too and then reached deep inside the pocket of his long cassock and withdrew a silver watch. He fiddled with its chain for a few seconds as if it were a rosary and then set off at a brisk pace across the little garden.

'OK, follow me.'

Harry followed his swinging skirts along the path, struggling to keep pace with him. 'The trouble with being approachable,' Peggy often said, 'is that people approach you.' He would never have time to make Bishop.

The parson said something to Harry over his shoulder but it was lost under the wheels of a train veering north into Cannon Street. Harry responded with an ambiguous laugh although his panic stirred again at the thought of having missed some crucial direction.

There was no need to panic because the parson walked him all the way to Southwark Street and then hugged him by the shoulder so that he could speak directly into his ear over the traffic.

'Straight on, OK!'

Then he clove the air three times with his outstretched hand, as if blessing Harry's journey.

'Straight on. Over Blackfriars Road. Straight down Stamford Street. God help you when you come to the roundabout.'

He patted Harry's back as he set off and then, hitching up his skirts, fled back to his Japanese tourists. It was one o'clock.

When he got to the arch the woman had gone. Her cubicle was still there but now it was occupied by a gang of fifth form girls who filled it with smoke from puffing fags and stared out at him with mild curiosity.

'Where is the woman who was here?'

No-one answered but they all looked him up and down.

'There was a woman here last night, with two kids.'

He intimated the heights of the kids with the flat of his hand.

'Boy and a girl.'

One of the girls stood up creakily to face him.

'She said we could have this place, alright!'

Harry noticed she was trembling slightly inside her woolly jumper, despite the heat of the day. He tried to cut through all the confusion with frantic waving.

'No! No! No! I just need to find her. Where did she go?'

'She didn't say. You could try Club Row, round the car park, or the church.'

'Shoreditch Church?'

'Fuck knows what it's called. Got any cigs?'

Harry withdrew one of Harold's tenners from his pocket and made a tiny fan of it. The girl watched it.

'You're sure you don't know where she went?'

'What's all the interest in her for?'

'What d' you mean?'

The girl withdrew a step. Harry stopped fanning with the tenner and held it out like bait. She came closer and shrugged her shoulders.

'You're the second fella to ask for her.'

'Who was the other one?'

'I don't know, do I? Nasty-looking. Her old man, I guess.'

The air under the arch became suddenly cold. Harry handed the girl the tenner and turned to go.

'She's only been gone an hour. She was waiting for someone but he didn't turn up.'

Harry nodded.

'I didn't tell the other one though. Told him fuck all. He's no idea.'

Her last remark gave him heart and he pedalled straight off for Shoreditch Church. Along Threadneedle Street and Bishopsgate he began to estimate her range. If she had been gone one hour, average speed with two kids; two miles per hour, at the most. There was still time to catch her.

'Why are you doing this?' his demon asked. 'You cannot succour all the ills of the world. Be reasonable.'

'Yes, yes, yes!' Harry said, aloud. A passing bank worker looked at him.

'That's true,' he went on. 'About the ills of the world.'

Harold could have confirmed this after one day in office. But the look of utter contempt the woman had cast on him when he had first offered his help stared at him again. He pedalled on.

As he passed Dirty Dick's, he thought he saw her jogging furtively down Middlesex Street with something stuffed up her jacket. He swerved across the path of a taxi and followed her swinging rat tails to the tiled doss-house, marooned on its own island in the one way traffic, but it turned out to be someone else. The woman approached a young man standing on a doorstep and half removed a parcel from her jacket. But looking round and spotting Harry watching her, she stuffed it back again.

'What you looking at?'

Harry pretended to fiddle with his front brake blocks but she was not deceived.

'Go on, piss off!'

He pissed off down Frying Pan Alley and up Commercial Street for Shoreditch.

Making a triangle of the three places that the girl under the arch had suggested, Harry combed the shambles in between.

On Club Row a boy in a khaki parka with a northern accent that Harry could not quite place, said he had seen her. But he was lying. When he made to leave, the boy clutched him by the tee shirt and hung on grimly, searching Harry's eyes for help.

'I've seen her, honest. Three kids.'

'Two.'

'That's right, two, two.'

He clung to Harry, even when he remounted the bike.

'I could help you look for her. I know the area.'

Harry's father had once bought him a little black mongrel on this very spot. The rogue of a vendor had sold it to them as a dog, skilfully tucking its tail between its legs to disguise its true gender. Harry had called it Prince for a week until his friend's granny, who knew about these things, lifted it up by the scruff of its neck and told him,

'You've got a little princess here, darling.'

Harry had renamed her Sally. There had been no beggars then.

'Bloody sweatshop of the world, Harry.'

But Harold had been wrong there. There was not even a sweat shop for this boy to toil in. Harry peeled off a second of Harold's tenners and gave it to the boy to make him let go.

'Get yourself something to eat.'

The pedant in him almost went on to lecture about not buying drugs but instead he took advantage of his loosened grip to tear himself free and shove off again. He dared not look back.

There were dozens of homeless people milling around the church and at the other end of the High Street dozens more squatting in cardboard shanties by the car park wall, but none of them had seen or heard of the woman.

He continued to pedal round the sides of the triangle, long after any hope of finding her had gone. Soon the rush hour traffic reminded him of his dinner date at the Russell and he set off back to Limehouse to borrow a suit.

'What are you? Forty, forty-two chest, thirty-four waist?'

Nogger flicked along a rail of suits. A tape measure hung round his neck.

'Thirty-two waist, Nogger.'

Harry tried to correct him but he had already selected a suit for him.

'There y'are. Try that.'

The dark blue, double breasted suit felt so expensive that Harry was alarmed by it. Nogger was pulling down the tail and dusting off his shoulders, professionally.

'Nice bit of stuff that is, Harry. Cloth's from up your end: Huddersfield fine worsted. Hand-stitched by Markovitz. None of your foreign shit. '

He wheeled up a long speckled mirror for Harry to admire himself in and went to rummage in a partially collapsed cardboard box.

'Harrod's wouldn't give you any change out of a grand for that, Harry. What size collar are you? Sixteen?'

He threw Harry a white shirt in a noisy cellophane wrapper.

'Pure silk.'

He nodded and pointed at his own chest.

'So don't drop your shackles and 'oop down it. I'll get you a nice red tie to go with it.'

He shot an anxious glance at Harry and stroked an imaginary tie.

'You are still wearing red? I don't really keep up with politics. I should, I know.'

'Red,' a PR man hired to purge the Party image of socialist features, had once told him, at a meeting, 'is found threatening by women.'

Peggy, who had been chairing the meeting, said, 'It's bastards like you we find threatening, not the colour red.'

The PR man had snapped his attaché case shut and stormed out. The memory made him shudder.

'Nice trilby and you could have dinner with the Queen.'

Nogger sized up Harry's bald dome with embarrassment.

'You've got a big head, like Charlie. Seven and half, he is. Here, try this.'

He brushed up the crown of a brown trilby on his sleeve and put it on Harry's head, pulling it slightly over his right eye.

'Sam Spade!'

Nogger was standing behind him, peering over his shoulder. Harry blushed. But he tried a casual hand in his trouser pocket, anyway.

'No.'

'Sam-fucking-Spade, I tell yer.'

He left Harry to admire himself in the mirror and picked up the invitation card which he began to scrutinize at arm's length.

'Says: 'decorations may be worn', Harry.'

'No, no, Nogger. Honest.'

'It's no good being bashful, Harry. The Tories will be there like fucking Christmas trees. They give each other gongs for sod all.

'Weren't we at Eton together, Claude? Why so we were, Charles. Well that must be worth an OBE. Well, if you insist...'

He mumbled the rest of his lines into the shoe box he was rummaging in.

'Mind you, OBEs are too big really. Vulgar. Now this.'

He withdrew a Victoria Cross on a faded ribbon and let it spin slowly over the open box.

'Definitely not, Nogger! Definitely not! They're for heroes.'

Nogger tutted into the box and replaced the medal.

'Trouble with you, Harry, if you don't mind me saying so, is you take this too seriously. It's a fancy dress party. I've got a DSM and bar here.'

'No!'

'DCM?'

'No!'

'World Cup Willy?'

'I'm sorry Nogger, but I'm having trouble carrying off the suit.'

Nogger made one last dip into the shoe box.

'There's a Croix de Guerre here. Beautiful piece. You won't see any of these in the Russell tonight. Go a treat with that suit, Harry. No? Pity, but there y'are.'

He brought Harry a generous hip flask filled with whisky and took him to the back door, packing him off like his mother had done.

'Don't get a cab back here, Harry. Get one to the Yuppie block on the wharf and come in the back way. OK?'

The sun was still withering the weeds in the back yard but Harry felt cool under his broad trilby. From the railway arch he looked back at Nogger standing in the shade of his doorway with the old yellow dog beside him and he felt a lump in his throat.

Harry could not bear the extravagance of London taxis so he walked to Stepney Green and took the Tube to Russell Square, which was dear enough. He was getting old.

Chapter 15

The lift at Russell Square was stiff with people up for the awards and heady with their cologne. The perfumes began to dispel Harry's vision of the woman and her kids and the knowledge of their plight. Perhaps he had imagined it all. The whole thing certainly seemed improbable now, strolling through the golden Bloomsbury evening to the hotel entrance.

He arrived at the same moment that two black limousines drew up containing the Prime Minister and his entourage who had turned up at short notice. In a shambles of security men with squawking radios he was placed behind the Prime Minister and his two aides.

'Keep with the party, please, sir.'

An ironical choice of words, really.

The Prime Minister walked through the lobby with inelegant haste, talking secretively to a perfumed young film star of a woman who carried his radio telephone for him. He almost walked past the manager and his assembled staff but just managed to pull himself and his impatient party back in time. The manager shook hands with him and exchanged a few words which ended in loud laughter and all the staff applauding. Bowing, the manager smiled a patronizing smile that seemed to foretell business as usual, very soon.

The party was ushered into a high-ceilinged room where the security men handed them over to the organizers and took up positions by the doors.

The Prime Minister was greeted with a large familiar handshake by a buffoon of a Labour peer who seemed already to be drunk. He offered a loud welcome in mock-Scots and received a whispered reply that turned him pale and sobered him instantly. He continued more formally with the introductions and Harry drifted off.

He managed to get through three large sherries before a young man with a clip board tracked him down and led him to his table where introductions were made to his fellow diners.

Jo and their local mayor came into view just as he was being introduced to the leader of the Tory group. Harry shook his hand with all the warmth reserved for formal enemies, clinging to it as long as he could for comfort. The Tory seemed, as Jo approached, a haven of propriety and predictable reactions.

In the gathering sherry-haze Harry thought, not for the first time, that if he had not been born a worker he would have made a good Tory politician himself. Like all politicos, he had a secret penchant for their brand of sycophancy and anyway it was so much easier. All the energy socialists required just to change the direction of society, they had available for politics. His demon joined him and they began to work on a thermodynamic equation involving political free energy and a component for the rate of change of social momentum in Newton when Jo's hand clasped his upper arm causing him to flinch and spill sherry down Nogger's trousers.

'Harry!' She hissed.

'You know the mayor, of course.'

They exchanged handshakes and embarrassed glances. The mayor asked, snidely,

'Been on any good walks lately, Harry?'

'Seen any good westerns, your worship?'

They left it there.

Jo began to move people around like chess pieces but she never let go of Harry's arm.

'You know Jim Wilkinson from Moorbank, don't you? Yes, of course you do. You were colleagues until last month, weren't you? Until you deserted them. Ha, ha, ha!'

She spoke the last words through clenched teeth and shook him like a ventriloquist's dummy until he answered her.

'Yes, yes. Ha, ha, ha! Deserter.'

Jim gave him a haggard, end-of-a-long-term smile and stood with his hands by his sides, grinning. Jo moved him aside to reveal two familiar third formers, although they were called year nine students now, of course, since the National Curriculum.

'And the stars of the whole occasion: two of the winning environmentalists from your old school. We're all very proud of them, aren't we, Mr Beamish?'

'Yes indeed. Yes indeed.'

He shook the small, cool hands of a boy and girl whose bright eyes glinted in the light from the chandeliers. He tried, desperately, to remember their names. The boy, he seemed to remember as a trouble-causer. Cunningly timing his remark to coincide with the announcement of dinner, Harry said,

'You must tell me all about your project.'

They began to drift to the dining hall. The boy walked beside him and sneered up at him.

'You don't even know our names, do you, sir?'

Harry had him now: Slade. But what was his first name? Began with N.

'Oh, I know you, Mr Slade.'

'Really. What's my first name then?'

Harry pretended not to hear him.

Jo was called to the telephone on their way to dinner and her tenure of his arm was taken over by their host, the director of Greener Europe PLC.

'Harry! Congratulations! Congratulations!'

He turned out to be a Tory ex-county councillor from a neighbouring constituency. He had been beached when his own government had abolished his council. They had found him this job as a reward for his loyalty during those difficult times. He was trying, with excruciating smiles, to ingratiate himself with incoming Government MPs.

'Spotted your victory in the results.'

He pulled himself up to Harry's ear and whispered confidentially.

'Between you and me, Harry. I wasn't surprised.'

Charlie would have told him to collect his cards and money and piss off but Harry could only manage a little frostiness as they sat down to dinner. The director oiled on about the old constituency.

'I'm sure we'll be able to work together on some local initiatives, Harry. What with our knowledge of the area. Your knowledge of the schools.'

'Remembered my first name yet, sir?'

'Norman?'

The boy sneered.

'Beats the chalk-face, doesn't it, Harry? You're well out of it, lad.'

It was Jim, his old teaching colleague who seemed on the point of tears. He was leering at a point about a foot in front of his nose and soliloquizing.

'Bloody mad-house, Harry. Bloody National Curriculum: midday bloody edition of. Bloody exams. Bloody truant lists. Records of bloody achievement. Little buggers with their bloody projects.'

The last indiscretion jolted him out of his trance and he smiled at the two students who ignored him.

The MC hammered out silence and some lord or other said the grace, for which, to outdo one another in piety, everyone stood.

Harry had not said grace, and then only seated, since his grandmother had moved out after a row with his mother forty-odd years ago, but it still seemed familiar. It made him feel strong and clean again, and resolute.

Late evening sun poured in through the high windows and he was a brand new boy at the grammar school again. He was back amongst short-haired boys in clean collars and long haired girls in crisp blouses. The other denominations were somewhere else and all the Anglo-Saxons were bashing out their Protestant hymns together. No multi-cultural nonsense then to paralyse them. A young man, strong among his strong tribe.

The grace ended and everyone sank back into their seats and began to crank up the hubbub of conversation again. But Harry still stood to attention, a smile on his face, listening to the old hymns and his demon whispering.

'You could have been a sea captain, Harry. *Nostromo's* Captain Mitchell. Harry Hornblower.'

His heart began to pound in a tribal frenzy. The corked-up genie of racial pride was out of the sherry bottle and coursing through his blood.

The boy tugged him back to reality by the sleeve.

'Sit down, sir.'

'I might have been a sea captain.'

He hadn't meant to say it, it just slipped out.

'Really, sir?'

The boy gave a quiet, supercilious, snort.

Harry turned towards Jo's vacant place, almost putting his nose between two creamy breasts, presented to him like avocado halves in a low velvet evening gown. After an initial shock he let his eyes wander up a naked arm, past a discreetly tattooed, or possibly just painted, bluebird. Past the ghosts of purple love bites under thick foundation, to a face that was, impossibly, familiar.

A voluptuous woman of about forty leaned over him and for one horror-struck moment he was afraid she was going to throw her leg over him there and then. Fortunately, the waiter refilling her glass raised his eyebrows censoriously and she fell slowly back into her seat like a praying mantis. Biding her time. She let the waiter fill her glass to the brim and then raised it to Harry with a whispered toast.

'To the revolution!'

As he slugged down his wine, Harry noticed the boy holding a very generous glass up to the light and saying to the girl,

'Looks like a decent Burgundy, at least.' Before dispatching it with astonishing speed. Harry wondered if he should he say something to him? But the woman was saying, 'You don't remember me, do you?'

Everyone seemed to be accusing him of neglect. She was smiling at him over the rim of her wine glass.

'I'm afraid not. You're face is familiar but I ...'

A memory was beginning to form in the mist. A memory of quite a different woman. She prompted.

'Ginny.'

'Ginny Booth. I came and spoke to your constituency on the unilateral position a couple of years ago. You were Chair at the time. I remember you. You're Peggy's old man. Congratulations, by the way.'

She drained a second glass and while the waiter refilled it she went on.

'I'm freelancing now. Bit of research. Defence still, mainly. But anything you need digging up.'

She handed him a business card that she seemed to conjure out of the ether. Nudging him in the ribs, she growled vampishly in his ear.

'Harry Beamish, MP. You're a sly old dog. I thought you were a school teacher.'

It occurred to him, for only the first time, put as bluntly as that, that he really must be a sly old dog, but the thought was barged out of his mind by the shock of recognizing her.

He had her now. She had stood on the platform beside him, wearing a man's suit, and waved one facile generalization about defence after another into the audience. And they had all been too cowardly to laugh. Trying out the same ideas on the doorstep in the general election, the electorate were not so restrained, or course. Shameful episode, that had been. She had worn a man's suit and a hint of a moustache in those days. Now she had shaved off her moustache and was playing a different game altogether, although with the same old self-assurance. A glow of admiration for her perseverance bloomed in his stomach with the wine and the sherry.

Keeping pace with the third former, Harry finished another glass and ran a lecherous eye up Ginny's legs when Jo's legs suddenly appeared beside them. They were scarred and muscular and twitching with the impatient shifting of her weight.

'Out!'

Jo jerked her thumb upwards. She was boiling dangerously in the humiliation of her black evening dress and the high heels that took her well over six feet. Ginny began a suave response to Jo's rudeness.

'Jo dear...'

But she was seized by the arm and hauled from her seat, force marched past two tables on the tips of her toes, and shoved out between the jaws of a sliding partition. She managed to say, in parting:

'I'll see you at the House, Harry.'

Jo threw herself into her seat, her skirt riding halfway up her thighs, and swigged down the remains of Ginny's wine.

'I've had enough of you. That was Lex on the phone. His office. Nine o'clock tomorrow.'

She took Harry's wine and drank that too.

'I've had enough of this fucking party. Of fucking men. And if you don't take your eyes off my legs I'll punch your fucking lights out, right now. What the fuck do you think you're doing?'

The dealing of the warm plates around the table spared him an answer. Instead he just smiled. Jo turned a dangerous crimson and he barely prevented himself from laying a comforting hand on her thigh.

The waiter kept their glasses brimming. This and the lamb tornados mellowed Jo, so that when she spoke again it was like her old pragmatic self.

'This Harold's a reasonable guy. I've offered him two grand expenses. He'll say nothing.'

She took another long swig of wine and began to smile disturbingly.

'We can always deny it if he blabs. Who'd believe him? I mean, it's too fucking fantastic to be true, for Christ's sake!'

She was shouting.

'Shh!'

Neighbouring tables had begun to bend towards their conversation and the buffoon of an MC was trying to get eye contact with Harry.

'Shh!'

Stuffing her mouth with lamb and wine, Jo chewed things over.

The MC introduced the Prime Minister who began by rudely checking his watch.

'So much to do. So little time in which to do it.'

'Ha, ha, ha!'

A polite ice-breaker of a laugh tinkled around the room. The Prime Minister waffled on, Jo chewed, the third formers drank and Harry could taste impending trouble like iron filings in the lovely Burgundy.

'...So I can assure all of you this evening, that efforts, such as yours here tonight, to raise community awareness of environmental issues, will have the full and generous support of the new Labour Government.'

There was a polite crackle of applause. Pausing for dramatic effect, the Prime Minister took up the list of award winners.

'And so it is with the greatest pleasure that I...'

'Wind up this whole shitty outfit because it is no more than a fucking Tory gravy train...'

Jo was talking aloud to herself between glasses of wine. A small ripple of tuts came from surrounding tables.

'...present tonight's splendid awards.'

He read out a catalogue of Tory Party benefactors and quangos. With false smiles all round, he presented awards to their jowly representatives who had temporarily delayed the plotting of his overthrow to collect their prizes.

In the tense atmosphere, brittle with insincerity, everyone seemed to be growing redder with the exertion of clapping and grinning. Harry felt his silk shirt flapping wetly against his side as he clapped and suspected that the air conditioning had packed up. People began to drink more and mutter. The wine waiter ordered more bottles to be opened.

All around him were men grown fat, that special fat of expense accounts. Fat of the land. Wasters of the land. Wasteland. He imagined he saw the haunted face of the woman under the arches moving between them for alms, unnoticed. An anger he recognized with inner sober alarm as drunken rage gripped him. Although part of the rage was for Jo's thighs. All rage from the same bottle.

'Moorbank School!'

There was more clapping and his table began to rise in a scraping of chairs. The third form girl steadied him by the elbow and led him towards the platform.

A photographer lined them up with the Prime Minister and flashed, flashed. Then the third formers went back to the table lugging an enormous trophy and Harry was left alone at the microphone to make the speech Lex had prepared and he had left at Nogger's. Anyhow he had something quite different for them. He swept the sea of sweating faces with the green jelly after-image of the flash bulbs hovering over them Pentacostally. He'd give them fiery tongues. The MC handed him a microphone.

'Thank you.'

The sound of his own voice over the PA startled him. Momentarily he caught the anxious eye of the director, standing at the back of the room, desperately trying to communicate comradeship with a sickly grin. Harry had no idea what he was going to say.

'Thank you, chairman, Prime Minister.'

Suddenly he remembered what a clever speaker he was. It all came quite naturally to him: how, he had never been able to figure out. It was coming naturally to him now and he found himself struggling to get off the slippery slope of civilized moderation that began to pour from his lips.

'Can I first thank our generous hosts this evening for a splendid dinner and...'

There were a few claps and one appreciative fart followed by giggles.

'...and compliment the hotel on its excellent cellar.'

Harry inclined his head towards the head waiter who inclined his own in return. The third form boy raised his glass and said,

'Hear, hear!'

And the whole dining hall raised their glasses in a ringing toast.

The head waiter blushed and the director seemed to relax for the first time in the evening. It seemed so gross to spoil their success. Perhaps, if he appealed to their better natures, they could fix the woman up with something. They seemed a decent lot really.

Braised leeks that had been served with the lamb began to turn uneasily in his stomach, as if resentful of the wine's praising. He felt himself go cold and his forehead began to sweat. The room gave a small lurch and he had to take a deep breath to steady himself. He recovered quickly.

'I couldn't help thinking, as I savoured that gorgeous Burgundy, of a woman I met the other day.'

The Prime Minister, who had been talking sub-aurally to his secretary, stopped.

Harry laid the microphone on the table so that it made a click over the PA. and then went on in his teacher's voice.

'She is living in a packing case with her two children, not two miles from here.'

There was a nervous silence while people tried to make up their minds whether or not it was the start of an off-beat after-dinner speech. Someone behind him asked the MC, 'Who is he?'

Harry continued.

'Her husband is trying to find her.'

He paused and smiles blossomed here and there in anticipation of a happy ending.

'He wants to kill her.'

All the smiles wilted but a couple of cameras flashed.

'She has nowhere to go. Nowhere to hide. She is a fugitive in an alien land. There is no safety and no rest for her.'

He caught the director's eye and addressed him.

'This is the green and pleasant land that has grown from the seeds you have sown in your terms of office.'

He showed him which land with a wide sweep of his open hand. One, tentative flashbulb triggered a chain reaction of them and a pack of paparazzi crept forward like Apaches under cover. A fat man in the audience said, in a patrician accent,

'The bloody fool.'

Harry turned a pulpit finger on him, from which spurted the Methodist fire of his grandmother.

'And as ye have sown, so should ye bloody well reap. This whole shitty gravy train of an organization...'

He caught sight of Jo's head, nodding amen.

'...should be wound up and its directors handed cardboard boxes to live in. That'd put you in touch with the bleedin' environment, that would.'

All semblance of civilization abandoned now: pure Cockney.

'You'd get some fucking lamb tournedos under the arches,' he roared.

'Be lucky to get a cup of Sally Army soup and a stale roll. Get some of that weight off you. Fat bastard!'

He added the last remark diminuendo. Sizeist really. But he didn't care.

The paparazzi flashed and when the Prime Minister injudiciously held his brow they blitzed. Harry was warming up. He stood with his knuckles on his hips and an insane grin on his face, nodding at the audience like a newsreel Hitler.

'Oh yes, the whole bloody pack of you.'

Flashbulb-blinded, he pointed at random into the blackened pack.

'Few nights on the street. Do you lot the world of good.'

There was an urgent shuffling beside him and Harry turned on the Prime Minister who was trying to make the best retreat he could.

'Before you go, Prime Minister.'

He stopped but his entourage moved on a few paces to be as far away from Harry as possible, in case his treasons hopped onto them like fleas. Fixing Harry with a look of anger and contempt, the Prime Minister said, quietly, 'I'll see you in the morning, when you're quite sober.'

The cameras whirred in a continuous rage of flashes. One paparazzo ran out of film and fumbling, dropped his replacement roll. He began to grovel on the floor for it, whimpering. His colleagues trampled him into the thick piled carpet to get nearer the Prime Minister. Security men moved in and held them back and the Premier left the dining hall. Harry shouted after him.

'If she can't count on your support, you can't count on mine.'

For a moment he wondered if he had got that right but knew that he had when the cameras turned on him.

The MC had retrieved the microphone and was trying to carry on as if nothing had happened.

'Moorbank School, ladies and gentlemen!'

A few stalwarts tried to drum up some applause but it was drowned out by a noisy scrum of reporters and irate Tories besieging Harry as he tried to make his way back.

People began to clutch at his arms. A military-looking man with a thin white moustache, wagged a finger at him and said, 'A time and a place, sir! Time and a damned place.'

He was swept away and his mild rebuke was succeeded by more sinister requests.

'Who is this mystery woman?'

'Interview with the *Guardian*, Mr Beamish?'

'The *Sun*, Harry, thousand pounds, cash, five minutes?'

The scrum was thickening and beginning to struggle amongst itself for a piece of his arm to hold onto.

'Have you had sex with her?'

'No, I have not!'

Flash, flash, flash.

'Harry!'

Jo was wading through the journalists, signing desperately to him to say nothing. She flicked through the headlines as she waded.

'MP denies sex with mystery single mum. Beamish bonking in Boxville? Left wing lecher lays low-life.'

The scrum now had a life of its own and oozed around the room like an amoeba with Harry as its nucleus. It squeezed between tables and ingested new people. It swallowed a big Geordie mayor who offered him his chain of office 'for the bairns, man' and new reporters with tape recorders. But always it moved steadily away from his table where Harry could see the rapt third formers grinning and drinking wine.

'Will you resign the Whip?'

'Harry! Harry!'

Jo had torn a way through the soft outer layer of reporters but she could not penetrate the hard core that contained Harry. Two of them, working as a team; one holding back the mob while the other poked a tape recorder up Harry's nose, had succeeded in pining him against a plaster column. They were demanding answers.

'Will you resign the Whip? What time are you seeing the Prime Minister tomorrow? Who is this woman? Where is she now?'

Someone at the back, presumably from a fashion magazine shouted,

'What colour's her hair?'

'Harry!'

Jo was only one row away from him now and she had managed to get her hand to her mouth and press her index finger to her lips.

'Shh!'

She was nodding in the direction of a fire exit. The reporter persisted.

'What did you mean by not supporting the PM?'

With a sudden surge in the crowd the recorder crashed into Harry's teeth and he tasted blood from a ballooning lip. For some reason the reporter was turning purple and seemed to be asking,

'Ek, ek, ek, ek?'

Now he seemed to be levitating before Harry's eyes. The braised leeks threatened to enter the fray.

Jo had managed to slide her hand down the back of the reporter's collar. Making a fist had cut off his awkward questions and now, with one superhuman heave, she tore him out of the crowd and shoved Harry through the gap his leaving left towards the fire exit.

He slipped out of the scrum which snapped shut again around Jo but someone inside was still clinging to his arm. With a sudden wrench Markovitz's hand-stitching gave way and Harry abandoned the arm of Nogger's suit to the mob and slipped through the fire exit.

In the doorway he caught a last glimpse of the scene. The MC was trying to present an award to a delegation of infant scholars who would not look at the photographer. Their eyes, like everyone's, were on Jo. With the straps of her evening dress gone she was standing tall and unencumbered, punching away reporters and photographers with beefy smacks.

Harry fled down a corridor lit dimly with red lamps and out into a small yard of tall, commercial dustbins.

Leaping onto the rubber top of one of the bins Harry discovered it had a cunning hinge mechanism. The lid simply slid off the bin with him aboard like a magic carpet. He began to fall and the whole binfull of kitchen waste followed him.

On his way down his demon appeared and began to explain that he had shifted the centre of gravity of the system. Altogether too much of that lately. Unstable equilibrium, it was called.

A gale of rotting cabbage-wind gasped from the open bin as if poured over Harry who sat, winded, on the concrete. As a nasty little afterthought, it dropped a trifle, still in its broken bowl, onto his forehead which raised a balloon on his eyebrow to match the one on his lip.

He scrambled out of the heap and got over the wall by way of a flimsy lean-to. Dropping to the pavement he limped into the balmy Bloomsbury evening.

In Bloomsbury Square he found a bench dedicated to an essayist he had never heard of. He sat on it and watched an indigo wash creep up the eastern sky.

As he scooped trifle from his collar and picked pieces of glass out of his hair he was overwhelmed by a desire to be in bed with Peggy, reading a detective story. He would have to see Lex and the PM now. The press would be full of tonight's fracas. He had ruined Nogger's suit and left his trilby in the cloakroom at the Russell, exposing his baldness again. Everything he had ever stood on seemed to be falling away, like the top of the bin. Unstable, that was the problem. He was overcome by a longing to cry.

Instead of crying he took a long pull at the whisky flask and then got up and began the trudge eastward to Nogger's place. He couldn't face the complication of hailing a cab.

Chapter 16

'I'm sorry about the suit, Nogger.'

Nogger waved the apology away.

'Don't worry about it. Have some more coffee.'

They were drinking coffee with Carnation milk and eating doorsteps with jam.

'Harry! You up Harry?'

Nogger nodded towards his mother's room and whispered:

'She saw you come in last night. I told her you got rolled down Catford Dogs.'

'Yes! Morning Mrs Howlett.'

'Come in here. Let me have a look at you.'

Harry went in and stood beside her bed. She spoke to him without taking her eyes off the television.

'Proper two an' eight you come home in, last night. You alright now? Is he feeding you? He's a bugger, is Norman. Norman! You feeding this boy?'

She reached up from her bed and gently turned his head to inspect the gash left by the trifle dish.

'You should have gone to Walthamstow. Fancy going over the water, to the dogs! Rough hole, Catford is. Always was. I told Liss I'd keep an eye on you. You watch yourself.'

This seemed contradictory to him, but he let it go in the euphoria of being called a boy.

'Stay on your own side of the water, alright?'

She turned back to the television.

'Alright, Mrs Howlett. Can I borrow your *Mirror*?'

She handed him the paper and shooed him away with it at the same time. He had spotted what was inevitable on the front page:

'PM's Fracas Fury.'

He spread the paper out on the kitchen table.

One of the paparazzi had sold a half page picture of the PM with his head in his hands then, Harry in the foreground, evangelical madness in his eyes, shaking his fist at an audience in the early stages of riot.

'A furious PM was today blaming the inflammatory speech of new Labour MP Harry Beamish for the ugly disturbance at an awards ceremony in a top London hotel yesterday. Violent scenes erupted after the left wing back-bencher accused the Greener Britain Corporation of being a 'shitty Tory gravy train' and responsible for the plight of homeless people.

'The outburst came as Beamish told the audience of a mystery woman he alleged was living in a packing case with her two children "not two miles" from the hotel. At one point he told the organizers of the gala dinner that they should all be sacked and given cardboard boxes to live in, adding it would "put them in touch with the bleeding environment."

'During an emotional exchange with the PM, Beamish threatened not to support the Government if it would not support the homeless woman. The Prime Minister said that the speech was regrettable.

"It was an award ceremony with young people present. He had been asked to speak about a project from his old school. The speech he gave was inappropriate in tone and content. I can only suppose it was the result of fatigue and emotion at the end of such a momentous election. I will be seeing Mr Beamish tomorrow." Beamish declined to elaborate on the identity or whereabouts of the mystery woman but denied any sexual relationship.'

Nogger turned the paper round on the table and read the story slowly, shaking his head. When he had finished he smoothed out the paper's creases and began a detailed study of the photograph.

'Handsome, that suit was,' he lamented involuntarily. And then, quickly, to show he was not harping on it:

'You'll need another one for this morning.'

'I'm sorry about this, Nogger. I'll settle up...'

But Nogger dismissed his apologies.

'I've got a nice lightweight linen. Sort of off-white. With a nice Panama. Just right for this weather. Very chic, Harry. I'll go and dig it out.'

Harry half raised his hand in a plea for something less conspicuous but Nogger waved it aside.

'It's alright, Harry. A pleasure.'

He rang Harold's Islington number and Jo answered.

'Deep shit, Harry. Deep.'

Her voice slid down an octave and rested as she considered the best way to describe the full depth of the shit to him. He assumed she was waiting for a cue.

'Why?'

He knew it was the wrong cue, of course, as soon as it was out of his mouth.

'Why! Well where shall I begin? You're the instigator of a conspiracy to impersonate an MP, remember? Harold took the oath for you. Mumbling into that fucking mask, sweat pouring off him like he had the fucking plague. He won't last another day. I've got a first in history you know.'

She was beginning to shout.

'Did you know that? And I've never heard of anything like it before. Never!'

He knew all this, and when he had time he would probably regret it, but right now he just wanted to get on with the job. This one last job. He began to wave away her digressions, a gesture lost over the telephone, of course. She went on.

'Lex came to see me. You, that is. He came, in person, to your office.'

She waited for the enormity of this irregularity to sink in but Harry was reflecting, in alarm, on his new found sense of purpose.

Grimly, he watched himself preparing for battle like a soldier: cold steel fixed in his heart, the last of his sanity shaken from his fingertips, all dissent suppressed again, until the war was over.

'Harry! Harry!'

He waved himself goodbye. It was the last he would see of Harry Beamish. Soft Harry, the fool: perhaps forever. The questions would never be answered now. Never put, really. Oh well, cry Harry! and over the top.

'Harry! Did you hear me?'

'What did he want?'

Jo seemed to sense his change and changed the tenor of her approach.

'There's still a chance we can get away with all this if you come home,' she corrected herself quickly, 'back. If you come back, now.'

Harry did not respond.

'He doesn't know but he suspects. He knows you're in some kind of trouble. He came to do you a favour for old times' sake.'

Her voice was soaring up towards hysteria.

'For fuck's sake, Harry, he's the Chief Whip with a majority of one and he came from Downing Street to see you in person.'

'Yes, but what did he want?'

Jo took a deep breath to steady herself then went on patiently.

'He wanted to be sure you'd stay the course till Thursday. And he asked Harold some very searching questions about the old days. If I hadn't been there. If Harold hadn't managed to get the mask on before he came in. Oh, Harry, for Christ's sake pack it in!'

It was Jo's turn to be silent. She had said too much: pleaded.

'Thanks for getting me out of there last night, Jo.'

'Story of my bloody life, that is.'

She sounded like Peggy.

'Are you alright? Those photographers looked ugly.'

'Some of them look a lot uglier now. Soft bastards!'

She said it with northern bravado and a little tinkle of laughter.

'Were the police involved?'

'Oh they made threats about charging me with affray, or something. All bollocks.'

She began to wander into details.

'Something about a photographer losing two teeth. I told them to lose one tooth might be regarded as misfortune; to lose two looked like carelessness on his part...'

They both began to giggle.

'Lost on the police, of course.'

'Norman! Norman!'

Delaying too long, Harry clamped his palm over the mouthpiece.

'Who's Norman?'

It was Jo, speaking with terrifying intelligence through the earpiece.

'Norman! Who's that on the phone?'

'It's alright, it's only me Mrs Howlett.'

'Oh!'

'Harry! Harry!'

'You still there, Jo? Must have been a crossed line.'

'Hmm!'

He could almost hear the word Norman turning over and over in her brain, making connections. She went on slowly, using the part of her brain not occupied with searching out Norman from her memory.

'Harold will meet you at Westminster Bridge, where you arranged, at a quarter to nine. He'll have your pass and the Order Paper and the Whip. Lex will have you met in the lobby at nine and taken to the PM's office.'

It might have been a morning briefing during the campaign.

'Oh, by the way, Peggy phoned. She might be going up to British Columbia for an extra week, some conference or other.'

The news infused him with a sense of divine benefaction. The gift of a sign.

'Or she might be home tomorrow.'

Definitely a sign.

As he lowered the phone, he heard Jo's voice squawk his name urgently over the receiver. He put it back to his ear.

'Norman Hoglett, Haglet, Howell. No, Howlett. Norman Howlett. Isn't he one of your brother's old mates? Lives in Deptford.'

'Yes, that's right, Deptford. Or Bermondsey.'

Anything to keep her on the wrong side of the river. But it was only Harry's London mind that was riven by the Thames. Jo's saw a low sprawling city, more of the nether lands than England. It was all one to her.

'No, Isle of Dogs. No, no, don't tell me. Where was it Fu Manchu hung out?'

With bitter admiration, he said:

'Limehouse.'

'Right, right. Limehouse. Deptford! That's on the wrong side of the river, Harry. I'm surprised at you. I'll look it up in my *A-Z*. Cheerio!'

Standing in front of the cracked mirror again in a pale colonial suit and a panama hat, waiting for Nogger to select from a bunch of bright floral ties, Harry could not make up his mind whether he looked like something off the cover of *Vogue* or a buffoon. Turning from one side to the other, he considered, philosophically, whether there was any intrinsic difference. Elegant? ridiculous? Elegant? ridiculous? No, it was no good, he would never know. Perhaps they were two sides of the same coin. Beauty and ugliness in the eye of the beholder. He felt an addition to the Great Speech itching at the back of his throat but Nogger had made a choice and was presenting him with a tie of tangerine silk.

'Japanese silk, that is, Harry.'

Satsuma then. It set off the suit perfectly, against his expectations, which reassured him. He tried the jacket buttoned and then unbuttoned. With and without a hand in one pocket. He walked towards the mirror and then away from it, looking over his shoulder at his retreating back. Arse a bit fat, but not unlike, he decided, the guy in *Sierra Madre* who presses the silver pesos into Dobbs' palm.

'This is the last you get from me. And just to make sure you don't forget your promise, here's another peso.'

'What was that?'

Harry coughed to cover up his soliloquizing.

'You're not getting this Eco-flu are you, Harry? There's a lot of it going about. I've just been reading about it in the paper. Epidemic, they're predicting.'

Nogger stuffed a silk handkerchief to match the tie into his top pocket and plucked it delicately into an orange bloom.

'There! Handsome! You could meet the Queen like that. Tea on the lawn, eh? Here boy!'

He called the dog to him and fastened a length of knotted string under his collar.

'Come on Harry, I'll walk down to the Commercial Road with you. I'm taking this old dog of yours for a run round the basin. Let him shit on the Yuppies' patch. He's an intelligent dog. What do you call him?'

'He's not my dog. He just latched onto me under Waterloo Bridge.'

'Don't you want him then?'

Whispering out of the corner of his mouth so as not to offend the dog, who was listening, Harry said:

'Not really.'

Nogger and the dog looked at one another with wet, brown eyes and the dog gave a yelp.

'I'll find you a box in the corner boy. Alright!'

The dog gave another yelp.

'I think I'll call him Harry, if you don't mind, Harry.'

'It's alright with me, if it's alright with him.'

The dog barked and barked and beat the back door with its tail and they all walked out into the hot midsummer sun, laughing.

A mile away in Wapping a fax lay on a sub-editor's desk and the journalist who had sent it was arguing over his mobile for the front page lead.

'I'm sure it's her. Sonia Smith, twenty-seven from Leatherhead. She's from up north originally, Cheshire. Two kids: Alison aged six, Daniel, five. Her old man's got a club in Brighton. Mad Mike, they call him and he's got a string of firearms offences. Nasty bit of work. She's tried to get away before but he's always found her. There's a Restraint Order in force but he doesn't give a monkey's. He's armed and dangerous and stalking her. Mad Mike, predator. It's a cracker, Arnie.

'It's thin, Dave. Where's the proof?'

'I've seen Mad Mike's old mum in Brighton. She says he's been looking for her in London for the past week. We'll have to move fast or we'll lose this one.'

The sub-editor breathed in through his teeth.

'If you can get a positive ID, Dave.'

'I got a family snap from the old lady.'

'Printable?'

'Definitely.'

There was another long intake of breath.

'Get Beamish to identify them from the picture and we'll go with it. OK?'

There was no reply but a click from Dave, for whom time was money.

Harold and Harry arrived together at the appointed spot near Westminster Bridge. They shook hands and then stood back admiring one another's summer suits.

'That's some tie, Harry. There'll not be two like that in the House.'

Harry waved the tie's end like Oliver Hardy and they both laughed. There was no need to add the catch phrase about the fine mess.

'It's all in here: Order Paper, Whip, a list of EDMs Jo thinks you should and shouldn't sign...'

Harold had placed his red attache case on the wall of the Embankment and flicked through its contents. Snow-white gulls, nosey as customs men, hovered over it, looking for pickings or snatchings.

'Here's your pass. Jo's made a copy but don't make me use it, Harry. I couldn't face another day in that mask.'

Harry took the pass but made no promises. Harold snapped the case shut and handed it over.

'There. The security people have given me some stick for that case, so you'd better have it. Oh well.'

His hands now empty, Harold flapped his arms freely by his sides as if he had a mind to join the Thames gulls and fly home up the Humber to Yorkshire.

Out in mid stream a tug hooted and Harold stopped his flapping and leant on the wall to watch it churn its way eastward.

'This has been something else, this has.'

'You've done a grand job, Harold.'

'I know.'

There was a long pause as the tug struggled the length of the old County Hall.

' I only come out for a packet of fags.'

They began to rumble with laughter and the tug churned under the Hungerford Bridge.

'Under different circumstances, Harry. You know, bit of training: constituencies and districts, council committees, wards, all that. I could have made a good MP. Don't laugh.'

'I wasn't laughing at you, Harold. I was laughing at how right you are.'

Released from the burden of wearing the mask, Harold expanded with the confidence he had last shown in the beer garden of the Collier's Arms. He leaned against the wall, hooking his thumbs in Russell's waist-band.

'I'll tell you one thing I've learnt, shall I? I haven't met one of them that gives a tinker's cuss for any bugger but himself. Although there may be some.'

He added this to be reasonable, then he waved a hand to show that this was only a digression and not the thing he had learned.

'What I've learned is that you could do anything you wanted to. Aught. All you have to do is...'

Straining on a word that would not come, even though he tried to fan it out of his lungs with flapping hands, he said, eventually:

'Do it. All you have to do is do it. Trouble with the Labour Party is you're all frightened of bogey men and dragons that lurk in the mists of Economics!'

He echoed the word for effect, then others.

'Economics! Market Forces! Fiscal Policies! Ooooh! You'll never do aught until you face these terrors.'

Harry looked at his watch.

'Harold.'

'Oh, I'm not saying they don't exist and that you don't have to be careful with them but...'

He was in full spate now, pointing up to the City and ahead to Big Ben, his gestures running ahead of his words.

'The market will respond to the reins right enough, you just have to have the right legislation. Be firm.'

Miming a charioteer, he hauled the market to a halt.

'There. Just do it.'

'I've got to go, Harold.'

But Harold was drunk with the release.

'Look how that dragon terrorized a whole kingdom till St George came along. He didn't fart about appeasing it, did he? He got stuck into it. Slew it.'

Bewildered by the conjured images, Harry patted him on the shoulder and turned to go.

'Superstition. That's what I mean. You're paralysed by superstition.'

Satisfied that he had had his say, Harold strolled with Harry as far as the entrance to New Palace Yard.

'Oh well, good luck. I'll see you in Yorkshire. Jo said she'll get me on the Council.'

'Well, good luck yourself in that case.'

They shook hands as Big Ben donged out nine and Lex swept past in his big black car, looking at them with a puzzled frown.

Harry went in without any problems and found his way to the Lobby. Two or three people, he noticed, were wearing dark glasses and masks, croaking to reporters and massaging their throats. He wondered if Jo had any sort of copyright on the concept.

The Lobby had not changed since he had last been there twenty years earlier when Lex had first been elected and he had been his agent. They had been revolutionaries in those days. He remembered how they had strolled round the building with their hands in their pockets, renaming parts after characters in the local Party, laughing at it all. Giving it a year at most. Harry had had a row with a Sergeant at Arms or some such red-faced brute on the very same spot where he now stood. The official had told him to take his cap off although he looked as if he would really have liked to take his head off.

'Would you remove your hat please, sir?'

Harry held the panama carefully by its brim and looked around the vestibule with its black and white tiled floor like a chess board and its filigreed stone recesses for conspirators to whisper in. Beside him, too close for comfort, the life-sized bronze of an oafish Winston Churchill sneered down at him from its pedestal. He moved away.

'Mr Beamish?'

By contrast it was a cherubic young man with choir boy straw hair and pink cheeks. He was smiling at Harry and holding out his hand for shaking.

'Dave Morrison, Child Poverty Action Group.'

Harry shook his hand warmly, trying to convey his respect for the organization.

'I read about your remarks at the Greener Britain dinner last night.'

They squeezed hands in comradeship and Harry blushed.

'Oh, I was just incensed at the bloody hypocrisy of it all.'

'Well we're very grateful.'

He reached inside his jacket pocket and showed Harry a postcard sized photograph.

'We've been trying to locate this woman, and the children, of course. Perhaps you can help us. Is er...'

'That's her! That's her!'

Harry was prodding at the photograph of a woman hugging two small children, herself hugged by a smiling husband in front of a sprawling bungalow.

'And the children?'

'Yes, yes, that's them. I've never seen the guy.'

'Thanks.'

The cherub stowed the photograph and left, waving over his shoulder.

'Thanks again!'

They would run with it.

'Harry!'

Lex was standing at the entrance to a corridor across the lobby. He was waving Harry towards him and shooing away reporters with the same hand.

'Ladies and gentlemen, please! You have my press release and the PM will see you at one o'clock. Now I really must insist.'

'Mr Beamish, what will you be saying to the PM?'

But Lex had him by the arm and was steering him down the corridor over tiles that echoed under their heels.

'Are these the Corridors of Power, Lex?'

'You're in the shite, lad. Cack up to here.'

He was whispering out of the corner of his mouth, the day's second prophecy of ordure.

Pausing outside the PM's office, his hand on the door knob, Lex began to fiddle with his tie and to whisper more dire prophecies.

'I had you set up. PPS in Education. That's...'

He indicated a nose-dive with his forefinger and whispered a discreet lip-fart.

'You've super-glued your arse to the back bench, Harry. And by the way, don't mention us and Militant, whatever happens.'

He opened the door on a grand office.

'Water under the bridge and all that.'

The office seemed empty. There was a secretary's desk in an alcove to Harry's left and a huge desk topped with green leather in front of him. This was piled high with bulging manilla folders all girdled with grubby thin ribbons, but there was no Prime Minister.

'Sit down there, Harry.'

Lex pushed him gently in the back and then withdrew. Perhaps, he thought in the instant before the door closed, they were playing him at his own game. Perhaps Lex was now rushing through some secret passage to appear behind the desk as the PM, wearing a mask and dark glasses. It could solve the problem of the thin majority; better than pairing. But as the door closed it revealed the Prime Minister standing at a window, staring out at the Thames.

Harry put his hat on the desk and sat down, although this meant craning his neck to look at the Prime Minister's back.

He was a small, plump man and with his hands clasped behind him he made a perfect pear of a silhouette against the morning sun. A ripe, prize-winning pear, polished and dressed for the judges at a show. He tapped out a slow rhythm on one buttock with the back of his hand.

Why was he not sitting behind his desk? Getting on with the job. Smoking a pipe, or whatever Labour Prime Ministers did nowadays. The pedagogue in Harry squinted at the fronts of the files with their columns of names all scratched through and initialled except the PM's. One or two were initialled by ministers fallen in the recent fray, now counting their loot in the Bahamas or somewhere. All their mess left for the domestic staff to clear up. Familiar enough to students of history, of course. Jo had written a pamphlet once: 'Inherited Crises' it had been called or something like that. Harry could never understand it.

The awful thought struck him that the PM simply didn't know where or how to start. They had been out of office so long now that their wardrobe of images had all faded or grown too tight round the waist. The man at the window had no more idea what a Labour Prime Minister should look like than anyone else had.

Somebody tapped on the door but the PM ignored it.

'On stage in five minutes, Prime Minister', it seemed to say. The Prime Minister spoke.

'How long can this wonderful weather last, Harry?'

Was the bollocking to take the form of a meteorological metaphor, then? Harry did not reply.

'Max Hastings said that if the weather had broken on polling day the Tories would still be in. Did you read that?'

Unseen, Harry shook his head.

'He's probably right. Oh well, as long as it sees us through to the recess.'

The PM raised a hand to his throat and coughed a gravelly cough.

' I hope I'm not going down with this Eco-flu, Harry. That really would be inconvenient, wouldn't it? Really throw a spanner in the workings of all our plans, wouldn't it?'

He turned a jowly profile on Harry.

'Hmm?'

'Yes, it would.'

Working his way round behind the desk, the PM sat down and stared at Harry across a pile of files. He smoothed a folded *Daily Mirror* with thoughtful strokes of his small hand.

'But we won't let that happen, will we? Can't let it happen. Too many people depending on us.'

The long silence that followed seemed to convince him of Harry's contrition and he glanced at his watch. His mind seemed elsewhere and when his gaze fell on Harry he seemed surprised to see him there. He stirred the air with the *Mirror* to wind things up. He seemed to have forgotten to mention the events of the previous evening. Perhaps it was enough to wave the article at him.

'So let's have no more of this sort of thing, Harry. I'm relying on men like you. We'll put it behind us now. This thing in the *Mirror* has already blown over.'

His face turned pale at the knowledge of what had blown it away but he did not expand on it. He seemed to have called Harry in to look at him and to make a judgement which was now made.

'OK, Harry, that's it. I'm briefing you all at ten. Good luck.'

Stretched across a desk too wide for his reach, the PM held out a hand and cranked up a grin. Harry did not move except to shift in his chair and slide the panama further into the middle of the table like a chess piece. The PM sat down again and looked at his watch. Three sharp raps sounded on the door.

'OK, let's have it.'

'It's very simple. It's the woman and kids in the box, on the streets. The ones I mentioned last night. I want them found and housed or I won't vote in the division on Thursday.'

The ultimatum rolled out prematurely onto the green table top like dice. They both sat, staring at them.

'This is ridiculous, Harry.'

'I know.'

'Then why...?'

Harry shrugged his shoulders like an adolescent which suddenly enraged the PM who slapped his hand on the table and began to colour up.

'You're a Labour MP, for Christ's sake! You wear Labour's colours.'

Harry slapped his own hand on the table and opposed the PM's red face with his own. They glowed, as if challenging each other's redness.

'Don't tell me about Labour's colours. I've carried them all my life. I won't haul them down.'

Pointing at his chest to show who would not haul down the colours Harry sat back in his chair.

'Not me.'

'Meaning what? Eh? Eh?'

The PM was leaning forward now on his knuckles, his face, alarmingly, the colour of a blackcurrant milk-shake. The knock at the door returned.

Harry had secretly feared this all along: they were not up to it. Squabbling when they ought to be doing statesman-like things.

'If you think I'm having every backbencher coming in here holding this Government to ransom for their own pet bloody hobby-horse, you're even dafter than you look.'

Moved by sheer mischief, Harry pushed the hat further towards the PM, as if it were a pawn aspiring to be a queen. The PM, beginning to shake in a mauve rage picked it up and threw it into Harry's lap.

'I will not have you making disreputable speeches in public and then swanning in here like Our bloody Man in Havana, threatening me. You vote against the Bill on Thursday. Go on! You'll be ruined. If they bring us down we'll be back with a real majority, with or without you. You think about that.'

He sat down and flicked an angry finger at the door. Harry did not move even when the door opened.

'Show Mr Beamish out, Nigel.'

But Mr Beamish sat and stared at his hat. The woman and her kids were moving on, she was shouting at them and the old man on the riverbank was saying:

'There in't a lot between them all I don't expect.'
'No, I don't suppose there is.'
'What?'
'He was right. There isn't much between us, is there? They've wandered the streets, terrified under the Tories and they'll wander the streets, terrified under Labour. Won't they?'
'Who will?'
'The woman and her kids.'

It was the secretary's turn to be waved out by the PM.
'You're addressing the PLP in five minutes, PM.'
He flapped his hand impatiently and the secretary withdrew.

'Harry.' The PM swept a hand over his bald head and took a deep breath for one last attempt at conciliation. 'Who is this woman?'
'I don't know her name.'
'Jesus Christ, Harry!'

The PM sprang up and went back to the window again, standing with his back to Harry and sweeping hand after hand over his head.

'Jesus Christ! Jesus Christ! You come down from Yorkshire. You see one woman vagrant. You don't even know her name but you're prepared to ruin your career for her. Even bring down the first Labour Government in fifteen years.'
'Yes.'
'Why?'

It was a good question and the PM, who was a good man, was entitled to a good answer. But he wasn't going to get one. Only the songs of Sirens wailed in Harry's head. It was the mention of coming down from Yorkshire that did it. Every face he had seen in his flight now wailed at him. The thin man was jigging up and down with the responsibility of a government on his shoulders, wailing. The old man on the canal bank was pointing at the bit of Axminster:

'There'd been a Labour Government in two years before we got a bit of carpet for the front room, now then!' And the woman was looking at him with contempt and distrust, shielding her kids from him. He felt himself beginning to sweat out every last ounce of energy from his body. The PM was looking at him with alarm.

'Are you ill?'

'No.'

'Then why on earth...?'

'Because...' HK was brushing flakes of samosa pastry off his trousers and saying:

'Women, Hari! They have no time for romance. Work! Work! Work! Ah well.'

'...because I promised.'

It was all he could manage: too tired.

The PM looked at his watch and came back to his seat. He took a file from a heap, slipped off its ribbon and pretended to read the last minute which was written in green ink. After a short while he returned to Harry on a new tack.

'Look!'

He put his elbows on the desk and presented Harry with an invisible roll of cloth or something. Harry looked.

'It's been a bitch of a campaign. We're all tired.'

They both nodded at the roll. Perhaps that was it. He was tired out by the election. It would be time to wake up soon. Go to his new office, find out what a Parliamentary Private Secretary did.

Nodding awake sharply, still in the PM's office, Harry sprang to his feet and threw the hat back onto the desk, like a challenge. He had almost been lulled to sleep.

'Anyhow, that's how it is.'

The PM closed the file, lifted it an inch or two and then let it fall onto the desk.

'These, are third world debt schedules.'

Harry had already seen that they were to do with Spanish herring quotas, but he was too tired to argue.

'I, we, the Party, have promised to cancel these. We can't do that in opposition.'

'If you, we, the Party cannot house one poor Englishwoman and her kids, we will not cancel any Third World debts. Believe me.'

The PM sprang to his feet too and shouted:

'You don't even know her name, man!'

'Then house them all!'

'By Thursday?'

'Yes!'

'Get out!'

The PM's fist crashed down through the crown of Nogger's hat, ensnaring itself in the straw. As he struggled to tear it off his wrist, he growled:

'Why didn't Lex tell me you were a lunatic. Here, now get out!'

The panama fluttered through the air and Harry caught it clumsily, breaking its brim. Defiantly he put it on and drew himself up to his full height, which was little more than the PM's. He said:

'Thursday.'

The PM shook his head slowly.

'God preserve the working class from posers.'

'I am the working class,' said Harry, who knew what he meant, even if the PM didn't.

He turned in the doorway, the crown of his hat flapping like a roughly opened bean tin, and faced the PM. To his horror his mother and father were standing beside the desk. His mother seemed proud of him at last and was giving an encouraging clenched fist salute but his father was shaking his head in exact time with the PM's. He shut the door on his headmaster's office and shivered. The secretary passed him on the way in, carrying a teetering load of files. He was hawking and holding his throat.

'Damned Eco-flu!'

Retracing his steps along the corridor, Harry became aware of a crowd shuffling along quietly behind him. It was his ancestors, holding their caps and smiling anarchically at him and at their own shipwreck. They stopped when he stopped and looked him up and down in awe: one of their own who spoke hard words to Prime Ministers and wore a sahib's suit. His Uncle Tom in his uniform from the Great War, broad shouldered and handsome, cap on the back of his head, a bit tipsy, winked at him. Harry shuddered from head to toe, shaking the vision to pieces so that only the smell of beery breath lingered in the corridor.

He took off his hat and ran the tangerine handkerchief over his sweating dome. This would have to stop. There had been visions before but nothing out of the ordinary. The occasional ghost at the back of a meeting perhaps. Nothing like this. Not one that came complete with smells and sounds.

Stowing the handkerchief, he took a deep breath, pulled himself together by the lapel bottoms and went on. The shuffling started up behind him again. His Uncle Tom, now quite pissed, his tunic open on his pale khaki braces, was offering him a swig from a bottle of brown ale.

'There y'are, Harry boy. Have a drop o' wallop.'

Someone sensible was saying:

'Shh! Tommy. Remember where you are.'

'I know where I am alright. A bloody easy billet, that's where I am.'

'Shh!'

'Never mind shh! They should try a spell over in Wipers instead of polishing them benches with their fat arses.'

The crowd began to murmur support.

'Get the buggers strung up like the Russians are doing.'

An icy Siberian cheer roared down the corridor. Why did there have to be so much blood?

'Bring them down, Harry. They're all the bloody same.'
'But this lot are ours. Workers.'
'Workers! Have you seen them?'

They all fell to rowing the old rows: blood everywhere. It was anarchy really, not socialism, just a rage against the rottenness of it all. Perhaps it was over and they could all breath a sigh of relief. Perhaps the thin, red vein in the bedrock of history had run out. Perhaps no more martyrs' hearts' blood need be shed for it. Perhaps they had lost. Perhaps...

Ginny was waiting for him in the Lobby. She was wearing a blue cotton dress so thin he could see the shape of her nipples through it. They seemed to be erect with anticipation of something.

'Harry, I've just seen Lex. He told me you were with the PM. Harry! You sly old dog.'

Her eye fell on the hat.

'What happened to your hat?'

He waved it absently by the brim.

'Oh, the PM put his fist through it.'

'Larking with the PM already.'

She shot her arm through his and clamped it to her side so that he could feel her breast trembling with excitement. He didn't need this. Not now.

'Harry, I've got to speak to you.'

He let her lead him out into the Westminster sunshine where she hollered for a cab in her hearty contralto and he let her shove him onto the back seat as soon as it arrived.

She gave the driver the name of a hotel in Chelsea and then flapped down the dicky-seat so that she could sit and face him, absently running her hands up and down the inside of his thighs. She squeaked with excitement.

'Harry, listen!'

She stopped rubbing and made quivering butterflies of her outstretched fingers as she prepared a deep breath to get something right.

'I know. I know the PM has offered you a PPS in Education. I heard the rumours and this morning confirms it.'

She was speaking to herself really but she glanced at Harry for confirmation before rushing on. Harry, sly old dog, nodded his head, and, ninety degrees out of phase, the crown of his hat.

'Harry!'

She seized both his knees.

'You've got to handle this correctly. You're a lucky bastard. People hang around here whole lifetimes and shuffle off with cardiacs and nobody ever gets to know their names. You've been here five minutes and you're front page news.'

She waved aside a protest that it was bad news.

'And now a PPS.'

Still holding his knees she began to muse as they went round Sloane Square and down the King's Road.

'I've seen these meteoric rises squandered, Harry. Do you remember Alun Jones?'

'No.'

'There you are. See?'

She gripped his knees in two vices.

'Harry, let me handle this. I can maximize your potential. This is colour supplement.'

She let go of his knees and opened the pages of a charade book.

'Cockney MP returns in triumph. You've got the North, South thing nicely, see. Picture of you in Yorkshire. One outside Westminster. One outside where you were born in Tottenham. It's perfect.'

She drifted into an anxious ecstasy.

'Chat shows. There's a paperback in this.'

It was Harry's turn to grasp her knees. He tried to break the bad news to her all in one breath.

'Ginny! I was not offered a PPS. The PM was bollocking me for the punch up last night and I was telling him that

I won't be in the House on Thursday for the Finance Bill because I have to find this woman and her kids. They're living on the streets somewhere over the river.'

She looked puzzled for a moment and Harry tried to wave away a full explanation with half-hearted hand gestures.

'It's a long story. I was sleeping rough when I first came down. Another long story. I met this woman with two kids. They're on the run from her old man and living in a packing case. At least they were but now they've moved on and I've got to find them before he does. Matter of honour.'

And running his eyes up and down her bulging thighs, he added:

'Matter of my manhood.'

She stared at him.

'Sir Galahad!'

She gasped in awe, and grabbing him by the lapels, pinned him to the back of the seat. Slowly, her eyes focused far away, she rose up and forced him down onto the seat, straddling him into submission. She was working herself into a frenzy with visions of success.

'Find her, Harry. Find her.'

With each command she bounced him on the seat by Nogger's creaking lapels.

'Minister in quest of honour. Minister risks all for his lady lost in cardboard jungle. My quest.'

She looked down at him with wild eyes.

'Christ, Harry! It's Arthurian. And she lowered herself onto him, filling his mouth with her muscular tongue.'

There was a message waiting for her in the lobby of her hotel and she read it avidly. As she read, she tightened her grip on Harry's wrist which she held as if he were a child she was afraid to lose.

'They've identified her.'

'Who?'

She waved the paper towards the river.

'Your woman. Sonia Smith. She's from up north too.'
'Who's identified her?'

Now she waved the paper eastwards.

'The Wapping lot. The rat-pack. They'll have her soon enough.'

She waved the paper at Harry's chest.

'You'd better hope they get to her before her old man does. It'll be front page tomorrow.'

For a moment she held the paper in one hand and Harry in the other and seemed to dither in some sort of choice between the two. Eventually she let go Harry's wrist and nodded to the desk.

'Room thirty-one. You go on up. I have to make a 'phone call, it can't wait.'

She shut herself in a little telephone booth and clattered out a number.

At the end of a corridor running back from the desk, Harry saw a door left open in the sweltering heat and for the second time in as many days he was through it and over the back wall while Ginny tried to sell his story in Wapping.

He walked along the Chelsea Embankment and got the Tube at Pimlico.

On the run up to Victoria an elegant young man with a pony tail got on. He was wearing dark glasses and a mask like Harold, except this mask had a sort of art deco oxygen cylinder attached to it with the logo of a famous mineral water company splashed across it. Harry's bones felt weary.

Rattling eastwards along the District line, he decided to get the bike out again and search for her himself. She had a name now: Sonia. The name rang a bell in his youth. They had had a student teacher called Sonia when he was at the grammar school. A tall voluptuous woman they had all drooled over. 'He's on yer, Sonia!' they had chanted at the back of the class. Innocent days. Not like these.

He watched his own reflection in the window opposite. Snakes of cables on the tunnel wall screamed behind his image. They seemed to be rushing through his head.

'In one ear and out the other. That's what happens to my advice, innit? Innit, my lad.'

Harry's father was lecturing him. He nodded in reply, 'Yes! yes! yes!' and dozed off. When he started awake again he was in Bow. He left the underground and took the long walk back to Limehouse in the blazing sun rather than face his own reflection again.

Chapter 17

'Sorry about your hat, Nogger.'

Nogger was absently turning the hat on his fist, trying to weave the battered crown back onto the rim with a thread of fine straw. He put it aside on the kitchen table when he realized he was embarrassing Harry and waved a dismissive hand over it.

'Don't worry about it. Here! Me and your Charlie once bought a gross of straw hats once off Hooky Bryman in Houndsditch. Just after the war, it was.'

Harry was sawing thoughtfully at a loaf of bread.

'I've got a feeling she's making her way north, up the Cambridge Road. I don't know why but I've got a feeling.'

'Pulled down now, of course.'

'I'll have another scout round the Lane, then I'll sweep up through Shoreditch, Dalston...'

He had finished sawing bread and was squinting at an A-Z spread open in the crumbs. Nogger began pouring lively beer from a can into two tumblers.

'We knocked them out down Southend one Bank Holiday Monday.

Took them on the train from Liverpool Street. Piled up to the bleeding ceiling, they were.'

'Trouble is, Nogger, I'm out of touch. I mean nobody lived in cardboard boxes when I left. Where would they be?'

'Half-a-crown apiece we sold them for.'

'Could she be in Hoxton, d'you think?'

'It was a scorcher, they went like hot cakes till it suddenly pissed heavens hard of rain and we ended up with armsful of wet straw. Laugh!'

'What about the canal? Do people sleep by the canal?'

'Charlie sold them to some old boy with a paper stall by the station. "They'll dry out a treat mate," he said. Bloody villain, your brother.'

'I can't make out half these streets, Nogger.'

Nogger finished pouring the beer and slid a glass across the table to Harry.

'The trouble with you, Harry, if you don't mind me saying so, and your old mum would back me up if she was sitting here now, is that you don't know if you want a shit or haircut.

He frowned regretfully on the sad state of things.

'I mean you go in for this MP lark, then you give it up right in the middle of winning, then you want to get back into it if you can find this what's-her-name. I mean, you've got to make your mind up.'

'I had, Nogger. I had made my mind up. Last Thursday I had this, this vision. Just a glimpse, but crystal clear. In a flash, I saw it all, just like that. All the shallowness and lies and deceit and sanctimony. All the egoism, the boastfulness, the bollocks. And the cliches! The cliches got to sound like.'

He was holding his ears, gob and eyes wide open like Munch's *Scream*.

'But I can't get out. It's become part of me. My brain or my body or in my genes. I'm dependent on it, Nogger. Like drugs.'

He took his hands from his ears and laid them both on the table, breathing deeply.

'But I will do this. It will consume me, I know that, but I will do this one thing. It will not roll past inexorably on its rails. It'll stop for her or I'll derail the fucker.'

Sweat was beginning to run down his neck and his breathing was fast and shallow.

Nogger put his arm round Harry's shoulder and squeezed him.

'Harry, Harry! What are we going to do with you? You take things too seriously. You always have. Drink your beer. Cheers!'

Harry drank a toast to not taking things seriously and Nogger went to the sideboard, and returned waving an enormous antique magnifying glass at Harry.

'Never mind the deceit and all that. Always been like that. Always will be. You want to stash yourself a few bob while you've got the chance, old son. That's what your old mum would tell you if she was sitting where I am now. Am I right or am I wrong? You know I'm right.'

Harry had begun to smile weakly at all this good sense and Nogger immediately turned the magnifying glass on him.

'What's this Watson? I think we're onto a smile here.'

He sat beside Harry and pulled the atlas into a space between them on the table.

'Come on then, let's have a look for her.'

They put their heads together and peered through the lens on Liverpool Street Station.

'And you've tried all round here: Bishopsgate, Club Row, Spitalfields, Aldgate? Christ, she could be anywhere, Harry. She could have gone back over the water or up the Cambridge Road. She could have gone west. She could be in the country. Anywhere.'

The magnifying glass waved over the map so that squares and roads and parks, in any one of which Sonia Smith could be huddled, loomed and receded giddily. 'He's on yer, Sonia,' Harry and his classmates chanted.

'It's bloody hopeless, Harry.'

But Harry's demon, like a spirit at a seance, was steadying the glass over Kingsland Basin on the Grand Union. Up it went, past Arbutus Street: 'My Love's an Arbutus', they had chanted that too. Not all bad. Over the Balls Pond Road, up through Stoke Newington to Stamford Hill where Charlie had lived in a miserable flat with his first wife. The demon forced the glass down again over Upper Clapton and made Harry tap it confidently.

'No. She was terrified of her old man. Absolutely terrified. If she's crossed the river it's because he's on the south side. She's making a clean break and going back up north. I know she is. And this is the natural route out of town.

'Why is it?'

Harry only nodded and grinned, although he had heard the question. Perhaps it was because he could still trust his demon to process the incoming data objectively, even if he couldn't do it himself. Perhaps it was the memory of a sepia photograph his mother had kept on the piano. She was standing beside a coster's barrow, piled high with a jumble of furniture. Her youngest brother, Harry's Uncle Fred, earmarked for death in Libya, was sitting on top, waving a Union Jack. They were all trekking north from Shoreditch to a promised council house in Edmonton just after the Great War. His mother's mother was holding the handle of the barrow and looking with proud defiance at the camera. She had known nothing but struggle. And her grandson had become an MP in a Government that should be building council houses. And instead he was...

'You alright Harry! Why don't you have a siesta? You look shagged out. It's this bloody heat that does it.'

'No thanks, I'm alright.'

He stood up and shivered in a chilly sweat.

'I'll take the bike and run out to Enfield, see if I can pick up a lead. I'll settle up when I get settled down.'

They grinned at the pun.

'Politician's honour?'

'No really, Nogger. I will.'

Harry set off feeling very unstable with a case of the Arabic corned beef lashed to the bike's carrier. Nogger and the dog shook their heads at him from the doorway.

Late afternoon Aldgate sweltered in a thickening heat haze but Harry continued to shiver in a cold sweat. Litter practised little swirling dances up and down the streets in the puffs of wind coming up from Kent: perhaps the weather was breaking. He got off the bike to wipe the sweat off his ribs with a handkerchief and shivered further with alarm at his shivering. Putting on Ernest's old jacket made him feel better and he pushed on northwards up Middlesex Street where he had drunk sarsaparilla from a stall with buckled bike wheels and one-legged old sailors had jangled their medals and begged for tanners in the old days. Or had they? Had he just seen it on an Ealing comedy? There were so many streets she could be in.

He ferreted about the streets up to Hackney Road before the light gave out and his legs began to tremble. If he did not eat soon he knew he would pass out so he pedalled up the Cambridge Road and found a quiet spot under a bridge over the canal. The spot turned out to be occupied already by two quietly chatting youngish men, sitting with their backs to the bricks of one of the bridge's supports. Harry thought about moving on but knew he couldn't make it any farther. He tore open one of the tins of corned beef and bit the meat straight from the metal in lumps. The two men stopped talking and stared at him, wincing as his lips grazed the sharp edges of the tin. He finished the last few pieces of meat sauced with his own blood. Then he lay, crucified in the gravel until he regained his composure.

'Would you, er...'

One of the men was squatting beside him, waving a litre bottle of expensive brandy in and out of his vision.

'...care to join us?'

Harry rocked himself up onto his elbows and tried a smile. The man looked exactly like Harry's eldest son and this produced in him a parental concern not to frighten the lad by continuing with his heart attack or stroke or whatever it was he was having.

'Thanks.'

He swallowed a good quarter litre and immediately felt repaired.

'Do you mind if Steve gets a couple of shots?'

'Shots?'

There was alarm in Harry's voice. The man tried to reassure him.

'Yes, few pickies, snaps, photos. Flash, bang, wallop! You know. For the papers.'

'No, no. I'm afraid not. Quite out of the question.'

But Steve was already snapping away. Harry put his hand over his face as Jo had taught him and the snapping stopped.

'You could be in the colour supplements.'

'No thank you.'

'There's a whole bottle in it for you.'

'Quite impossible.'

'Why?'

'A matter of some delicacy.'

This was exactly the wrong thing to have said to a journalist, Harry knew, but he had said it now and he was stuck with it. His mind searched desperately for a way out.

'Do you mind?'

Harry indicated the bottle again.

'No, no, here.'

The journalist thrust the bottle at him, a bit over-eagerly.

'You drink up, there's plenty more where that came from.'

What was it about journalists and booze? Getting at the truth, perhaps. In vino veritas. He doubted it.

'Truth is,' Harry lied, 'I'm a journalist myself.'

'Which paper?'

'Oh, freelance.'

'Shit.'

Steve put his camera back in its bag and they all sat by the canal's edge and watched the sun go down in Islington. The real journalist said:

'We're on a job on for one of the Sundays. Cardboard city thing. The real and shocking extent of it. You know: what's the Labour Government going to do about it? Editors have been covering it up for fifteen years, now they've developed a social conscience all of a sudden. Wicked old world, innit?'

They all took thoughtful swigs from the bottle and Harry said:

'I'm on the Sonia Smith story, myself. Paper up north in her home town's commissioned it.'

They looked at him oddly and he wondered if commissioned it was right.

'Sonia Smith?'

'Yes, the mystery woman this MP's threatening the Government over. I'm trying to find her.'

'Oh that. Is that her name then?'

They seemed only mildly impressed that he had snouted out the name.

'You haven't seen or heard anything about her on your travels, I don't suppose?'

The journalist shook his head. The photographer shook his too, then added:

'Wouldn't mind a few pix though. If you're not working with a photographer.'

He handed Harry his card.

'There's my mobile number. Give me a bell if you find her and I'll do the shots. We can work something out; see what it earns.'

The two men looked at their watches. Steve said:

'We'll just finish this and then we're off down the Strand. You?'

'No, I'm going north. Kind of a half-lead.'

When the brandy was finished the journalist threw the bottle into the canal and they all took turns in trying to sink it with pebbles but no-one could and it simply floated off into the night.

Chapter 18

At midnight Harold was still sitting on the backbenches, crammed onto the end of a row of Yorkshire MPs by the Regional Whip who passed urgent notes up and down their length. He sat gloomily with his arms folded as best he could manage in the crush and sulked into his mask.

He had let Jo bully him too easily into one last stint in the mask and he was regretting it.

For a while he followed the order paper but it was torn from his hand in one of the divisions and he lost what little heart he had. After that he just sat and watched the proceedings and listened to the Regional Whip trying to trade Select Committee places for votes in some sort of PLP elections on the side. It might all have been, he thought, a scene from a Hogarth print. Or from his memory of fifth form science lessons in his secondary modern. Speakers spoke but absolutely no-one listened. They were all carrying on their own conversations, some shouting. Some exchanged furtive notes like betting slips, others yawned and scratched their stomachs. On the bench in front someone farted villainously and his row furiously wafted the vapours towards the opposition with their order papers, cheering and guffawing. The speaker called hopelessly for order.

During a long boring speech from the Chancellor he tried to name the Tory front bench to himself but choked in the middle on their unrepentant arrogance. They lounged with their hands in their pockets and their legs stretched out, the fat of the land rolling over their waistbands. Occasionally they hooted,

'Haw, haw haw!'

One or two of them played pocket billiards, oblivious of the TV cameras.

The rage was not good for him. Only a limited supply of the chamber's worn-out air came in through the mask and if he got excited he grew faint. He settled on the sedentary distraction of counting the number of other Eco-flu masks. There were three on the opposition benches, including the Shadow Environment Minister, very quick off the mark he had been. And there were four on his own benches: one upside down on a dozing member sleeping off an inter-divisional snifter.

He thought pityingly of daft Harry, scouring the streets. He was in another world. Certainly not in this one.

A new edition of notes were being passed back and forth now. They were coded messages about a threatened left-wing mutiny. They said the tabloids had wind of it. Harry's small story had been blown away already.

Yet another note arrived and he passed it on. It came back rapidly and he handed it to the Regional Whip who handed it back. For a while they exchanged it in a sort of pass-the-parcel frenzy until the Whip said:

'It's for you.'

Harold unfolded it and read, on the Chief Whip's notepaper:

'My office, immediately after last division. L.L.'

He looked about nervously for a way out but the Regional Whip said, as if he knew everything:

'Don't worry, I'll take you along to his office.'

Escorted through the stampede of released members by the regional whip, Harold arrived at Lex's office just as Lex arrived himself.

'It's alright, George, this won't take long. You get some sleep.'

Lex sat down at his desk and waved Harold towards a chair.

'I think we've earned a gill, don't you?

He poured out two generous glasses of House of Lords whisky and pushed one across the desk to Harold.

'Cheers!'

Raising the glass to his lips he looked across the rim, into Harold's eyes.

'Come on, drink up. It's safe to take the mask off in here, Harold.'

They chinked glasses, sportingly.

'Cheers!'

Chapter 19

Harry slept fitfully under the bridge through an airless night of many dreams and turnings. Although it was hot he shivered awake from time to time into vivid hallucinations. Once Sonia Smith was standing in front of him, her two kids angelically holding hands beside her. She was thanking him in sarcastic mock gratitude.

'Thank you so much, kind sir, for setting the press on our heels. We'll just wander off the stage now. No, don't bother to get up.'

But he was up, teetering on the canal's edge. He went back to the foot of the bridge and curled up tightly in the gravel until Peggy came for him. She led him by the hand, very gently considering how he had behaved. He began to weep with gratitude and relief.

'I did my best, Peg.'

He was standing in the middle of the tow path, Ernest's coat clutched around him and tears making mud of the dust on his cheeks.

Later a bit of a wind got up, making it easier to breath and he managed to sleep the rest of the night more easily, although the dreams played almost continuously.

Sonia Smith and her kids were kneeling down and being shot in the back of the head like on an old newsreel of Nazi murders he had once seen, but the executioner was not a Nazi nor Mad Mike but Harry himself. He tried to laugh the imagery to scorn for its triteness but it just went on and on. Then he was a boy again, riding down to Broxbourne on his father's shoulders, happy as the bank holiday larks. Then the shootings began again. His demon wandered through the dreams, shaking his head and looking very worried.

It was mid morning when he awoke properly. Traffic was roaring over the bridge quite normally but something was wrong with the light: it was the colour of guilt. It was slept-in-too-late-for-work bedroom light, filtered through blinds. It was the good Lord's light of his Methodist childhood, wilfully shut out. It was self-blinding.

He mounted the bike and rode through Dalston without even pausing to brush the gravel from himself. Perhaps, if he acted normally, no-one would notice he was late for work.

Over the Balls Pond Road, wobbling up through Stoke Newington, Harry began to look desperately for Sonia Smith. She was everywhere. Going into video shops. Lugging kids out of newsagents by their skinny arms. Sitting behind the dirty windows of cafés, staring out, stirring tea. Talking with dark men from the eastern Mediterranean outside betting shops.

The foreignness of it all oppressed him and the fact that the foreigners all spoke with his own accent alarmed him. The accent had become his own property, living in the North. It identified him. He felt as if something had been stolen from him. He was alarmed at the incorrectness of his feelings.

'This is a very rash enterprise for a man of your age.'

Even his demon seemed alarmed. Like Conrad's captain in *Heart of Darkness*: hand on his holster, war drums on the riverbanks.

'Sanity is a frail craft, Harry.'

'I know, I know.'

He was talking aloud to himself now, just another old madman on a push-bike. Some Black kids, leaning on a rail by traffic lights gave him a clench fisted salute.

'Yo, man! Say it like it is!'

They fell into each others' arms, laughing themselves hollow. The air was darkening around him again.

He pedalled up Stamford Hill in a lather and reached the crossroads at the top, gasping for air. Dizzy.

'You must rest now and eat.'

His demon was writing something on a clip board and smiling at him patronizingly.

'Quickly!'

Dumping the bike in the gutter Harry staggered into the Salt Beef Bar and managed to stay on his feet long enough to take some kosher fish and a glass of lemon tea to a marble-topped table by the window. He sat and fainted in and out of consciousness until he had enough composure to scoop down the fish and begin on the tea.

The nourishing effect of the kosher meal was so complete that Harry began to wonder somewhere in all the xenophobic turmoil, whether he might be Jewish himself. Outside, on the pavement, two Hasidic men with dark ringlets springing from their Homburgs, hands clasped behind their long frock coats, carried on a conversation by nodding their heads and looking everywhere but at each other. They both spotted Harry's alien face peering at them and turned their backs on him too. They continued their conversation by nodding at the traffic as it crawled down to South Tottenham. An illogical sense of rejection came over him.

'Trouble with the Labour Party,' someone on a doorstep in Cleckheaton once said to him , 'is that you want to suffer with everyone. And that's daft.'

One of the Hasidic men burst into a flurry of arm waving and his friend, following a 127 down to Ponder's End, nodded and nodded and nodded in agreement. He could only be confirming the general rottenness of the world. The solace of the ill-used everywhere and always. Harry nodded with him, attracting an old woman with a glass of tea to his table.

'Anyone sitting here, darling?'

He turned to shaking his head.

'Bleedin 'ot, innit?'

She fanned herself with an abandoned paper from a neighbouring table.

'Oi, oi, oi!'

Harry felt more himself and started to sketch out a piece for the Great Speech. On the nature of anti-semitism.

Something to do with the sheer antiquity of the faith. His own anti-semitism was of the mild English variety which was becoming disturbingly fashionable on the left wing. But he had never understood it. It had just come with the baggage of language and religion. A sort of free and unwanted gift. He decided to scratch this bit of the Great Speech.

'Here, look at this!'

The old woman was pointing at a headline she was keeping to herself.

'Gets more like America every day. Too many guns, that's the bleeding trouble. Look at this!'

'What?'

'This!'

She was nodding angrily at the front page as if Harry ought to have known what was on it.

'This bloody maniac looking to shoot his missus and kids for no fucking reason at all as far as I can make out. They want their whatsits chopped off.'

She made a razor slash across her crotch with her thumb nail and threw an imaginary bolas of testicles out of the window. Harry felt faint again.

'Best for everybody, really.'

Harry's cooled brain throbbed with fever again.

'Show me!'

He cleared his dish onto another table to make room for the paper which blazoned the Sonia Smith story on its front page.

'Death Race.'

The photograph Harry had identified in the Lobby was blown up and stuck on the right. Mad Mike had been removed from it for star billing in his own black box on the left. The story ran over two pages.

'Leatherhead nightclub owner and convicted gunman "Mad Mike" Smith is stalking London's cardboard cities for his estranged wife Sonia and their children Daniel and Alison so that he can kill them according to his mother

Mrs Bessie Smith of Brighton.'Michael's always been highly strung,' she said,'but when Sonia left with the kids, he just snapped. I know he's armed and I'm frightened he'll do something he'll regret forever. I'm appealing to him to go to the nearest police station and give up the gun before it's too late."

Police said they believed Smith had traced his wife to an area of north London where they were now making house to house inquiries. Earlier this week, new left-wing Labour MP Harry Beamish threatened the PM's fragile majority in tomorrow's Finance Bill if she was not found and housed.

"He seems to have made it an acid test of the Government's credibility," said a senior Labour figure. "Although why he should have chosen this is beyond me. These things are best left to the police."

'The Government Whip's office refused to comment on rumours that Beamish is missing and searching for Sonia Smith himself in what has become a macabre death race. They would only say that they were assured Beamish would vote in Thursday's division. Mr Beamish was not available for comment.'

Death race. Two cold syllables. Like the cocking of a gun.

'Terrible, innit?'

The old woman, who was sweating heavily, foraged in her bag for a handkerchief and began to mop her bare arms with it.

'I wish this storm'd get a bloody move on and break.'

She flapped the neck of her blouse. Then she put her finger on the front page story and tapped it.

'They're down at White Hart Lane, now.'

'Who are?'

'This lot. The police.'

On cue a police car and a couple of ambulances whooped by outside, their blue lights a portent of lightning in the darkening afternoon.

'I came past on the bus just now. They've got a road sealed off down there. It's this bloke, Mad what's-his-bloody-name. Shut himself up in a house, by all accounts. They've got those coppers there with the black berets and the what's its.'

She squinted along the sights of a rifle, levelled at the backs of the Hasidic men outside.

'They'll kill him, of course. Don't know if he's got her with him.'

She prodded the photograph of Sonia and her kids again.

'Poor cow.'

Harry left her prodding the paper and sped off towards Seven Sisters after the sirens. The clouds were black and boiling now, tuning up their kettle drums for the big Wagnerian bash to come. One large cloud lit up like a dirty Chinese lantern with internal cracks of lightning. Confused, the street lights came on and a few random gobs of rain smacked onto the dry tarmac. Sizzling.

By the time he reached High Cross, hot and cold winds were fighting it out on the streets. bowling plastic pizza cartons along the gutter and sending cats for cover with their ears down and their tails between their legs. It was all down-hill now.

A glimmer of lightning animated a silent movie clip of Sonia Smith on a hording for him. She was mouthing, silently, the words in his dream.

'Thank you, kind sir...'

No need to mock him. He had done his best. He wasn't after her to kill her. That was another guy. He was trying to save her. Another flash projected her onto the tarmac, her skin blotched with leprous rain-freckles. She was mocking him and her husband in the same scornful laugh. Harry would not stand for this. He shouted:

'I will not stand for this.'

A small crowd of women, sheltering in a shop doorway with their carrier bags, followed his career down the hill.

He was haranguing the tarmac and the bill hoardings now, taking his hands off the handlebars to emphasize points.

'We're not all the same. I reject all that original sin crap.'

A parson, tying trestle tables onto the roof rack of his ancient Volvo, looked up suspiciously at the sound of theological dispute.

'I'm a bloody Labour man!'

The storm exploded overhead and Harry fell off the bike. He rolled along the pavement like a badly fastened roll of lino for a few yards and then came to a halt, face upwards, outside a kebab house. He closed his eyes against the torrent of rain and lightning.

It was not long before a rivulet found its way up his trouser leg and crept round the elastic of his underpants.

'Capillary action, Harry,' his demon pointed out.

The thought of leaping up and running for shelter crossed his mind but was never going to be taken seriously. He doubted anyway if he could make himself get up any more. Or even if he could make himself make himself get up. A sense of relief even greater than when he had fled on polling day crept over him as if by capillary action: the relief of pissing himself in the pissing rain. He smiled.

The parson arrived and knelt beside him. His straw hat was already battered shapeless by the rain, and he clutched his jacket collar round his throat. Looking over Harry's wreckage with the ill-disguised weariness of a professional carer, he said:

'Oh dear!'

A flicker of the fear of Harry's madness reflected from face to face with the lightning.

'Er, don't try to move yourself now, I'll get an ambulance.

As if in a film or dream, a siren sounded on the road beside him, but it was only a police car: headlights on, windshield wipers in a frenzy, crawling through the deluge. A parody of haste.

While the priest was gone, Harry and his demon settled to estimating the rate of water flow around him. One centimetre deep, say, two metres wide. Speed, gauged by a passing fag packet: one metre per second. That was twenty litres or kilos per second. More than a tonne or two hundred gallons a minute.

'Ah, Harry!' his demon lamented. 'We could have gone on like this for ever. Thinking up questions for your students. There's a work sheet in this. A man lies on the pavement...'

Another police car came past, wading up the hill this time, its siren almost sobbing with frustration. It was followed by an ambulance which was followed by the parson, waving his umbrella in a vain attempt to get it to stop. A volley of hail pelted down and Harry curled himself into a foetal position and shielded his face with his forearms. The parson came back and knelt down with the umbrella held charitably over Harry's head.

'I've called an ambulance. It won't be long, although this siege is holding things up, of course.'

Harry's foetal position was worrying the parson, who had seen it too often before. He put a hand on Harry's shoulder and tried to roll him over but his firm resistance confirmed his worst fears. He gave up and squatted down for a long wait.

'Are you in pain?'

Harry half shook his head.

'Would you like a cigarette?'

Harry shook again.

'Well, I think I'll have one myself. If you don't mind, that is.'

He settled to making a little cloud of blue smoke under the umbrella.

'Shouldn't really,' he coughed. 'Dreadfully bad for the health. There seems to a new horror revealed every singleday: lungs, heart, thrombosis, strokes and now this Eco-flu.'

He spotted his tactless drift and altered course.

'I just haven't got the will power to give it up. It gets me through the day. A crutch, I suppose, really.'

He waved away the smoke and the shop-talk and peered over Harry 's arm, trying to see if his eyes were open. Harry closed them.

'Are your eyes alright?'

Harry made no answer.

'Can you not open them?'

Still he made no answer.

'Is there something you don't want to see?' He asked perceptively.

'I've seen enough,' Harry echoed from the cave of his elbows.

The parson sighed and looked at his watch. The rain had reached his underpants too.

'This can't keep up, surely,' he wondered aloud, and then, to Harry.

'It's my youngest son's birthday today. We were going to have the party outside because of the heat. I was just putting some trestle tables on the roof rack when I spotted you. I should be putting them up under the cherry tree right now.'

'Don't let me keep you,' said Harry, uncharitably.

'Well they won't be wanting them now, will they?'

He puffed out a few more clouds of smoke.

'Funny, really, isn't it?'

'Funny?'

'Yes. The way things work themselves out.'

'What do you mean? Work themselves out.'

'Well it's as if things have arranged themselves so that I can be here with you.'

Harry almost let it go. This was where he had come in. Cause and effect all ballsed-up in half-baked theories. He wanted to drift away on the torrent in the gutter. Dissolve in the rain-mist. But his clockwork ticked inexorably on.

'Arranged themselves, Vicar?'

'Well, been arranged, then.'

'By whom?'

The old clockwork was manoeuvring the priest into a philosophical tight corner. Cruel, really. It was not this good priest's fault that Sonia Smith had been cast out and shot like a dog. But that was soft.

'Too bloody soft, you lot.' Charlie said.

The Church had let her be cast out and shot with its half-baked sentimental dereliction as much as the Party had. Too much pity. Pity spareth many an evil thing. Causeth the forests to fail. Slayeth my nymphs. Slayeth our women. Pity.

The priest stretched out one leg after the other to relieve the rising cramps in his thighs but still managed to keep the umbrella over Harry. He was a good Christian and Harry felt easier about persecuting him.

'Well, God, of course.'

He did not evade the question but he sounded uncertain. The meaning of the words seemed worn away by repeated use. Words, words, words, both their stocks in trade. Harry was sick of words but they slipped out of the corner of his mouth anyway.

'God should have arranged for that poor woman,' he nodded over his shoulder towards White Hart Lane, 'to be safe with her kids and not shot like a dog by a bloody madman.'

This sounded like madness and he fumbled to qualify it.

'That woman in the papers. Sonia Smith. The one the MP was making all the fuss about...'

The priest butted in, unable to contain the triumph of a rare piece of tangible evidence.

'Oh, He arranged that this morning. That's her husband barricaded in the house. He let her and the children go. Not all bad, I suppose. Seems as if things are coming to a violent end. Poor man.'

He seemed un-shocked by the violence but he said 'poor man' with weary sadness.

A mute ambulance splashed up the hill towards them and the parson waded ankle deep into the road to flag it down.

Two paramedics in short-sleeved bum-freezers made quick and probably unprofessional work of wrapping him in a red blanket. They strapped him onto an aluminium stretcher and then slid him into the ambulance like a Sunday joint.

'You coming too, Padre?'

The parson heaved himself into the ambulance and sat at Harry's feet thinking up an excuse for his family. One of the paramedics slammed the door and hammered on the driver's partition and they set off, their siren remote in the hammering hail.

'What happened?' One of the paramedics asked the parson.

'Oh, he fell off his bicycle in the storm.'

'Anything broken, d'you know?'

'No, I don't think so.'

There was silence in which Harry imagined the parson screwing his forefinger into his temple.

'Oh!' said the paramedic.

Another silence followed.

'You were very quick.'

The parson tried to make complimentary conversation.

'Well, we were on our way back from this siege business down the road.'

'Is it over now, then?'

'Sure is. He's gone on ahead in the other...'

'Is he...?'

'As a doornail. Sniper got him through the head.'

'Poor man! Poor man! And all for the television and the newspapers.'

Everbody, including Harry, nodded. The air in the casualty bay still buzzed with the arrival of Mad Mike.

Harry was transferred to a trolley and wheeled to the psychiatric unit. The parson walked with him through a ruck of newshounds who shot mutes of Harry, just in case.

'Is he involved in this, er...?'

'Get out!'

The parson raised a sudden angry fist and a photographer snapped him eagerly.

'You'll never be a bishop, you know,' said Harry, from his darkness.

'I know.'

They put him between clean sheets and injected him with something and he fell into a deep and unremembered sleep.

Chapter 20

He awoke to a cool morning breeze, blowing in through the barred windows at the end of his bed.

Stretching his toes down into the crisp sheets he felt a perfect peace. But it dissolved as it was recognized. He sighed. In the instant it had taken his memory to move back into its attic room with all its lumber of guilt and fears, he had been an innocent boy again. He sat up and smacked his lips. He was no longer a boy but he seemed to have woken with a boy's appetite.

It was the breakfast trolley, tinkling on its rounds that had woken him.

He was given a plastic bowl of corn flakes and a square of thinly greased toast with its own tiny pot of marmalade. These he wolfed down without decorum, scraping so desperately for the last sugary sediment in the bowl that he fired the top of his plastic spoon into the next bed. He stopped only long enough to shrug a blameless apology to his neighbour who held up the spoon top between a finger and thumb. The toast could not be cut with the blunt, maniac-proof knife, so he just heaped on the marmalade and made a roulade of it which he scoffed in two bites. Licking his fingers, he looked around greedily for more.

'Tea'll be round in a bit,' said his neighbour, very sanely.

Before the tea trolley appeared, a tall, military-looking old man in a silk dressing gown approached Harry at a slow march. He came to a parade-ground halt at the foot of the bed and looked carefully up and down the ward. When he seemed sure the coast was clear he stepped briskly up to Harry and put his hand into his dressing gown pocket.

'Quick, hold out your hand.'

Harry obeyed and the man placed some tiny, imaginary object in the palm and rolled his fingers over it, patting them gently, satisfied that the thing was safe.

'Can't be too careful. Not many of us left. Agents everywhere.'

He turned to Harry's neighbour who had started to read the *Guardian*.

'Still got yours, Sergeant-Major?'

'Yes, Major.'

'Good man. Carry on!'

Turning on his slippered heel, he marched back down the ward. Harry looked at the bars on the windows and at the muscular Black nurse at his desk by the door and felt uneasy. Now that the tranquillity of his waking had passed there was a whiff of menace in the air whose acquaintance he vaguely dreaded. He wanted his clothes now; to say 'cheerio' and be off to the House; a new man and MP. He swung his legs out of bed and walked confidently up to the nurse, whose muscles seemed even bigger close up.

'Could I have my clothes now, please? I need to be off.'

Harry smiled, trying not to leer. The nurse looked up from his paperwork but said nothing.

'I need to er...'

He had to be careful what he said next. Under the circumstances, it might be wiser to edit the truth a little.

'...get to work.'

Nothing but the truth there. The nurse seemed unimpressed and Harry began to babble.

'I've got an important job on today. So if I could just have my clothes please and whatever papers I have to sign...'

'The doctor will be round after lunch. You'll have to ask him.'

The nurse went back to his form filling.

'But I must get to work this morning.'

'I'm sorry, I can't authorize your discharge. You'll have to wait for the doctor.'

Harry began to explain patiently.

'Look, I simply can't wait here all day. Grave matters depend on me being out of here soon.'

Wrong, wrong, wrong. He shouldn't have said that. The nurse nodded him back to his bed.

'If you'd like to go back to your bed and wait, I'll make a note for the doctor.'

Harry began to simmer with rage.

'Get my clothes! At once!'

'There are some magazines in the rest room, the nurse suggested.'

Harry's rage boiled over.

'I don't want a fucking magazine! I'm a member of the fucking Government. And if I don't vote in the Finance Bill division today, the fucking Government will fall. Alright? Now get my fucking clothes or telephone the Whip's office and let them know where I am.'

He tried to give it some governmental aplomb by standing up straight and pulling his stomach in but this only caused his anti-suicide, cordless pyjamas to slide to his knees, exposing him cruelly. No-one seemed in the least concerned.

He regretted the whole outburst now, especially all the 'fucks' but at least it had resolved matters. The nurse looked much easier. This was more like it. He held up two pale palms to Harry.

'Hey! Unwind yourself, man.'

Harry doubted if this was a psychiatric nursing term but there was much wisdom in it. He went back to his bed and sat on the end of it. A crow outside in the gardens laughed itself hoarse.

His neighbour tossed him a fluttering *Guardian* Europe supplement and Harry read about terrible things happening in Bosnia. The word Sarejevo cast a chill over him. He was too old to be starting in politics. What little he knew already was too much. He could foretell that the Habsburgs would be back soon, the Bourbons too, probably. Napoleon's work undone, never mind Lenin's.

He knew it by a weary certainty that came with age. Then he noticed the date on the paper.

'Hey! This is last Friday's.'

Instantly, he remembered where he was. Perhaps such things were just not noticed. He added, quickly:

'But interesting, nevertheless. This Bosnia business; terrible.'

Harry's *Guardian*-reading neighbour, whom, he now noticed with unease, was wearing convict-arrowed pyjamas, pushed his reading glasses up the bridge of his nose and looked at him sternly.

'If you would trouble yourself to look carefully at the date, you will see that it is this Friday's copy. That is to say, today's.'

'No, no,' Harry corrected patiently. 'Today is Thursday. I came in on Wednesday and this is Thursday.'

'That you came in on Wednesday,' his neighbour replied, looking over the tops of his glasses which had slipped again, 'is not in dispute. But you spent Thursday in the arms of Morpheus.'

Harry was stunned to silence. The man continued with languid pedantry.

'Or more correctly, in the arms of Barbituus, a cheap derivative. Yes...'

He laid the *Guardian* over his crossed legs, took off his glasses and looked up at the magnolia ceiling.

'...I see Barbituus as the Titan brat of *Morpheus and Barbara*, a Hollywood demi-goddess. Morpheus and Barbara proudly announce the birth of their son, Barbituus: an ignoble panacea for a plebian age. There's a Broadway musical there. Morpheus and the Barbitones; I can see it in lights.'

He picked up his paper again and hummed snatches of experimental songs into it, smiling at some private joke.

'Barbara, Barbara...'

Harry checked the date again and again until he began to doubt the year, but here was no mistake: he had lost a whole day. So what had happened in the vote? He had to get hold of the main part of the *Guardian*. But how? Simply to seize it would probably be unwise under the circumstances. The nurse had already made an ominous telephone call, looking at him all the time and nodding knowingly into the receiver to some distant authority. Harry decided to win his neighbour's confidence with a cunning display of perspicacity. The man's full name: John McCrea, was pencilled helpfully on a grubby calling card, slotted into his metal bed-head.

'So, where do you teach, John?'

It was the wrong thing again. John flung himself back onto his pillows and let the *Guardian* glide to the floor. Harry prevented it from floating under the bed with his foot. Halfway there, if brutally.

'I'm sorry.'

Wrong again.

'No, no, no. Don't be sorry for me. Pity is the most despicable of sentiments.'

He covered his face with his cupped hands and drew in long, sobbing draughts of air. Harry tried to turn the *Guardian* to its front page with his toes.

'You must know, since, presumably, you are in the same line of business yourself: we are like sardines in tins in these places, that one no longer teaches anywhere. One presents a circus act to be pilloried and humiliated. Laughably I presented classics in a Haringey comprehensive.'

He laughed bitterly.

'Ironically I presented it largely to the heirs of Byzantium who preferred their own, contemporaneous course in loud farting. Ah well!'

He clasped his hands behind his head and crossed his ankles, stretching in a mime of relaxation.

'Someone else's job now, I quit. I shall concentrate on my writing. I need only peace and quiet and a pencil for that.'

Harry almost added paper but restrained himself. He was learning.

Under the bed, Harry managed to find the front page but the headline was ambiguous and he strained to read the first, bold paragraph.

'I have contributed several verse plays for schools to a well respected anthology, you know. No advance and three hundred and seventy-five pounds in royalties. Still, they are there.'

He smiled wanly and licked his lips with scholarly satisfaction.

'Rejected in my own authority, of course, since it required the little bastards to sit still and read for more than five seconds at a stretch. And that would never do.'

Very reactionary, that. Harry should have tutted, at least. But he was beginning to focus on the lead story.

'Government whips managed to muster every one of their three hundred and twenty-six votes in the Commons yesterday to squeeze through the controversial Finance Bill with a majority of one. Threats of rebellion in the Labour ranks came to nought as the extent of the opposition to the *carte blanche* provisions of the Bill became clear. At least fifty Eco-flu sufferers were packed into the divisions after attempts by the Government Chief Whip, Lex Latham, to secure pairing for the afflicted was rejected by the Opposition.'

"Last night we laid the foundation stone of Britain's economic recovery,' Mr Latham said. 'And it will take more than a flu epidemic to prevent Labour MPs going on to build that recovery. In case anyone has forgotten, Labour means business..."'

Harry picked up the paper and read it frankly. This could not be right. Perhaps they printed a special, psychiatric edition with all the exciting news euphemized in the reader's best interests. No, he had to face the facts that were there before him. There had been no pairing. There was even a breakdown of how the parties had voted. He was being impersonated. There was no other explanation.

He sat down on his bed and flung the paper rudely back to his neighbour who was reciting:

'Achilles' wrath, the direful spring
Of woes unnumber'd, heavenly goddess, sing!'

Chapter 21

Harry sat at the head of his bed and listened gloomily to Mr Yates, the consultant psychiatrist, who sat at the foot, picking fluff off the coverlet and sprinkling it into the space between the beds like spice into a stew. He seemed to be on the edge of a nervous breakdown himself. He spoke with a faintly Welsh accent that Harry could not quite place.

'You've got some important friends, Harold.'

He smiled at Harry who glowered back.

'Mr Beamish, the MP, telephoned to ask after you.'

He looked with disappointment at Harry's stony face.

'He's hoping to get along later, when the House rises. It must be very difficult for them. The Government, that is.'

He was babbling.

'You a Labour man, Harold? Mr Sutcliffe?'

'Yes, I am a Labour man,' Harry replied, in his sanest, and therefore most suspicious voice. 'I am the Labour MP, Harry Beamish.'

The psychiatrist smiled and began to explain, patiently:

'Mr Beamish telephoned...'

But Harry cut him off with a waving hand and his own smile.

'There is a rather bizarre mix up here, that's all. I,' he prodded his chest with all ten stretched fingers, so that there could be no doubt, 'am Mr Beamish.'

The psychiatrist sighed and Harry lost his thread and began to declaim.

'Do I sound like a Harold Sutcliffe? Eh? Do I? Harold is a Yorkshireman. I am a Cockney.'

He pointed at his own chest again.

'I am branded on the tongue. As you are.'

He pointed at his tongue and then at the psychiatrist.

'You are Mr Yates from Wales. I am Mr Beamish from London. The MP,' he added for clarification, 'and Harold is from Yorkshire. And I am not. Harold, that is. Nor from Yorkshire.'

The case, such as it was, he presented in two open palms. A bit bitty and the evidence circumstantial, of course, but he was becoming darkly aware of the lack of any other kind. The psychiatrist peered at it and dismissed it with a sniff.

'But there is your wallet with your name in it. And your library card.'

He smiled apologetically at the vulgarity of introducing such concrete evidence.

'And London and Cardiff,' he glanced accusingly at Harry, as if his origins were a medical secret, not to be divulged, 'are big cities: ports...'

'Yes, yes, yes, alright!'

Harry waved away the lecture, conceding a faulty argument and they both settled to picking fluff from their respective ends of the bed, in silence.

'Let's say,' Harry opened, 'just for the sake of argument that I am Harold Sutcliffe. Just for argument's sake, you understand.'

'Of course, of course, of course!'

Mr Yates nodded and nodded in encouragement.

'How soon could I be released? Discharged, that is.'

The psychiatrist stopped picking fluff, stood up and began pacing the aisle between the beds.

'Ah!'

He stopped at the barred windows and spoke to Harry over his shoulder.

'There's a bit of red tape there, I'm afraid.'

Outside in the gardens a lone blackbird sang its heart out.

'Red tape?'

'Yes. Nothing important, of course. You've been sectioned, that's all. A sub-committee of the authority will have to authorize your discharge.'

'Sectioned?' Harry asked, naively.

The psychiatrist sat down again on the foot of the bed and sketched out a rectangle on the cover. Pointing to the top left hand corner, as if beginning a report, he said:

'A committal order has been made for you.'

Harry felt the blood drain from his face.

'Don't be alarmed,' the psychiatrist said, alarmed. 'It simply means that I have to make a report to the sub-committee for them to consider your discharge. That's all. We just need to convince them that you are not a threat. With a bit of cooperation, I'm sure we can make that report.'

'We?'

'Yes, you and me.'

'I see. Incidentally, to whom am I considered a threat?'

Mr Yates raised a knee, cradled it in a basket of his fingers and began to tell Harry a story.

'Well, Mr Beamish has made a statement.'

He dragged down the corners of his mouth in mock horror at the use of such a formal, legal term.

'He says that you have been following him ever since his election.'

Now he opened his eyes wide in amazement at such a suggestion.

'He says that you were involved in a serious disturbance at a gala dinner and that there has been an attempt on his life.'

'That's very serious,' Harry butted in, very seriously. Anxious to be on the side of the sane majority. Just like politics really, he'd soon get the hang of it. He rubbed his hands together, warming to the game.

'Yes indeed.'

The psychiatrist seemed cautiously hopeful. For a while, they sat in silence.

'What do you suggest I, we,' he corrected himself quickly, with a false smile, 'do?'

'Well. Mr Beamish has kindly offered to give us some of his time this evening.'

Mr Yates smiled manically and Harry ground his own teeth into a grin.

'So I suggest we all have a chat and straighten things out.'

'Confront the problem, so to speak?'

Harry offered this in the spirit of cooperation. Encouraged, the psychiatrist decide to press home his advance.

'Quite. But it would be a tremendous start if you could just acknowledge your name. If you feel you can, of course. It would be a big step towards your discharge.'

He smiled a real smile.

'Very good.'

Harry gulped.

'I am Harold Sutcliffe.'

'Are you quite sure now?'

Mr Yates smiled again. He was relaxing. Almost there now. Harry breathed very deeply to control himself and hissed from between tightly smiling lips:

'I should know who I am.'

Without any warning the psychiatrist sprang to his feet, crimson with rage.

'Are you taking the piss?' he shouted and stormed out of the ward, very unprofessionally, Harry felt.

He laid back against the bed-head and closed his eyes. The blackbird in the garden, ran up and down his scales. He had to think carefully. The Health Authority chairs would have been replaced by Party nominees by now. The committal order would not be rescinded or whatever they did with them. He would have to think. Think. But all he could think of was a time when he had been a boy, hitch-hiking in Scandinavia.

A young man was giving him a lift into Oslo or it might have been Trondheim. The driver had asked:

'Where are you from?'

Harry had replied, honestly:

'London.'

'You lying bastard, you're a Swede.'

The rudeness of the driver had shocked Harry. But he had the perfect alibi for not being Swedish and he trotted it out, triumphantly.

'But I can't speak Swedish.'

The driver had looked at him and sneered.

'Yea, sure!'

All the way into Oslo or Trondheim, Harry had wrestled with the frustration of proving he could not speak Swedish. He could taste the memory of that frustration now. Fresh as the day it was minted.

'I'd advise you not to upset him.'

John McCrea was sitting upright again in his convict pyjamas, doing the quick crossword.

'Why not?'

Harry was disturbed by the note of fear in his neighbour's voice.

'American brimstone: s something, something, f, two blanks.

'Sulfur. With an f. Why not?'

'Because he's mad. Colour of dead leaves, seven letters, begins with f.'

'Filemot. Mad, really?'

'Of course, of course, feuille mort, from Latin via French. I should have got that one.'

There was a hint of accusation in his voice and Harry decided not to be so clever if he asked him another.

'Oh yes. Raving. Paranoid delusions, to take just one symptom. You saw him just now. He accused me of being pedantically obstructive just to annoy him. Labour PM six letters.'

'Wilson.' Harry couldn't stop himself.

'Of course. Few enough of them, after all. No offence, of course. I pointed out that, as he should know, pedantry was an occupational hazard of the pedagogue. He exploded just as he did with you, just now. Quite unstable.'

Harry shook his head and tutted; already the old lag.

'Unstable,' McCrea repeated. 'I seven blanks, t,e.'

Harry tried to hold back irresolute, but it just rolled of his tongue.

'Yes, could be, yes, that's very good. Not too sure it's quite the same thing but it fits. He's also spiteful. Beware!'

'Caution, avoid, eschew, perhaps? Not really the same thing.'

'No, no! Beneath that soft, blond hair is a hard and spiteful man.'

He took off his glasses and looked across at Harry with tears welling up. Harry's heart went out to him. He was being heroic. Warning him like this. Nobody, clearly, had warned him.

'Play him very carefully, or you'll wind up in a residential. You must think for him.'

The tears were spreading round the rims of his eyes.

'Anticipate what he wants to hear and let him think he's got it out of you with a respectable effort. He's supposed to be a psychiatrist, after all. Professional pride, and all that. Only reasonable really.'

He told Harry all this with the desperate reason of insanity. Harry nodded gloomily.

Chapter 22

After a lunch of decaying fish and boiled-out potatoes, Jo visited. She looked subdued.

'This is heavy stuff, Harry.'

'I know.'

They sat for a long while in silence, staring at a colourful copy of *Labour News* that Jo had laid on the bed between them. It might have been a prop in some half-hearted attempt at rehabilitation.

'What were you thinking of? One! A fucking majority of one, and you sodding around like a schoolboy. These are hard times, Harry.'

She was on her feet now with the magazine, wringing it in frustration. She was wild with anger at her own subjugation, at her own powerlessness. She walked up to the barred window and looked out onto the gardens.

'Why? Why did you do it?'

Harry shrugged his shoulders, a wasted gesture since she had her back to him but he just could not remember the answer.

'I'd just had...' Enough was not enough, somehow. He pushed away an invisible mess in front of him.

'...too much. I'd just had too much.'

Jo began to tap the rolled up magazine against her thigh and Harry's neighbour shuffled off for a diplomatic pee, holding up his cordless pants by a handful of the waist.

'I've seen Lex.'

She held the magazine in both hands behind her back and wrung it until its pages split.

'What do they want?'

'They want to stay in office. What do you think they want?'

She was angry now, her knuckles showing white around the magazine. Harry went on, innocently.

'No, I mean what do they want me to do?'

Jo's hands became still.

'They want you to stay in here.'

Panic, like ice water down his pyjamas.

'They can't keep me in here. This isn't Russia. We don't keep dissidents in asylums.'

He knew it was an out-dated analogy as soon as he made it but it was out.

'Dissident! Dissident! You're not a dissident. You're a bloody nuisance.'

She sounded like his father, poor woman. The weight of the world on her shoulders and so few of its pleasures. They were two of a kind really: deadly serious and sincere: a kind of insanity in itself really. Perhaps they were both in the right place, after all. Jo half raised her arms and let them flop to her side again with a sigh.

'Don't you think I'd like to give up sometimes?'

Harry was angry at the triteness of the remark.

'Why don't you then?'

'Because of the struggle: the cause.'

She said it to a crow in the garden who laughed in her face: haw! haw! haw!

Harry knew it was childish to ask what cause. He knew too much altogether. He knew the asking of questions was childish.

He knew too what the struggle was. It was the struggle of their youth, of all youth, that was passing beyond them: later than for most, but the harder for that.

'What cause, Jo?'

'The cause of the working class, Harry. Remember?'

But it had all gone. What had been sacred was really sentimental. The myths and legends that had sustained him were now phantoms. Tales from a tiny room, told long ago, before the window was burst open by the wind.

'Jo,' he said, condescendingly. 'Ginny offered to market me the other day. That's what the struggle has come to.'

'Ginny is a political whore.'

The last word broke on a sob and she gasped in air to control herself. Harry should have desisted, but went on.

'You didn't always think so.'

'I did. I did, you swine. I did.'

She was crying now in open rage. Soft Harry wanted to change the subject but his demon was spurring him on:

'There's been too much of this Harry and too little scientific rigour. Too much building on crooked bases of double standards and short measures. No wonder the whole edifice is creaking.'

'Then why did you nominate her for the seat.'

He found himself posing the question with real venom although it had all been had out long ago.

'I didn't.'

'You did.'

'I didn't, you bastard. I didn't.'

She had turned on her heel to face him, bawling openly, the magazine raised like a truncheon.

'You can cry all you like,' he said, unwisely. 'But you proposed her for the seat, just because she wore a man's suit and pretended to be a ... It was as simple as that. Don't talk to me about the cause.'

He spat the last words onto the floor, badly cleaned by some private contractors.

'You bastard!'

She had suddenly stopped crying and was drawing in a mighty breath, growing menacingly. He tried to get off the bed before the blows landed but she was too quick.

'Bastard! Bastard! Bastard!'

With every 'bastard' she hit him so hard with the magazine that his brain struck little blue sparks off the inside of his skull. The sparks set off a feeling of nausea but he managed to struggle to his feet and grope blindly for the flailing weapon. By chance he managed to wrest it from her grip and cast it, unfolding in flight like a bird of paradise, into the middle of the ward. The old military man put his foot on it to prevent it flying away again and looked disapprovingly on all the violence.

They both sat silently at opposite ends of the bed, breathing heavily in a sort of post coital calm and watched the Major pick up the journal and read its front page. He read it for a while without expression and then, walking slowly with it, as if trooping the colours, dropped it on the bed between them.

'My father was a Labour man.'

He said it with a wealth of sadness. Jo and Harry nodded sadly at the floor.

'Lot of water under the bridge since then, Major.'

Harry smiled a grim, soldier's smile up at the tall figure.

'Lot of water.'

A bit of *Casablanca* dialogue, that was, although for once Harry could not be bothered to place it. There had been a lot of water altogether recently: canals, rivers, drenchings in torrential storms. Pathetic fallacy, perhaps. Nature trying to tell him something: baptism and rebirth. He looked down at his feet on the grubby floor; perhaps it was the end of a line. The Major left at a slow march, humming a dirge.

'Why? Why did you do it, Harry?'

Jo began again, accidentally; sighed, stopped and then went on anyway.

'You must have known it couldn't work. And why this homeless what's-her-name? God knows the Labour Party has always been about compromise. Swallowing camels, not choking on hairs.'

She lost control of the metaphor and waved it away, impatiently.

'You know what I mean.'

'We've swallowed too much. All of us. You and me, for one, two.'

He swung a limp pendular finger from himself to Jo and back again as if showing his students what a single oscillation was.

'Well, you've swallowed too much. At least I'm an MP.'

He hesitated and looked at her. She was shaking her head.

'Well, sort of MP, then. But what have you got for twenty years work in the Party? Eh? My PA? At best.'

He added the last bit for pedantic accuracy.

'Is that it? PA to a sort of MP.'

He stared at the floor again. For once he had no idea what he would say next. He waited for the words to come.

'You could have been Vice-Principal by now, if you'd stayed at the college. Principal even. Nice little place in Tuscany. You and Jack. Easter Frascati by the Arno in Florence, before the tourists arrive. His mind was wandering over old memories of Florence, the English name so much nicer than the Italian, for once. He was with Peggy and they were walking by the river. She was holding his hand. Oh dear, how hard they had all made the world.

They both blubbed quietly as a cool breeze stirred the gardens and blew in through the bars. More rain on the way by the smell of it. Perhaps the final act was coming: of this play, at least.

'How am I going to get out of here, Jo?'

'I don't know.'

She answered kindly, eschewing the obvious, bitter response. They shuffled their soles over the gritty floor.

'You'll have to tell them.'

'Tell them what?'

'Tell them the truth.'

'What makes you think they'd believe me?'

'They'll believe you...'

He tailed off into a silence that grew as they worked out the scenario together. Jo broke the silence.

'Yes, they'll believe me. They'll love to believe me because you and me and half the fucking CLP officers will go down and the Government will fall in disgrace.'

Her voice rose, out of control.

'Shh!'

The nurse was eyeing them with disturbingly intelligent suspicion. Harry screwed his finger into his temple to throw him off the scent but instead of being distracted the nurse picked up the telephone and spoke into it quietly, his eyes on Harry all the time. Wrong again. Why did he do these things?

When he had finished on the phone, the nurse walked over to Jo and spoke to her in a whisper. Harry noticed, jealously, how young and handsome he was.

'You'll have to go now, I'm afraid. Official visiting time's at seven. You can come back then, if you like. OK?'

Jo smiled up at him and blushed as they walked off together, talking very quietly.

As soon as Jo had gone the medicine trolley came in, as if it had been waiting off stage and her exit was its cue to enter. It squeaked its rounds escorted by the Major who stood to attention at the foot of each bed and said:

'Sick parade. Fall in!'

He was ignored by each patient and by the patient nurse who wheeled the trolley.

McCrea, Harry noticed with pity, gulped down his rattling half beaker of pills ravenously and sighed. Harry held his own large yellow capsule under his tongue and swallowed heavily on tepid water with a skill unpractised since childhood but still perfect. He managed to get the capsule out before its cover dissolved and smeared it between the pages of *Labour New*s where it would be at home amongst the other opiates. Then he pretended to doze, as he imagined was expected of him, and to eye things anxiously through half closed lids.

Chemically inspired, McCrea was sitting up with an exercise book propped against his knee, writing a novel that would never be finished nor read. He was a man of his time. The idea sandbagged Harry that he was ending up amongst his own kind, the whole tangled mess resolving itself into a perfect and predestined knot. He had fallen between so many pairs of stools on his way down: man and woman, proletarian and bourgeois, hero and coward, proud and ashamed of his own tribe. A sense of shame overwhelmed him so totally that he wondered if some of the drug had managed to leak out of the capsule and why, if it had, it should be a shame drug. But things were happening in the ward.

The duty nurses had just changed over and before the new one could settle the doctor arrived on his rounds. He seemed to be in a hurry, waving aside the duty nurse's offer to accompany him.

'You carry on, nurse.'

There was something odd about the doctor. For a start he seemed too old for a hospital doctor. And there was his large, Gladstone bag. He seemed, as he stood at the end of each bed, eyeing patients over their charts and saying: 'Mmm' and 'aah,' to be more like a doctor in a fifties comedy film, which, being Harry's brother Charlie, he was, in a way.

He stopped at Harry's bed and called for the screens. The duty nurse looked up, puzzled, from his interrupted paperwork.

'Quickly! Quickly!'

Charlie checked his watch impatiently as the screens were rattled round the bed. As soon as the nurse had gone Charlie dumped the Gladstone on the bed and pulled out shirt, tie, trousers, shoes and a white coat, like his own. He looked at his watch again, this time holding it at arm's length to focus the minute hand.

'Get this fucking clobber on; chop, chop!'

Harry dressed as quickly as he could in the narrow margin between the bed and the screens as Charlie bollocked him as if nothing had changed since their pipe-fitting days on Canvey Island.

'I told you it'd come to this, didn't I? Well, didn't I?'

Harry nodded.

'Fucking politics, politics. Done your fucking head in, politics has. Come on, hurry up!'

He was looking at his watch, trying to make out the minutes and rebuke Harry at the same time.

'You could have been anything, with your brains. Engineer, chemist, doctor even.'

He indicated himself by running his hands up and down his white coat.

'Real one,' he clarified.

Harry shrugged.

'Fucking about in politics. I told you it would come to this, didn't I?'

The theme recurred.

'Didn't I?'

He shoved Harry's arm into the white coat, buttoned it up and settled the collar.

'This is a fucking nuthouse, this is.'

Charlie pointed to the floor between his feet and lolled his tongue out of the side of his mouth, miming an imbecile.

'You know that, don't you?'

Harry nodded.

'Fucking nuthouse!'

Charlie looked at his watch again as a commotion broke out at the other end of the ward. Harry could hear Nogger shouting, 'What's this bastard doing in my bed? Nurse!'

There was a loud crash as a bedside cabinet went over and then general shouting. Charlie followed the proceedings through a chink in the screens.

'Right,' he said, over his shoulder, 'when I give you the off, straight to the main entrance. Turn left. My van's parked opposite. There's a pair of overalls in the cab.'

He held Harry back with an outstretched hand as he watched the mayhem gather momentum. Then he suddenly opened the screens.

'OK. Go!'

As soon as Harry was clear of the ward, Charlie joined the fracas around Nogger and extracted him firmly by the arm.

230

'Now then, George, What's all this? I am disappointed.'

Nogger calmed instantly and everyone looked on Charlie with awe and gratitude.

'It's alright nurse, I'll deal with this.'

He led Nogger, now improvising quiet monkey noises, towards the door.

'By the way, let Sutcliffe have the screens for another half hour, will you, nurse?'

'Very good, doctor.'

Chapter 23

The two older men bounced on their seats, roaring with laughter as they drove eastward through the afternoon traffic on the North Circular. Harry sat between them in overalls that reeked of plumbers' flux, ungratefully sulking.

Nogger cupped his hands to his mouth and announced with echoing drama:

'Dick Barton, special agent!' And they both sang, bouncing out the rhythm:

'Dah, dah, dah! Dah, dah, dah!'Until tears blinded them and Charlie drove up the central reservation, which made them even worse.

'Zorro! Zzz! Zzz!'

Charlie slashed rapier zeds on the windscreen with his biro.

'The masked, fucking avenger!'

Nogger became suddenly solemn.

'You look fucking handsome in that white coat though, Charlie. No, straight up. I reckon you'd make a good doctor. Just like plumbing, really, innit?'

He looked to Harry for support.

'Pipes, an' all that.'

They roared with laughter again.

'You want a check up then? I've got my ferret in the bag.'

They were off again, screaming with laughter, turning purple. Nogger began to choke alarmingly, gasping and crying.

Harry watched Epping Forest flash by. They were somewhere near that bastard Tebbit's turf, weren't they. Chingford, or somewhere like that?

How easily those shits had beaten them all. For all their huff and puff, their harmless witty barbs, their isolated braveries drumming crossly against their enemy's chest. The tops of his ears reddened with shame at the memory.

They had planned their strategies on the wrong maps. No wonder they had been outmanoeuvred so easily for so long. They really should have checked.

Stalin had done something similar in the war, hadn't he? Planned on a globe instead of a map, or something. Sent the Red Army to the wrong place. He'd had innocent generals shot too. Done him no good in the long run, of course: his dynasty gone with the Romanovs now; water thinner than blood, after all. Mother Russia had gobbled them all up insatiably and was already smacking her lips in anticipation of the next course. Just a bridging snack, hopefully; the days of banquets gone with the Czar.

A sense of foreboding crept over his skin and he had a too late longing to be back in the staff room, reading history books and arguing with the Tories in the history department. It was a mistake to get mixed up with history. Especially as he had done. Taking the piss out of her, as it were. What was he going to do?

'You remember Dougie Skinner?' Charlie asked. 'And that fucking greyhound of his?'

It was the cue for unrestrained hysteria and the van swerved off the road into the quiet thudding ruts of the forest. It lurched from one side to the other, tools crashing everywhere and the two silly old sods whimpering with laughter, clutching themselves incontinently and screaming.

Charlie brought the van to a halt inside an elderberry bush.

'He said to me: "I'm going to race this dog at Walthamstow." I said: "You'll probably beat the fucker. Harr!"'

He clutched his side in pain and wept and gasped in air, inflating like a balloon, little whimperings leaking out of both ends: prrp! winding them up even more.

Nogger just managed to gasp in a full breath but squandered it all on one falsetto scream.

'Ahh!'

Charlie struggled for enough breath to snort out:

'You'd better drive, Harry. Go through West Ham and cut back.'

This sent them back into convulsions.

Harry got the van back onto the North Circular and pushed on more soberly, hoping he would recognize the way to West Ham.

They passed sun baked water holes, lakes, they had been when Charlie had taken him fishing there in the summer afternoons after the war. Carefree days: smoking roll-ups, chewing the fat, telling tall tales.

The other two were getting over their hysteria like a bout of crying, blowing their noses on oily rags from under the dashboard, drawing in shuddering breaths, giggling and shaking their heads at the floor, afraid that eye contact would set them off again.

'We done some fishing there, Nogger, eh?'

Nogger hawked and gobbed out of the open window. Charlie asked:

'Did I ever take you there, Harry? No, I don't think I did.'

So Charlie's mind was going first. It was some consolation for his waves of thick, brown hair. But not much of one.

Harry was wounded that he had not remembered their fishing trips and he was jealous of Nogger.

'Of course you took me there, senile old sod. Often.'

The two friends, huddled by the passenger door, their arms interlocked like schoolgirls, giddy with nostalgia, prepared themselves for another bout of giggling.

'Senile old sod! Shall we take him back, Nogger?'

But their laughter was just exhausted wheezes now. Charlie said:

'Pull up at this cafe, Harry. This one! Here! 'Fore I piss myself.'

The mention of piss aroused the serpent of prostate trouble in the older men who bundled themselves out of the van and stood jigging on the car park, trying to hurry Harry.

'Come on, Harry, move yourself. I've got to lock the motor. Property's not safe nowadays. Not with a fucking Labour Government in.'

Just rasping little whimpers for laughs now and their legs buckling as they carried each other into the café, giggling. Harry followed them, still sulking.

He no longer took milk or sugar in his tea but he got it here, they all did. They also got cheesecakes, little almond tartlets with shocks of coconut hair that Harry had quite forgotten. Nogger took his teeth out to eat.

'Fucking coconut gets under my plates.'

They all munched and slobbered in silence.

'Trouble with you, Harry, is...'

Charlie raised a piece of over-sodden cheesecake to his mouth when it dropped off and he chased after it, catching it in mid air, his reflexes hardly blunted. He began again.

'Trouble with you is you don't know if you want a shit or haircut. Never have. Just like the fucking Labour Party.'

'I told him that, Charlie. My exact words. And your old mum would say the same if she was sitting here too, wouldn't she? Am I right, Charlie?'

Nogger shoved his oar in, stirring it. He was probably right. Charlie had always known how to please their mother, even if he seldom had; Harry had never had a clue.

Charlie finished his cheesecake and rubbed his hands clean on his thighs. Then, holding out one hand, palm upwards, bending back the little finger with the index finger of the other, he began to enumerate Harry's shortcomings, although first addressing those of the Labour Party.

'One. What the fuck do you lot believe in? Eh?'

Harry cocked his head to one side to begin mincing words but Charlie waved them aside and went on.

'Two. Are you an MP or a fucking revolutionary? Christ knows it's a cushy enough number. All on taxpayers' money.'

He added the last bit sharply and both the older men shook their heads with the grave piety of inveterate tax-dodgers. Harry smiled.

'It's nothing to fucking laugh at. People who pay their taxes expect...'

Nogger began to titter and Charlie gave him a look of pained betrayal.

'Alright! Alright! I didn't say I paid, did I? I said people who paid.'

Nogger now laughed until he slobbered out a porridge of cheesecake. Charlie said:

'You want to listen properly. Going fucking deaf you are.'

He abandoned the fiscal theme and began to bend over a third finger.

'Three. Three!' he repeated to quell the tittering, a bit angry now, breathing hard through his teeth. 'All this Black business.'

Harry groaned and Charlie expanded.

'Pakis, Africans, Palestinians, Ben-bloody-galis, any bugger but your own. You know what I'm talking about.'

He leaned back in his chair and got his breathing under control.

'I'm not prejudiced, Harry. You know that. But you lot think more about foreigners than you do your own people.'

Nogger was confirming this to Harry with regretful nodding.

'The only thing you seem certain of is that Britain is always wrong.'

He had strayed, somehow into foreign policy, where Harry had taken more than enough stick from the far left for being patriotic. Carrying the white man's burden, he had been accused of once by Ginny. A very marketable line these days. He was about to respond, although he was not sure how, when Charlie bent over a fourth finger and moved down the agenda.

'Four. What the fuck do you want?'

Ah, there was the rub, of course. That should have been number one really, that should. Get that right and the rest just followed on, no problem.

Nogger gargled the coconut off his palate with tea and put his teeth back in, testing them out with a few reptilian snaps at imaginary flies.

'What do any of us want?' he snapped, philosophically, 'Eh, Charlie?'

After a silence, Charlie summed up.

'Well, there y'are!'

They all nodded assent. Carried then: 'There y'are.'

Back in the van, Charlie drove, quarrelling quietly with Nogger about immigration and Harry dozed, half listening to the radio. The strain of recent events was catching up with him, draining him.

He found himself wondering how the Whips had found out, although he was too tired right now to consider it properly. The idea that the Party was not daft floated across his mind, followed by a little glow of pride that warmed him like a hot water bottle. Sleep, that was what he wanted. Some fool on the radio was going on about the election being in October when it had been in June. Bloody sloppy research that. He'd write to the BBC. Get an EDM down, or something. He slipped off.

He was wakened by Big Ben tolling loudly over the radio and more quietly through the open window, to the west.

'Dong! BBC news at four o'clock. Four Labour MPs die when their light aircraft crashes at East Midlands airport. PM calls general election for October the eighth. Dong!'

Chapter 24

Harry's attention wandered out of his first class carriage window and onto a King's Cross platform that had begun to walk, ever so slowly, southwards.

'Tell us Mr Einstein,' his demon was saying. 'when does New York Central stop at the next train?'

No more relativity jokes with the sixth form, then. All innocence flown now. A commission note for the Sonia Smith story from a tabloid editor, hidden, unknown to Jo, in his inside pocket. Nogger's inside pocket really.

He watched the Rastafarian driver of a little baggage truck stop to rekindle a Winston Churchill-sized joint and then puff on his way again like the ghost of some old LNER loco. No wonder they had lost the Empire. Although, paradoxically, he felt sure the Edwardians would have approved of all this. He could see Sherlock Holmes nodding away by the news stand, his own meerschaum stuffed with more than Gold Flake. They had all grown so tame.

'Are you paying attention to this?'

Jo waved her hand sideways over a heap of papers on their table top. Harry searched desperately for a displacement activity.

'I need some coffee. Anyone else? I'll get it.'

'Sit down!'

Jo had collected the travel warrants from the office herself and she kept them in the side pocket of her jacket where she felt for them from time to time with a little rustle. She had also used Harold to box Harry into a window seat and then put her leg up in case he tried to crawl out under the table. She was pointing to a table of MP's allowances.

'You can afford to take Harold on in the constituency office.'

His treachery over the committal order forgotten. This compromising job his reward.

'Even though I'd earmarked that for Jackie!'

She made the aside with such venom that both men flinched.

'Still, you can put some part-time work her way. You know: part-time work, women's work.'

She snarled this quietly and then shouted:

'Bastards!' so loudly that they both pushed themselves back in the plaid and other passengers peered over crosswords and round seats at them.

The train was drawing clear of the platform, shimmying over the rails with a shake of its hips. Getting back on the right track. Metaphors again.

Lex had told him, in a song of metaphors, that bygones were to be left as bygones, water was under the bridge, hatchets buried, sleeping dogs left to lie, cans of worms unopened and anyhow it could all be denied. Who would believe it, after all?

'Will you look, at least. Look!'

She was calmer now, biroing a line under the secretarial allowance figure. Harry looked. It looked astronomical. Reading his thoughts, Jo said:

'It's not as much as it looks, but it'll pay for Harold in the office and me in London. I'll shuttle between until he gets the hang of it. Probably best to have some new blood in the constituency anyway: above the factions.'

She was wandering. Rationalizing things.

'We'll put you up for Moorbank Ward,' she said, turning to Harold who pretended to be surprised. As if it hadn't all been part of the package of reconciliation.

'It's safe enough. We'll have you on the Council for May.'

He rubbed his hands in naive anticipation and Jo grinned at him through clenched teeth.

'We could do with someone sane in the Group.'

His hands stopped their rubbing and he looked anxiously at Jo, who bellowed, her anger not quite blown out:

'Although I'm not sure you qualify on that fucking score!'

The back gardens of north London were cantering past now so Jo lowered her restraining leg and cleared the papers from the table top.

'You can order breakfast now,' she said and gave Harry back his wallet and his beloved credit cards.

Dozy on fat bacon and eggs, Harry pretended to look out at the embankment that made a mirror back for the window. Really he looked at Jo. She was knocking a sheaf of papers into shape on the table and her unrestrained breasts were jostling one another under her tee shirt. A whiff of the regret he had felt on polling day stirred again but he dismissed it resolutely and turned his attention to the table top where Jo was beginning to knock the new campaign into shape. That was all behind him now. He was a new man.

'The *Messenger* gave your homeless woman escapade some pasta, as you can imagine.'

She dealt out three lead articles.

'Not all bad though. This one's a peach. Nice picture.'

She tapped the article thoughtfully.

'We'll have to go on it. Put a homeless slot on the back of the main leaflet. Dig out some homeless single mum the Council's just housed. Nice picky over the endorsement. "I know I can trust Harry to stand up for the homeless, blah, blah, blah." Other slots as before, I think. This has got to be camera ready for Thursday, so we don't want too many alterations. I'll work in the brave Government tragically interrupted in its mission theme into the bit on the back.'

She began to tick a list of her own making.

'Yes, yes, yes. Right.'

She turned round a pre-printed campaign schedule for the other two to see and ran her biro down it, stabbing each deadline in turn.

'Intro leaflet to printer. Main leaflet to printer. Intro leaflet out. Nominations deadline.'

She stabbed all round this last item and boxed it in three times before she went on.

'Postal votes go out. Harold can get started on the pee vees tomorrow. We'll run the labels off the old discs. There'll be a supplement out but it'll be nought. Anyhow, we'll not be short by a handful of postal votes. We should piss this one.'

Harry nodded, watching her lips moving.

The familiar words were working on him like a lullaby. But somebody was turning down her volume. She was fading out and another voice was fading in.

'Map itself don't show if this is swamp or desert.'

She had a gold map on her knee now and was pointing at the Sierra Madre. In a Lincolnshire back garden two small boys took aim at the carriage with their cap guns and for a minute the bullets were buzzing in the carriage like a swarm of bees and Harry was shooting bandits off their horses like Coke cans, although he couldn't get his demon who rode with the bandits and wore a gold hat.

'I got three, credit me with three. How many d'you get?'

'Three? Three what?'

'Sorry. Sorry. I must have dozed off. It's the heat through the window.'

He smacked his cheeks and shuddered himself awake. Nothing to worry about. He cleared a little patch on the table and began to sketch on the back of a leaflet.

'What we really need to do now is rough out a diary of events so that we can plan the themes of our press releases.'

The others were looking at him with the old confidence. He could feel his seized machinery beginning to turn again in all the familiar grooves.

'Try to control the agenda. Get into the driving seat. The locomotive of history,' he quipped.

They all laughed.

'Right, what's coming up?'

He rubbed his hands like a gourmet. Taking charge. The old machinery beginning to hum nicely again. Responding to the throttle. He was his old self. His demon had ridden off with the bandits, his wits were restored and he was back in reality. It had been a close shave, but he had made it.

He fell on the candidates' mailout like a long lost friend and turned up the TV broadcast themes. These he tapped with his pen.

'Ideally we should aim for our local stories to peak around these broadcasts. Our theme a local expression of the national theme. The national suggests, the local confirms. It's an illusion really.'

He was lecturing Harold with one thumb in his waistband and the other hand waving up illusions. Even Jo, though his rehabilitation should have been the cue for her to vent her righteous anger, was nodding in appreciation. A warm glow of satisfaction with his own cleverness began to creep over him followed quickly by an urgent need to pee. He sprang to his feet.

'Excuse me.'

Jo's eyes followed him warily along the carriage to the toilet.

Blinded to the illuminated engaged sign by the pressing urgency, Harry rattled the door until the terrified occupant whimpered:

'It's engaged!'

'Sorry! Sorry!'

His panic mounted. He had promised his bladder relief: a rash politician's promise as it turned out. His bladder promised immediate rebellion. He pelted through the next carriage, leaking into his underpants.

'Fuck! Fuck! Fuck!'

A few 'tuts' followed him, cursing, to the next toilet. It was also engaged. He rattled the door anyway, as if to show his bladder he was doing his best. A little squeal escaped him. He must not think of flood gates opening, he thought, walking with his knees together through the next carriage. No toilet at all here but a buffet car where a barman deliberately poured a tonic water slowly onto tinkling ice. A dark stain began to spread over the crotch of Nogger's trousers.

'Fuck!'

'Tut, tut!'

The next carriage was empty and its toilet unoccupied but the electric gadget that opened it seemed to be confused. When Harry pressed the big 'open' button it clicked, made as if to open, then sighed and thought better of it.

Click, sigh, click, sigh. Harry hammered the button with one hand and clamped the end of his dick with the other.

Two men were swaying down the carriage towards him. One of them, a dapper young man, took in Harry at a glance. He was the PR man from Leeds and to Harry's horror he seemed to recognise him. He was talking with a fat man who brushed ash from his shirt front and belched his responses in the conversation. Harry placed him as a Tory Regional Whip.

Click, click, click. The door gasped open and he squeezed between its rubbery gums while it was still opening. He pressed the 'close' button and the door closed almost completely.

Ecstasy. Harry leaned against the wall and peed in and around the basin as the brakes went on for Grantham, his bliss marred only slightly by the disappointment that he had not hung on long enough to piss on Lady Thatcher's birthplace.

'Ahh!'

A sigh of rapture escaped him. Hadn't St Thomas More said that micturition was one of the two fundamental carnal pleasures? Utopia, or somewhere. Very wise observation, that had been: worthy of canonization in itself.

'The trick will be to give them just enough rope to hang themselves.'

This was not St Thomas More but the PR man, right outside the door, talking to the Tory Whip.

Harry tried not to thunder into the basin so that he could hear what he had to say but it was lost as the brakes went on sharp and the train stopped outside Grantham station.

Squeezing his eye into the gap in the door Harry watched them make their way back along the carriage, nodding to one another.

He made a handsome codpiece of bog roll in his Y fronts and shook his head at all this duplicity.

He buttoned up and admired himself in the mirror, practising a few sound bites for interviews.

'Sonia Smith? I'm afraid I was incensed by her plight. She was living proof of the neglect of the previous government...'

No, he had to be careful there, thin ice.

'There is so much to be done. It would be tragic if this interruption...'

No.

'Perhaps some good can come from this tragedy if the Labour Government returns with the majority it needs to...'

Something like that. He brushed aside the need for rehearsals. Words would come. They always did. All his confidence had returned. The past two weeks simply rolled away in his wake. He decided to have an early drink in the bar. Repeal the prohibitions of his Methodist childhood. Put the past behind him. One last look in the mirror.

'Here's looking at you, kid.'

Casablanca, Warner Brothers, nineteen forty-two. That was something he had to stop too. He was not Humphrey

Bogart, he was Harry Beamish the MP and that was good enough. Same initials, though. He had never noticed it before. Incredible. Harry Bogart. Humphrey Beamish. He shrugged Nogger's white jacket higher onto his shoulders. Rick Blane.

'Are my eyes really brown?'

No, they were not, they were blue. Still, no harm in a bit of nostalgia, was there? He left that question unanswered and after checking that Jan and her boyfriend had gone, made his way to the bar. The wet patch at his crotch was drying nicely.

He would tell Peggy that the Eco-flu had left his memory of the past fortnight hazy. Might even grow to believe it himself.

In the bar everyone looked vaguely familiar. It was like a small home-coming for him. Peggy had once said that the main line from London to Leeds was like a village high street on wheels. You soon got to know everybody on it.

Harry nodded to a regional trade union official of brief acquaintance, shiftily making deals at the bar with a man in a pin-striped suit. He also caught the ambiguous glance of one of a couple of young men at the bar whom he vaguely remembered from Westminster. The young man had an Eco-flu mask hung casually around his neck while he drank a gin and tonic and talked politics. From the pastiche of sound-bites that floated towards him Harry could not make out which side he was on. A candidate probably. Or a professional agent. Harry rubbed his hands with delight.

The spacious end of the bar was occupied by a group standing around bags stuffed with papers. They were talking education. Hardened drinkers of the conference circuit by the looks of them, drinking coffees laced with brandy from an army of dead miniatures. A young man in the group seemed to recognize him. Harry ordered a coffee and a scotch.

The conference-goers were all swapping gossip of adulteries and chuckling lecherously. Somebody began a tale of the PR man Harry had so narrowly escaped. They all fell to disparaging him when he suddenly arrived. They stopped and grinned shamelessly like sharks.

The PR man's grin fell on Harry. For an instant it set hard as he tried to weigh up his value and then it spread across his handsome face.

'Harry!'

He beckoned him into their circle with both hands as if he were an aeroplane trying to land on a carrier.

'This is Harry Beamish, MP. He's your MP in fact, John.'

Harry got in a bit of early handshaking with his constituent.

'Not an MP yet. Just a candidate.'

'He's a rising star,' he went on, moving one of the women's bags so that he could be placed centre stage.'

'Of course! Of course!'

Everyone recognized him now and he got on with his handshaking amidst backslapping and wishes of good luck.

The PR man broke in loudly.

'I was talking to the Secretary of State yesterday.'

All other talk stalled momentarily. The young men at the bar stopped talking and the one with the mask fondled it nervously. Harry asked, although he never really meant to put it so rudely:

'Which one?'

'Leonard, of course. Spoke very highly of you. Said you were in line for a PPS.'

He took Harry by the elbow and moved him towards the bar as the group rearranged itself into pairs. He lowered his voice.

'I must say, I admired your stand on the homeless woman.'

Harry smirked modestly.

'You'll have sold the story.'

He seemed to be looking through Nogger's jacket to the tabloid contract. Harry touched it involuntarily and tried to make an ambiguous noise but it was unnecessary.

'You should get incorporated.'

'Get what?'

'Yes, it's the only sensible way to minimize tax losses on your extras. It's all the rage. Half the Left's doing it. What's-his-name...'

He clicked his fingers impatiently a couple of times and then came up with the name of the famous left-winger Harry had met in Parliament Square a week earlier.

'...Of course, he's got his chat show, but you have to be prepared for these things. It makes sense. Harry Beamish MP PLC. What are you drinking?'

Harry tried to pretend to himself that he had not already worked out the tax on the contract and lamented its loss. And someone had told him regional TV paid at least two hundred pounds an appearance. There were several in the offing. Perhaps he should be looking ahead.

'You're joking, of course.'

'Never joke about money, Harry. Cheers!'

'Harry!'

It was Jo, calling him angrily from the entrance to the bar. He waved her in but she stood resolutely on the threshold like a disapproving teetotaller. Glaring at all the afternoon licence.

'Harry, we were in the middle of...'

'Coming, coming.'

He waved his whisky at the PR man.

'My agent, Jo Firsby.'

The PR man was eyeing her with a look of chilly recognition. He nodded towards the doorway.

'Jo.'

'Jeff.'

The train sat for a long while outside Grantham. Long enough for the two whiskies to soak in and lead Harry's thoughts out of the window, away from the kaleidoscope of forms and leaflets that swam on the table top. Flat country, this was. Big sky country. People looked up here and away to the future. This was Cromwell's and Newton's country. No-nonsense men's country.

The train rolled slowly into the station and sat there. Just outside his window a fidgety sparrow perched on the back of a bench and crapped liberally onto its spars.

Jo had once told him that the benches on Grantham station had been painted blue in honour of Mrs Thatcher but they were red again now. All things passed, then. The sparrow seemed to be making a poetic statement.

'Behold! I put white full stops to the song of your glorious deeds.'

Never really had any sense of rhythm. He was a prosaic man.

A whistle blew and rose-pink young people with back packs ran down the platform, shouting urgently and laughing. The party in the bar were laughing. Jo was laughing over something. Everyone was laughing.

All the stored-up shock of the last ten day's turmoil came upon him at once. He leaned back and closed his eyes on tears of gratitude. He had come so close to disaster. He watched the characters of the drama line up like actors for a curtain call. They were all there, holding hands. The old man in the cabin with his Communist Manifesto, the thin man with his worries. Sonia Smith with her two children, looking bewildered. Harry with his arms round them for the cameras, smiling. Everyone was smiling and laughing.

They were laughing for Harry's triumph. Harry Beamish MP PLC. Tears squeezed out under his lids and he stood up, stumbling over Harold's legs into the aisle.

'Not again, Harry?'

'Sorry, Jo. Matter of some urgency.'